The Autograph Hound's name is Benny Walsh and he's the original Nowhere Man. He's a mediocre busboy and a worse lover. When he tries to sell his body to a hospital, they won't take it.

But Benny Walsh knows what living is. It's prowling with pen and pad through the haunts of the rich, the famous, the beautiful. It's cornering Orson Welles, Bea Lillie and Buffalo Bob Smith all in one ecstatic night on Broadway. It's dashing past the cameramen to get signatures from Johnny Carson and Joe Namath right there on nationwide TV. It's all the zany scenes and wild schemes of a man who has 2,376 autographs and is gunning for more!

"John Lahr has captured something alive and writhing...a sense of human failure at its clownish worst that runs just beneath the polyester surface." —*Chicago Sun-Times*

THE AUTOGRAPH HOUND
was originally published by Alfred A. Knopf, Inc.

John Lahr

THE AUTOGRAPH HOUND

 A POCKET BOOK EDITION published by
Simon & Schuster of Canada, Ltd. • Richmond Hill, Ontario, Canada
Registered User of the Trademark

THE AUTOGRAPH HOUND

Knopf edition published 1973

POCKET BOOK edition published June, 1974
2nd printing..........April, 1974

This POCKET BOOK edition includes every word contained in the original, higher-priced edition. It is printed from brand-new plates made from completely reset, clear, easy-to-read type. POCKET BOOK editions are published by POCKET BOOKS, a division of Simon & Schuster of Canada, Ltd., 330 Steelcase Road, Markham, Ontario L3R 2M1. Trademarks registered in Canada and other countries.

Standard Book Number: 671-78361-0.
Library of Congress Catalog Card Number: 72-6776.

Cover photograph by Terry McKee.

Printed in Canada.

Lyrics from "I Want to Take You Higher" by Sylvester Stewart used by permission of Warner Bros. Music. Copyright © 1968 by Daly City Music. All Rights Reserved.

Lyrics from "They All Laughed" used by permission of Gershwin Publishing Corporation. Copyright 1937 by Gershwin Publishing Corporation. Copyright renewed.

The author wishes to thank the Rockefeller Foundation and its Villa Serbelloni, where this novel began.

To Mike Magzis
&
John Hancock
&
Anthea
With love and gratitude

"Why do they come and see me? I don't know what they want to know."

JANIS JOPLIN

LOOK AT GARCIA. For a man in his position, he's got no style. A Stetson should be tilted and squared like Lash La-Rue, not stuck in a Hoot Gibson hump with a crease down the middle. The handles of his six-shooters are pointed forwards. In a gun battle he'd be slaughtered. The maître d' before him—Levy—he was no fancy pants. One gun (handle pointing backwards), chaps, no phony rodeo necktie with a silver holder. Everybody liked working for him. He used to let me off early before the Broadway shows broke. If there was a special premiere, he'd fix it so I could make up the hours. He was the best maître d' The Homestead ever had. Nobody talks about him now.

Garcia gets so uppity. Two nights ago, one of the waiters decided to add a little color to his uniform. He put on an Apache scabbard. Customers noticed it. It helped with tips. But Garcia made him take it off.

Busboys don't wear uniforms, just The Homestead brand—the Flying H—on their white jackets. I could've been a waiter. I know I'm not strong, but I'm strong enough. I know my eyes are bad, but I've got a great memory for detail. Waiting table's too much responsibility. When it gets hot, my glasses start to fog up and my head buzzes. I slip into the bathroom next to the time clock and sit on the toilet until it goes away. If I was a waiter, I'd have to keep working. There's no letup. You walk into the kitchen at rush hour and Zambrozzi's there in his white hat, his chest hairs like clumps of broccoli creeping over his T-shirt, screaming his dago skull off, banging the bell. *Fai presto! Fai presto! Pane! Insalata!* There's so much to do, and so little time to do it.

Zambrozzi is to restaurants what Vince Lombardi is to

9

football. He's what the New York *Post* calls a "task-master." The Homestead has been in the *Cue* Guide to Dining for three years running, and last month, the restaurant was rereviewed by *The New York Times*. Zambrozzi, Garcia, and the Boss were mentioned. I have the clipping in my wallet. The *Times* liked the antipasto, but felt the zabaglione lacked "e-c-l-a-t."

The good busboy does his job so quietly that no one knows he's around. Of course, everyone would like to be mentioned in the *Times*, but they're only interested in the results, not the behind-the-scenes activity that gets the food to the table. I could've told them a lot about The Homestead. I keep a scrapbook. But he didn't sit at my station (number 4). Water, bread, butter, plates—once in a while a trip to the front of the house to get cigarettes from Louise, the hat-check girl. Busing's not as glamorous as being a waiter, but it has its advantages. You're out on the floor. You see people. You make their acquaintance.

I work hard. The restaurant is known for its service. I guess that's me. I want people to come here. I remember the old days when we were serving only steak and lobster with two kinds of vegetables. That was eight years ago. Now The Homestead seats two hundred. There's a bar and painting of the Wild West and drink holders in the shape of the beaded saddle standing by the cash register. The saddle belonged to Buffalo Bill. He's about the only person who doesn't come in here. Every night there's somebody new, somebody you've read about in *Variety* or *Sports Illustrated* or somewhere.

You can always tell a celebrity. They stand apart. They're friendly without being snooty. They chew their food but don't make noise. Sometimes I just walk right up and say, "Are you famous?" I'm not wrong very often. I've been collecting autographs since I was ten—one quarter of a century. The celebrities are generous. They smile and answer my questions and sign my book. I don't take up their time. They've earned their privacy. Only the small-timers are wise guys and don't look at you when you ask a question. But with these types, I don't listen either. I let them sign my pad (you never know who's going to be valuable in a few years) and then walk away.

10

Of course, I know many of the faces right off the bat. Rosalind Russell, Stella Stevens, Zero Mostel, Ralph Nader, Anthony Franciosa, Teddy Kennedy. I only let them sign in ball-point. The celebrities write with such energy. Even when the letters are scribbled together, their signature is so . . . *them*. For instance, Zero signs his name in big, round swirls like his face and Teddy Kennedy is so busy that he draws a straight line with a few bumps along the way for the *T* and *K*. Myself, I don't write too well. But in my business you don't have much writing to do—union cards, health policies, that sort of thing. I write to my mother almost ten times a year now. I feel sorry for her since they took the sainthood away from Christopher and Philomena—her two favorites. She wrote and said the Church found no evidence they existed. I wrote back: "From now on, don't believe anything you haven't seen." That's difficult for her. She's blind in one eye, and how many celebrities come to an old-age home in Asbury Park? She keeps pestering me about who I've seen. Every *P.S.* is the same: "Good contacts are good business." When I was just starting in New York, she wouldn't give my signatures the time of day. "Nobodies," she'd say when I'd show her my Carmine Basilio or my George "Shotgun" Shuba of the Brooklyn Dodgers. "These are nobodies! In my day, we had real stars—big, big people. Valentino, Paul Whiteman, Bill 'Bojangles' Robinson, Bobby Breen." Sometimes I write her in the styles of my friends. Last month, I tried Namath's hand—the butterfly *J*, the oversized *N*. It wasn't bad. But I don't have the power in my fingers that Joe has.

The Homestead's good for autographs. It's better lighted than Trader Vic's, and where "21" also gets a late night crowd, there are five headwaiters hovering around. At The Homestead there's only Garcia to worry about. That's enough. But Garcia's usually at the front of the house chatting up the reserved tables, keeping single women out, taking the tips that pay for his '56 Thunderbird with bucket seats and hand-carved wooden steering wheel. He can't keep his eyes on the busboys. The waiters are supposed to report any funny stuff, but they hate him, too. So, at the back of the restaurant, I have freedom many

11

others don't. Sometimes when other busboys have a famous person at their station, we pull a Cain and Abel—football talk for switching assignments—so I can get the autograph. That's why my collection has grown so fast and why some people, like Louis Sypher at the Waldorf, don't do so well. My collection must be worth $20,000, but I'm not in it for the money. The Waldorf crowd is all Italian singers—Sergio Franchi, Julius La Rosa, Eydie Gorme, Liza Minnelli. They're hot now, but wait a few years. Louis gets $20 a book. With him, it's slam-bam-thank-you-ma'am. He doesn't follow his people. He doesn't really care. That's what makes great athletes or great anything—care.

Nobody wants to just give away his autograph. You've got to feel the mood. You've got to red-dog into a conversation when the star's relaxed and when you're confident you can handle the situation. You've got to read a lot. You don't go up to Willie Mays and start talking b.o. —box office, in show-biz lingo. You talk to Mays about himself. The first year in the minors with Trenton when he hit .353, or how he likes living in Hillsborough, California, next door to the publisher of the *San Francisco Chronicle*. I buy all the magazines and trade papers. Mom says I shouldn't pay $40 a month for such things. But how else can I keep up? Most people read *The New York Times* for its obituaries. But once a famous person is dead, he's of no use to me. *Variety, Hollywood Reporter, Sports Illustrated, Baseball News* give me the facts and figures that never get into the *Times*. Take Jackie Kennedy. I've seen her walking along Madison Avenue with John-John. I've also seen her with unidentified older men. The *Times'* stories always invade her privacy. I wouldn't think of doing what they do. How that woman has suffered! But the *Times* only talks about her when she's been embarrassed by some snooper or has lost her jewelry (they're still looking for the $12,000 diamond stolen from her Fifth Avenue apartment). There's so much to the woman—all those cooks and servants and children and famous-people parties. Why doesn't the *Times* report that! They treat her like Garcia treats me. When I saw her on the street, I couldn't take my eyes away. Her hair had

12

that lovely two-tone quality—gold and bronze like a Chevy Impala. Her eyes were hidden by sunglasses. Nobody knew her but me. She stopped to look at an art gallery. She lifted her glasses on the top of her head like in *Vogue*. Then, out of the corner of my eye, I saw Macready. He works Park and Madison during the day and hangs out around Sardi's at night. I've heard his pitch a hundred times. "Excuse me, ma'am, could you spare some change? I got separated from my platoon." Now Jackie's the kind of woman who gets things free. If I were a cabdriver, it'd be my honor to give her a lift. She doesn't need to carry money—everybody knows her. But Macready's bad. You don't panhandle the ex-First Lady, somebody who knows politics, whose husband (may he rest in peace) was separated from his platoon himself and swam nine miles dragging a wounded buddy on his back. I saw Macready and walked up to him to block the way. I asked him for a cigarette. Under his breath, he says: "Fuck off, Walsh."

My voice got loud: "Do you have the time?"

"Fuck off, creep. That's Kennedy's old lady."

I saw Jackie notice Macready. She turned and walked inside the gallery. Just before she opened the door, I saw her look back and smile at me. I walked away fast. (Macready's much bigger than me.) I'd protected Jackie from another intruder. If she comes to the restaurant, I'll get her autograph. I'm sure she'll be nice. I'm sure she'll remember.

"Stop yapping, Walsh. Table thirty-two's a mess!"

Garcia reminds me of Edward G. Robinson.

"You want I call the Boss, Walsh?"

"I'm going. I'm going."

The kitchen's steaming. My neck gets prickly. The noise is too much—plates dropping, silverware crashing in the bins, hot air hissing up from the vats. I scald my hand. I've got a right to stand somewhere and let it cool. Garcia has it easy. He doesn't have to go into the kitchen if he doesn't want. He doesn't have to scrape plates or haul garbage. He stands by the telephone talking in his best English. The celebrities call him by his first name, Enrique. He whispers to them, he does them little favors and brings them the red phone for special calls. I don't have that chance. More butter, more rolls, water, a napkin. That's all I'm allowed to do. It's not much in their eyes, but the work's ten times harder than the maître d's. I told that to Garcia after our last fight. He said I couldn't carry my autograph pad in my hip pocket. He said Boss's orders. Now I hide it in the freezer, and when somebody comes in I sneak it out.

Garcia makes me feel like I'm in enemy territory.

It's been a slow night. Louise told me that George Segal stopped by for a drink at the bar.

My hand still hurts. My legs ache. The waiters pile as many plates as they want on a busboy's tray. I'm no Chaplin. Fall down with a tray of plates and it's not so easy to get up. These swinging doors are murder. Zambrozzi's laughing. The first time I've seen him smile all night.

"Eh, Benny, *che succede!*"

I wish he'd speak English. The assistant chefs—Anthony and Victor—keep making faces. Anthony clowns around. "Sophia Loren . . . Monica Vitti . . . Rossano Brazzi . . ." Everyone thinks he's funny, but the stars are no laughing matter.

I put the plates down and start to scrape. One of the waiters comes rushing back. Ike and Tina Turner are at station four. I can't hardly believe it. Victor and Anthony want to know who Tina Turner is. They spend their lives listening to Mantovani and Liberace. I sing a few lines of Miss Turner's latest hit. It's number 64 on the charts, but rising:

> *"I'm a bad, bad woman—ooh*
> *And I need a bad, bad man . . ."*

Anthony and Victor—those mambo dancers—laugh at the song. Ignorance is bliss.

I can see the party of seven through the window of the kitchen door. Six men and Miss Turner. Ike's hair is very smooth and shiny. You can tell he's the leader. The others have the same style clothes, but he's the only one in green. Their hair is matted and high like the guys who hang out and harmonize around my house on 102nd Street. But Ike and his friends are a team, not a gang.

Tina's wearing a pants suit. Except for Marlene Dietrich, Garcia almost never allows women in slacks into the restaurant. But nobody sasses Tina. She's got Garcia tipping his ten-gallon hat. He doesn't want an incident. Black people are getting angry. It's in all the papers. The Homestead never had these sit-ins or strikes. We've served blacks from the beginning—Sammy Davis, Jr., Harry Belafonte, Sidney Poitier, Roy Campanella. If Garcia insulted Tina, there's no telling what could happen. Demonstrations. Riots. And all because Garcia won't keep up with the times. But he's smiling at her. He's letting Ike twirl the six-shooter. On my block, blacks and Puerto Ricans don't get on this good.

Garcia's spurs jingle as he hurries back into the kitchen. He goes over to the Chef. Zambrozzi's pushing side orders onto the counter. His face is shiny with sweat.

"*Siete* fried chicken," Garcia says, holding up seven fingers.

Zambrozzi pretends not to hear.

"And home fries."

Zambrozzi throws his hat on the floor. "Veal *piccata*. Veal *parmigiana*. Veal *zingara*. I learn cooking since I was ten. I win prizes. I no change my menu for Carlo Ponti."

"*Cágate en tu madre.*"

"Zambrozzi's no short-order cook. Remember that, Garcia."

"They're up and coming in *Cashbox* this week. They bring business. Publicity. We can put their picture in the window."

"I no come here to work a hash house."

Garcia stares at Zambrozzi. I know that look. So does Zambrozzi. He picks up his chef's hat and mumbles something to his helpers. He returns back to the stove. Zambrozzi thinks he's an artist, but his cooking couldn't gross $212,000 in two weeks at the Dunes, the way Ike and

15

Tina did this Christmas. He may be the best cook in midtown Manhattan, but I don't see people waiting on line four hours to get into the restaurant. Ike and Tina earn whatever they ask for.

Garcia sees me by the door. "Get out there, Walsh. The Turners need bread and water. They got no napkins!"

Garcia slaps his hands at me. He thinks he's Desi Arnaz.

I take my pad out of the freezer and put it under the roll basket on my tray.

From the window, I see they're laughing. Ike holds out both hands—very flat, very straight. They all slap his palms. It's the best time for information. When the stars are relaxed, they talk freely. They don't notice you, you can hear what they say and write it down on the spot. I put their words on the back of their autograph. That makes it more valuable.

Ike's saying, "They got more bread than sense. This dude wants us to sign with Epic. We produce our own thing. They promote. We sing. Three hundred Gs, if you please."

Everything Ike says turns out poetry. "Do the deal! That's better than Janis Joplin on Columbia or Jimi Hendrix on Reprise."

"Whatchou say, boy?"

"I didn't say anything."

"Don't jive wit' us, baby."

"I think it's great, Ike. I think you're great. I love the custom-made guitar table in your living room. I wish you all the success in the world."

"Give us the bread and butter. And get lost."

"Would you sign my autograph book?"

"Man, not in our food. Dig it, Ike, that book's in our food."

I laugh back. I hold out my hands—very flat, very straight. They don't slap them.

"You messin' wit' the King and Queen of Soul, jim."

"I know. Could I have your autograph?"

One of Ike's sidekicks pushes up from the table. He

16

pokes me in the shoulder with his finger. "Get lost, motherfucker." My shoulder feels like there's a hole in it.

"I happen to be a fan of Miss Turner's. I know her whole story, Ike's too. Annie Mae Bullock, Brownsville, Tennessee. Ike Turner, Clarkson, Mississippi. Ike discovered her one night at a club where he was playing the organ. She was with her sister. The drummer handed the microphone to Tina's sister and asked her to sing. She wouldn't. Tina grabbed the mike and started to sing. Ike was shocked. After that he asked her to join the group. Listen to this—

> *"Thrill me*
> *Kill me*
> *Fill me*
> *With your love—uumh*
> *Your sweet love . . .*

"That's what Tina sang. It could've made the charts."

The man shoves me. My pad drops on the table. A glass of water spills on Miss Turner.

"Sheeit," she says.

Ike's friends try and mop it up. I'd stay and help, but I hear Garcia coming.

Garcia orders me into the pantry. He glares at me. His silences are worse than his noise.

"I tell the Boss . . ."

"But, Mr. Garcia . . ."

"Ass-wipe," he says. "Go to station twelve. I want Fosburg on four."

His mouth's full of gold teeth. His Sen-Sen breath makes my nose itch.

"I want to serve the Turners."

"Fosburg takes the Turners."

"He's only been here a week. He used to work at Nedick's. Station twelve's roller derby stars and theater parties. I've been here longer than you, Mr. Garcia. I know this place."

"Bite the bullet, Walsh."

17

He bangs the door open with the square toe of his boot and walks back to his post.

Black fingers on my shoulder.

I put my tray back on the stand. I hold it with both hands.

"Hey, baby, sorry for jivin' witchou. That flaky cowboy's a heavy trip."

"He says I'm not allowed to talk to customers."

"Eleven o'clock tonight. Fillmore East. It's on Tina."

A yellow ticket slides on my tray.

In the kitchen. Victor and Anthony are joking. They must've seen. Anthony puts two potatoes in his T-shirt. "Sign my spuds, bud," he says to me in a high voice. Anthony rubs against my shoulder with his potato chest.

> *"I'm a bad, bad Boogie*
> *And I need my big, bad Benny, man."*

"Hey, Benny, get much?" laughs Victor.

"Yes," I say and show them the ticket.

The good thing about subways is they run all night. It's too expensive to get to the Fillmore East by taxi—anyway, who do you see in a cab but yourself?

I took a cab once and asked the driver if he ever carried any big names. That driver was a real nut. He kept singing songs to himself—"Swinging Down the Lane," "I've Got the World on a String," "Chicago." After every song, he'd turn back to me and ask, "Don't you think I look like him?"

"Who?"

He put on a felt hat and tilted the brim over his forehead so he could hardly see. He kept showing me his profile while he drove, asking me to guess. It was dangerous. Finally, at a traffic light, he turned back and crooned with his hands held out like a dead fish. He looked like Mickey Mantle running to first base. He kept singing. He gave me clues. "F. S.," he said.

"I give up."

18

As we pulled up to my stop, he gave me a rough look. "Frank Sinatra, schmuck."

I didn't give him a tip.

"Don't you have anything for the driver?"

I took out my penknife and slashed his seats. I ran out of the cab down into the subway.

As Ziegfeld said, "Talent will out."

It's very quiet underneath the city at this hour. I can sing to myself and hear the echo. I can play the gum machines and read what's been written over the GET OUT OF VIETNAM stickers. I look good in my Mets cap, I've broken in the crown just right. Anthony and Victor think I could pass for Yogi Berra (as a catcher, not a coach). I'm short and heavy. I've got thick hands for the knuckleball. I'm not afraid of getting dirty or hurt—after all, I'm a New Yorker. When nobody's around, like tonight, I can put my face close to the mirror over the candy machine and practice how I'd coax Tom Seaver on the mound. I was in the bleachers while he was up and coming. I worked hard for his victories. "Fire it in there, Tom, big fella! How you chuck! Put some spaghetti on it, Tom baby—let it dangle!" He's got my sign. Here's the pitch. Strike three. The Mets are one closer to the pennant.

The crowd goes wild.

The doors of the subway slam shut.

"This is your subway car. Keep it clean. When you leave, take all papers with you. Over and out."

My only paper is my brown bag, and that's for the autograph book. I'm not leaving it anywhere.

"Thirty-fourth Street next stop. Pennsylvania Station. Madison Square Garden. Change for the QB and the F. Have a pleasant journey."

The door opens. A man with a wooden board for legs rolls himself into the car. He steers with his hands. There's only half of him left. He stops at each passenger and clanks his cup.

I pretend to be reading my paperbag. He won't go away. They should lock these types in the slammer. They

19

should keep them off the streets, make them work for a living.

"Change, mister."

I show him what I have in my pockets—two tokens and a ticket.

"Change."

"Seaver's going for number fourteen tomorrow. The miracle Mets. They're a sure bet for first."

He rattles his cup.

"Put your money on the Mets. At seven to one you could make thousands."

"May God have mercy on you," he says, and pushes his raft down the aisle. Ungrateful.

Out at Eighth Street. Cool air smelling of incense and onions. Crowded streets. I like uptown better—you meet a more mature class of person. Here they bump you. Kids mainly—weirdos dressed like Indians or Hunters or African Warriors or Buddhist types who look you in the eye and sing to you. None of them famous.

One Buddhist comes up to me. He holds out a sea-shell filled with calling cards. "Krishna consciousness," he says. "The Empire State of ecstasy. It works as advertised."

I take a card.

"It's like going to the top by elevator instead of the stairs. You hit the sublime in no time."

He dances away, singing.

I toss the card into the gutter. Nothing good comes easy.

The Fillmore East is no Winter Garden. The ushers are grown men with beards, not nice old ladies in white collars. They don't show you to your seat, they just point. They don't tip you off to the big names in the audience.

On Broadway you see women—at the Fillmore, girls of all ages. They won't behave. A program and a seat's not enough. They walk up and down the aisles in the darkness. They brush against you. They don't care. Their bosoms jiggle. Their nipples poke up like pug noses.

I'm fifth row on the aisle. It's safer sitting down.

An arm reaches over my shoulder. Warm breath and a bottle. "Have a swig, Benny."

"Moonstone. It's a public place."

"I can't handle that uptown hustle every day, man. Sypher wanted me to hang out at the Opera opening. He promised a fifty-fifty split. A lot of heavies—Leontyne Price, Nureyev, Leonard Bernstein, Rudolf Bing . . . I mean I can't take that shit, Benny. I mean it's the Age of Aquarius. I'm only collecting the ones in my orbit. I wanted the real juice tonight."

"Forget about Bernstein, he's always around."

"Don't get me wrong. You guys have taught me a lot. But there's a time to work and a time to play. Dig?"

"You'll never be big if you don't concentrate."

"A brandy high's the only thing for Tina. Smooth and sweet. Gets the buzz going."

"You can't drink in the theater."

"Belly up to the bar and have a few. It's party time."

He shoves the bottle at me. I push it away.

"Rock stars come and go, Moonstone. They're not stable. You can't put all your time into flash-in-the-pans."

"That's the beauty part, man. I dig change."

"You're crazy."

"Why are you here?"

"Tina gave me a ticket."

"Sure. Paul McCartney sent mine special delivery from Apple."

"McCartney's in New York, Moonstone."

"Where?"

"The Plaza."

"How do you know?"

"Read *Variety*. Europe to New York. Pay the fifty cents, it's worth it."

"The old time, Benny. There's got to be new rules. I mean it's so corny. I'm into people, not grosses."

"You gotta have the whole picture. They say the Beatles may split."

"Yeah, and Snow White snorts C. Don't be a downer, Benny. Tonight it's Tits 'n' Ass."

"Show some respect, Moonstone."

21

"If I was seventeen again, I wouldn't have dropped out."

"You're only twenty-four. The world's your oyster."

"I wouldn't have joined up with Uncle Sam. 'See the world,' my ass."

"At your age, you could do anything. I was still slaving in the composing room of the *Asbury Park Press* at twenty-four."

"I'd be a lead guitarist. The Feds would never find me underneath those groupies. One-night stands all over the country. I'd have money. A rep. Hard dope and fucking—what a life!"

"You couldn't be a star with that attitude."

"I'd be great. I got rhythm and I got blues."

The musicians take their time coming on stage. Don't they know people are waiting? They check the amplifiers.

"Tina's gonna grease your tracks, Benny. She likes to make you suffer. Know what I mean?"

Moonstone doesn't even know Tina. He keeps poking my shoulder until I turn around.

"Look at that!"

He doesn't have to point. The lady stands out like Mary Martin across a crowded room. She takes a seat a few rows behind us. She doesn't chew. She doesn't stomp the ground or clap for the show to begin. She's wearing a long red dress down to her ankles, a veil hangs from her hat. Her skin seems very white, her lips very red. Her nails and toes are painted the same color. She's got to be Broadway, maybe Hollywood. She's not reading the program but a book—a large one she rests on her lap. Hardback. Shiny pages.

"Where have I seen her? She's very Joan Crawford."

"Let's lay a drink on her. If she's here, she swings."

"She's somebody."

The band starts to warm up. Moonstone sits back in his seat. "There's only one woman," he says. "Wait for it."

"And now straight from a record-breaking five months in Las Vegas—the Ike and Tina Turner Revue."

I get comfortable. I push my knees against the back of the seat.

The Ikettes bounce into the light. White dresses with fringes wiggling with them. Legs like breadsticks.

"Easier than bangin' H, eh Benny?"

"Sssh!"

The Ikettes are going to sing golden goodies. The first's "Under the Boardwalk." Everybody applauds. I don't—just mentioning the beach makes me feel sand in my shoes. The Ikettes sing about warm nights and love—but that's only three months of the year. Somebody should tell them about the rest. Booths boarded up. Wind too strong for sand castles. Old folks talking to their dogs. Pee dripping through the cracks, stinking up the sand. No radios, no kids . . . just Ma by the pavilion at five yelling for me to come home.

"Twist and Shout" is next. The minute they say "shout" I picture Garcia, or Mom by the staircase telling me I forgot to flush. But the Ikettes make screaming fun. They are loose, not tight. Their hair falls in front of their faces, their hands flap like wings. They get carried away, but not at you. I feel like laughing.

"Just a cocktease," says Moonstone.

It's no time for conversation. The Ikettes are sliding sideways—knees high, hands waving as if they held spears. "Who can do the Tinaroo?" They keep singing the question over and over. Of course they can't do it—they're not Tina.

Tina jumps out from the wings. She does the dance. The Ikettes can't touch her. It's dangerous. Tina could hurt herself.

She grabs the microphone. "Hi, everybody!"

"I'm here, Tina. I'm here. Slip it to me—I need it!"

"Sit down, Moonstone!"

"C'mon, you can do better than that. I'm gonna yell it one more time—Hi, everybody!"

"Hi, Tina."

She remembers me.

She says, "We don't do nothin' nice 'n' easy—we do things nice 'n' rough."

The lights go down. You can hardly see the Ikettes bopping behind her. She's in a purple glow. She sings about being a honky-tonk woman and how she needs a honky-tonk man. First she looks at Ike, then at us. It hasn't made the charts yet, but when you're with Tina everything feels like a smash.

Tina gurgles into the microphone, "Shuggabugga. Shuggabugga."

I swear I used to say those words to myself in the dark. She whispers, "What you hear is what you get."

I can hear her nylons scrape the microphone. They're silver. They sparkle as she sings. Her knees nudge the long stand. Her legs are all muscle. They bulge. They shine. Everything's tight and fresh. If she were a steak, she'd be too tough to chew.

I put my cap in my lap.

The lights are way down. It's better to shut your eyes and imagine Tina.

She says, "Now, I'm gonna be serious. I'm gonna sing this for the men."

Everybody's very quiet.

Tina says, "I want you to give it to me . . ."

Ike says, "Oooh, shit baby . . ."

I have to see this. Flat palms working their way up the head of the mike. She never touches it. Just her sharp nails and long fingers. Her hands seem to be singing.

Tina is

> a pony
> a panther
> a Cadillac convertible.

She is standing bowlegged, singing—

> *"I wanna take you higher*
> *Higher*
> *Higher*
> *Higher . . ."*

She does her sidestep. She's bucking. The strobe lights start to click. Tina turns silver. You have to squint to see her. A cloud of smoke bursts from the floor.

24

"TINA TURNER! TINA TURNER! TINA TURNER! TINA TURNER! TINA TURNER! TINA TURNER!"

When the voice stops, the smoke has cleared.

Tina has vanished.

"Outtasight," says Moonstone.

The audience's standing on their seats, yelling for Tina, asking for more.

This is the way it should be with the stars. You should see them. Then they should disappear.

Moonstone's on home ground. He knows a shortcut. He leads me through a small room by the side of the stage and onto the street.

I can see Ike and Tina's bus. The crowd presses close to it. One man stands on the bus's fender, holding onto the rearview mirror for balance.

We angle in toward the stage door. Moonstone's good at running interference. He talks right into people's faces. "Did you see Bob Dylan? On the corner. Bob Fucking Dylan."

People turn, standing on tiptoes to get a look.

We slip closer to the door.

The Fillmore stage door doesn't have your bronze Broadway polish or the lettering. It's black and rusting. The Fillmore door slides open, the Broadway stage doors open out. It's more dramatic. You see the iron staircases. You hear the vibrations of the stars hurrying down on their way to Sardi's. The doorman's at his table—the bulletin board with telegrams saying BREAK A LEG is right under your nose. The Fillmore's a letdown. There's nothing to see backstage—no sets, no stars. The stage managers are as hairy as the musicians. Sometimes the door slides open and a familiar face peeps out. The crowd pushes forward. The face disappears. Rock stars spend too much time in recording studios, they don't know how to treat their public.

Moonstone puts his head against the door and talks through a small crack. "A cat here wants Tina to do a riff on his pad for auld lang syne."

"Tina's not seeing anybody."

25

"She brought him down here. His maiden voyage. Noonan sent me."

Moonstone waves me close. He takes my pen and pad and pushes it through the door. "Benny Walsh."

"Is he a relation?"

Moonstone starts to tell a lie. I stop him.

"Just sing this to her—Kill me. Thrill me. Chill me with your sweet love . . ."

The door clamps shut.

"Tell her to say 'To Benny.' "

The bolt thumps down on the latch.

"Didn't you want one, Moonstone?"

"I'm on vacation."

After a few minutes, the door opens again.

"Make way." A Hell's Angel type waves the people back. He's got my pen and pad in his hand. Moonstone grabs them back. He's learning fast.

Suddenly, a whole wedge of bodies, a human wall, rushes out of the door. Ike and Tina in the middle. "Clear the way!"

The people won't budge. They fight to keep their places. It's hard to get a look. I see a hand reach out over the guards' leather jackets and grab at Ike's tie. There seems to be a fight. Somebody's hooting, waving Tina's scarf in the air. He shoves it into his blue jeans.

"Sypher has green fringe from Little Richard's bolero jacket. He's a hot shit."

"Get wise, Moonstone. That stuff's worthless. I mean you can't prove it's his."

The lights on the bus go on. The engine turns over. The man on the front fender won't get off. He's staring right over the windshield wipers at Tina. His pants slap against the flat front of the bus. He's leading the crowd. They yell, "WE WANT TINA." The crowd rocks the bus. The driver honks his horn until the man jumps off the fender. The bus creeps down the street.

They follow it.

Both of us hear the scream. *My book! Somebody help!*

The crowd's a forest of elbows and ankles. Then I see

26

her—Moonstone's well-dressed lady—on her hands and knees. She can't get her balance. Feet ram the book and kick it aside. It slides under the fire escape by the ash cans.

"Let's get out of here," says Moonstone.

"Wait a minute."

"Haven't you ever been in a riot? Keep on the outside of the crowd."

I work my way over to the ash cans.

"Wanna get trampled, Benny?"

I pick up the book. I push into the crowd and help the lady up.

"Thank God you found it," she says. "Are the pages dirty?"

"They stepped on it."

"Thirteen eighty-five for a *Players' Guide*. Five hundred and twenty-four pages, five pictures to a page. Why won't they stop pushing?"

"C'mon, Walsh!"

"No upbringing. They treat you like Bette Davis," she says, looking at her broken shoe. *"You're all pigs.* Not you."

"Are you all right, ma'am?"

"All right? Of course, I'm all right. Don't I look all right?"

"The crowd's murder."

"Look at my hands—they're scraped. And my nail! Ecch. Don't look at me."

"I saw you at the concert."

"These people act like animals."

"Let's get across the street."

She holds the book to her chest. I step in front of her to lead the way. "Don't look at me," she says. "I'm not composed. I'm a mess."

I put her book on the hood of a '68 GTO called "The Eliminator."

She leans against the car and buckles her shoe. "The only Joan Crawford 'Chase Me' shoes in New York. Took a month to find them. Three-inch heels. Open toe. None of these imitation fat heels. Stiletto, see. The real thing."

27

"They don't pay much attention in a rough crowd like that."

"You'd think they'd show some respect. Where have you seen platform shoes, cinch belts, padded shoulders, real silk stockings?"

"In the movies."

"I've been wearing these kind of clothes fifteen years. Boutiques are just catching up with my style. Are my seams straight now?"

"Yes, ma'am. Very Joan Crawford."

"You've got a better eye than your friend. That's because you're older. You've been around."

"C'mon, Benny, let's split."

"I know your type—Bette Davis fans. You applaud when she walks out on Leslie Howard in *Of Human Bondage*. So what if he had a club foot? Leslie Howard would've made an excellent husband. He was kind and talented. He had the bedside manner. The minute he looked down Bette's throat, Leslie knew it was her lungs."

Moonstone pulls me aside. "Benny, this broad's a bomb."

"I heard that."

"He's just a kid, lady. He don't know how to act around grown-ups."

"What's your name, Mr. Know-It-All?"

"Moonstone."

"Mr. Moonstone, what do you do in case of an atomic conflict?"

"You gotta be kidding, lady."

"One. Never look at the sight of the blast. Two. Turn your head away from the shock wave. Three. Get as close to the ground as possible. Four. Cover your head to avoid debris."

"Can we split now?"

"The number-one rule of safety, and he doesn't know it."

"Who cares?"

I give Moonstone the elbow. He's been hanging out with Sypher too much. You don't talk back to performers. You listen.

"The new actors have a method. They get background for their parts."

"Do you play nurses or something?"

"Is there any place around here where a girl can make herself pretty?"

"I'm new down here, too."

"First time?"

"It was worth it for Tina's autograph."

"You got it?" she says.

"Uh-huh." I show her the name.

"For your information, that's Benny Walsh. He has more autographs than anybody in New York. He's the Motown of signatures."

"Really?"

Moonstone whispers, "She's jeffing us, Benny. If she's in movies, what's she doin' waiting for Tina to sign?"

"Lady, if you're in movies, what were you doing getting Tina's autograph?"

"Part of my research. I study film types. Tina just finished her third movie."

"What movies have I seen you in?"

"I'm working my way up."

"That's the only way. Color or black and white?"

"The works—close-ups, middle-long shot, take four."

"I'm sorry, miss," says Moonstone. "There's a mirror at the luncheonette around the corner."

"I've been an actress nearly five years. I also sing. I'm not boring you, am I?"

"My name's Benny Walsh."

"I'm Gloria."

We shake on it.

Moonstone leans across the linoleum tabletop. "Take it, Benny. Go on. It's gossamer tip. The best."

"Are you crazy? She'll be out of the Ladies any second."

"I'm telling you she's hot to trot. She's wide open."

"You said you were sorry."

"Starlets, man. They get to the top on their backs. That's the rules."

The soda jerk brings our orders. Moonstone gets the

29

banana split. I'm the egg cream. The BLT on diet bread, butter not margarine, is for her.

Gloria arrives back in time. Her perfume makes it hard to smell the egg cream.

"May we start?" says Moonstone.

"Well . . . how do I look?"

"Very nice."

"Is it an improvement?"

"The tricks of the trade, right?" Moonstone says, kicking me.

"I pencil under the iris. The black line is what gave Joan's eyes their size. She never had an operation, she was just a master of makeup. You'll notice I have real eyebrows, too. You can take this penciling too far. I'm not falling into the same trap as Lana Turner when she shaved them off for *Marco Polo* and they never grew back."

"You mean Lana's not all there?" says Moonstone.

Gloria's cheeks are so rouged it's hard to tell if she's blushing. She looks down at her food.

"What he meant was—it must be very tough breaking into movies."

"You've got to be very, very careful. Don't overeat. Don't undereat. Don't use water on your skin. Don't wear unmatched colors. Don't use bad grammar. Don't be bad mannered. Don't forget to brush your hair seventy times a night before going to bed."

"Seventy?" says Moonstone.

"It's a beauty tip," says Gloria.

"Well, it works."

Gloria smiles at me.

"What are you waiting for?" she says. "Eat."

Moonstone makes a mess. He uses his spoon like an oar. He stirs everything up. "I'm into color," he says. Whipped cream drops on his pants. "I'm creaming." He laughs and digs back in.

"Other people are eating, you know."

"He's trying to be the life of the party."

"I've lost my appetite," Gloria says, pushing her plate away.

Gloria stares past me. She reminds me of Mom waiting for me to finish dinner, tapping the Lucky Strike song on the table while I chew each piece of meat twelve times. "You wanna talk, Ma?" "Sure." "What'll we talk about?" "Anything." "You start." "You asked first," she'd say and cross her arms, waiting. Finally, I discovered how to break the ice. I'd slap my face like Milton Berle—a real hit. "I sweah I'w kiw you. I'w kiw you a miwion times." I even picked my teeth with my pinky. Mom would start to laugh. Each time I'd hit myself, she'd laugh harder. "The fourth Ritz Brother!" she'd wheeze. It was great—the two of us entertaining ourselves like friends. Sometimes she'd get up, and hurry into the other room. When she came back, she'd say "Whaddya want, Ben?" "I dunno." *"Makeup!"* she'd scream, and whack me with a fluffy powder puff. A white cloud would hang all around me. I could taste the powder in my teeth. She'd shake with laughter (this was before she started shaking for real). "My son the actor," she'd say, and pat my head.

But Gloria's too New York for slapstick.

"So long," says Moonstone, slapping something flat and rubbery in my hand as he slips out of the booth. "It's for your tip."

Moonstone puts on his sunglasses and bows to Gloria.

"Good riddance to bad trash," she says.

At the door, Moonstone turns. "Sticks and stones."

The waiter puts the check in the middle of the table. Gloria acts like she doesn't see it. The check flops off the table. I pick it up and put it back.

"I hope you're not insulted?"

"I'm not frowning, am I? Do you see any wrinkles?"

"Or upset?"

"In my business, you do your crying in the dressing room. Once you walk out that door, you show nothing. You hold it in. Nobody wants an emotional actress."

"It's this kind of thing I'm after. I'll file it under Miscellaneous."

"But *I* told it to you."

"I'll keep it on a card for when you're famous."

"I've got you pegged. The Don Ameche. First, you get a girl to tell you everything. You give her the bum's rush

—flattery, promises, the whole thing. Then you take advantage."

"Your information's safe with me. I got two thousand, three hundred and seventy-six autographs, five hundred and fifty-two doubles. All locked tight in my apartment."

"Really?"

"Someday my collection will be famous."

"All you do is collect women."

"And men, too."

"I don't wish to know about that."

"What's it like being under the lights?"

"No comment."

Gloria pushes the check over to me.

I push it back.

"Don't be fresh," she says.

"I thought you were treating."

"Who said?"

"You're the one in the movies. You're the one with a *Players' Guide* instead of a pad."

"Moonstone gave you money. I saw him."

"No, he didn't." I drop Moonstone's present and put my sneaker over it. I hold out my hands to prove nothing's in them.

Gloria pulls the veil down from her hat. "A lady's not supposed to pay for herself. That's the man's job. And, for your information, the lady's not supposed to even see the check. I don't want to see it."

"Well, it's two dollars and five cents."

"Money doesn't grow on trees, you know."

"But you're so well dressed."

"I have to shop very carefully. In show business, you've got to save for the dry periods."

"Give me your address. I'll send you my share."

"I should never talk to strangers."

She takes the money out of her purse and hands it to me under the table.

"You pay," she says.

The soda jerk comes from behind the counter to collect. He won't go away.

"What about a tip, Gloria?"

She puts more change on the table. She shakes her head. "The way you start with a man's the way you end."

"Is that another movie saying?"

"Forget it," she says, handing me her overcoat.

Gloria stops and stares at every ad on the subway platform. With me she's quiet as a tomb—but a picture of a Motorola television console gets her talking. "Isn't it lovely," she says. She stands back like Chef from his pastry, then moves slowly forward for careful inspection until the next ad catches her eye. "I'm old-fashioned about clothes, but very modern when it comes to appliances."

Gloria has the makings of a first-rate collector. She wants to acquire. It's the tip-off to talent. She looks presentable. She doesn't beat around the bush. She gives as much as she takes. In fact, she's got three out of Coach Lombardi's Big Four—Determination, Energy, and the Will to Win. But she's crude—no Discipline.

"You should work harder on your autographs. You could be good."

"My goal is to complete my *Players' Guide*."

"But that's just for actors. Don't you want to widen your horizons?"

"I want to study film people. Not everyone can get a *Players' Guide*. You've got to qualify."

"How did you get it?"

"I got it."

"The Academy Award winners—the envelope performers—aren't in the book. They don't need to remind people what they look like. Everybody remembers."

"You're trying to make me wrong."

"Look around, Gloria. People who never went to Hollywood are getting bigger all the time."

"The *Players' Guide*'s a very important publication in our business."

"The *Players' Guide* weighs five pounds. It's a drag."

"I think Amy Vanderbilt knows a little more about autographs than you."

"Does she have over two thousand signatures?"

"Amy Vanderbilt's influenced thousands of America's

finest families. She wrote a book. Daddy gave it to me. 'Do as she says, not as we do.' "

"Does she talk about her big signatures?"

"She's no collector."

"Then, what does *she* know?"

" 'Autographs given freely to all and sundry have no value either historically or momentarily. The rare ones are the good ones. To ask a really important person to sign an autograph book full of names of nobodies is to insult him.' Amy Vanderbilt."

"If they're insulted, they won't sign. They usually sign."

"Feel this paper—High Gloss. Look at the type—Bodoni Bold. The *Players' Guide* is heavier than the complete works of William Shakespeare."

"Too many pictures."

"Every face belongs to Equity. You're not being rude if you ask an actor to sign."

"No room for comments."

"Who gives comments?"

"Mickey Mantle."

"Who's he?"

"Number seven. They retired the number for life when he hung up his spikes. He was a New York Yankee. He's a millionaire now. Insurance. He's hard to get. Even in the old days, he'd sit in the locker room and only sign baseballs. Nothing on paper. He signed my pad, 'Keep smiling, Mickey.' "

"He said that?"

"You never know when somebody's going to become rare. This Vanderbilt doesn't even know. Suddenly they can retire or be killed, lose their show or go to jail. There's so much happening. Opportunity only knocks once."

"You mean a strike-while-the-iron's-hot technique."

"Right."

"Aren't you embarrassed to hand somebody a scrap of paper when they've just stepped out of a Cadillac limousine, when they say Tiffany all over them. There's such a thing as self-respect. Paper might be okay for a ballplayer, but a movie star with a long-term contract or a hit commercial? You'd be a laughingstock."

"Would you believe Nanette Fabray, Yvonne De Carlo, Mrs. Bing Crosby?"

The subway screeches to a stop. Gloria and I step in. Gloria takes a newspaper from the seat and dusts off a place for herself. The headline says—

CONTINENTAL DRIFT CARRIES
STATES FARTHER FROM EUROPE

We don't talk. We look at the ads. These are the ones I like, faces you can depend on.

"Arthur Godfrey. Got him. Buddy Hackett. Got him. The Ronzoni Brothers, including the three not pictured—got them."

Gloria smiles. "You think I'd be good?"

Shubert Alley's like home plate, the first and last spot an autograph collector touches every day. But Gloria isn't paying attention.

"Just go up to them and say, 'Are you famous?' "

"Benny, let me take the *Guide*. I can't ask somebody I don't know."

"Try it anyway."

"No. It's not right."

"We made a bet. It's the test."

"In auditions, you're allowed to hold the book."

"Don't worry. You look very nice."

"What if they're not actors?"

"Are you kidding? That's Sardi's."

"I'm not used to hanging around in alleys."

"It happens to be a city landmark. By law, nobody can build over it—ever. I'll wait here."

"I don't get anything out of this bet. If I lose, you don't pay for the ice cream and soda. If I win, all I get is autographs I don't know and a 'surprise.' "

"You said you wanted to be good."

"How do I know you won't take my *Guide*?"

"Would I want someone else's signatures?"

Gloria starts toward Sardi's. She turns around.

"Are my seams straight?"

"Go ahead."

It feels nice leaning against the rave reviews. Gloria's not interested in history, but our crowd's had some good times here—the greatest shortcut in Manhattan. Shubert Alley's where Sypher got Greta Garbo, and I hit for Orson Welles, Bea Lillie, and Buffalo Bob Smith. The wind can really work itself up in the winter. But it's not as bad as Dustin Hoffman made it out to be in *Midnight Cowboy*— that was Hollywood.

Horn & Hardart's is around the corner, but once in a while it's fun to camp out. Sometimes the construction workers leave a steel drum lying around. Moonstone and Sypher tip it up and fill it with paper. *The New York Times* is across the street, and leftover Sunday supplements burn like birch bark. We get a pretty good fire going. We take turns keeping watch—one person at each end of the alley. That way, on 44th Street we cover Sardi's, the Playbill Bar and Grill, and the Royal Manhattan, and on 45th Street the Piccadilly, the Theatre Bar, and the Scandia. The stories they tell around the fire! Somebody should write them up, like the time we roasted marshmallows on the aerial from George Hamilton's Mercedes 300SL.

Gloria hurries across the street. "I got Janice Rule and Ben Gazzara quicker than you could say Jackie Robinson. I'm fainting."

"They're husband and wife."

"Ben Gazzara was Channel Four. I watched him all the time. The doctor told him he'd only one year to live, so he runs for his life all over the world."

"The show's Neilson rating was nineteen point one in 'sixty-five. It dropped to eleven point five in 'sixty-eight."

"He lives it up before it's too late. Can he dance!"

"I've never watched the show."

"What's my surprise present?" says Gloria.

Somebody's yelling at us from across the street.

"You got my Ben! Give me my Ben!"

It's Della. She's hobbling towards us. She's a disgrace. She's dressed like a shadow—black shawl, black gloves, black hairnet, black skirt, black sneakers.

"I'm scared, Benny."

"Relax, Gloria. Hunchbacks can't hurt you."

Della's got the guts of a bandit. She comes right up to us. Even her teeth are black.

"Don't pretend I'm not here. I'm here. I saw. Ben was one of my first before the robbery. And Janice. She was just off the train from Cinci. Now they won't look my way. They don't remember. Please, lady—you're young—spare a Gazzara."

"Get lost, Della."

"Benny, I'll give her—"

"Stay out of this."

"George Segal was in The Homestead tonight," Della says. "Mr. Sypher told me. He said you'd struck it big lately. He said you'd have something for me."

"You never learn, Della. Anybody stupid enough to carry their autographs around with them deserves what they get."

"I've turned over a new leaf, Benny." She lifts up two bags. "See? Alexander's Plastic. They're tied to my wrists with rope. No jigaboo's gonna steal them this time."

"Charity begins at home, Della. Do yourself a favor. Scram."

"I reported everything to the Precinct. I gave them my list. I just need some signatures to tide me over. I've got so many to catch up."

"That's the way the cookie crumbles."

"I know you've got extras, Benny. Have a heart."

"It's not the size of the dog in the fight, Della. It's the size of the fight in the dog."

"You've all got your noses up the devil's ass."

Della walks away.

"You're tough," says Gloria.

"You're as good as what you earn."

The room's just the way I left it. Shade pulled almost to the bottom of the window by the fire escape so burglars can see my Protecto-grate. Pan still soaking off the scrambled egg in the sink. *Variety* opened at "Legit Bits" on the bed. It's all the same. Only the clock has changed from when I left for work. It was 10:05 in the morning. Now it's nearly 1:30.

"Benny, there's bugs in the hallway."

37

"Just a second, Gloria. I'm not letting you in until everything's just right."

"A deal's a deal."

" 'Cleanliness is next to godliness.' You're the one who said it."

"No funny business. I'm no chippie. I earned my surprise. And I happen to have Guardian in my pocketbook, for your information."

I take the keys out of the seashell on the dresser. I open the grating locks and push the grate back. I roll up the shade. The moon's over the playground. The dust on the windows gives it a nice misty look. I stack the magazines on their piles. I smooth the green felt on my autograph table. I unlock my files.

"The instructions say . . . Benny? Can you hear me?"

"I'm sticking a picture back on the wall."

"You're very quiet in there."

"Gloria, would you mind taking your 'Chase Me' shoes off? The heels are very sharp . . ."

"The instruction says—'Immediately renders attacker harmless when sprayed directly into the face of assailant. Also sprays identifying dye for police identification.' So keep your distance."

I put out the file trays so Gloria can see how tightly packed and colorful they are. The index cards are straight as soldiers. No dog-ears in the bunch. I hide the key back in the shell and put Mom's letter under it, along with her others.

"It's very rude, Benny. The girl's supposed to go into a room before the man."

I stand back in the corner by the TV for one last look. The room isn't much. Nobody'd pay to see it like I did to walk through Truman Capote's. Of course, Capote makes fourteen cents a word. But someday these autographs will be worth a fortune. Maybe a million dollars. Sometimes, I sit in my easy chair thinking about the value. I can almost feel it growing. Then I get nervous and stop thinking. Where could I get a room twenty-five sneakers by fifty-two sneakers for the same rent?

I open the door. "Make yourself at home."

After all her complaining, Gloria won't come in right away. She stands in the doorway and looks around.

"Did you do this by yourself?"

"With a stepladder."

"This should be in a magazine."

"Why waste space is what I say."

"How did you get all these pictures on the ceiling?"

"Tape. Glue makes them bumpy. Anyway, Mrs. Berado won't permit glue on the walls. Says it pulls down the plaster."

"How many do you have up there?"

"I guess about two hundred and thirty-seven."

Gloria walks right by me with her head in the air. "You could spend hours just looking at the ceiling."

"Days."

"That's Virginia Mayo. And, let's see, Ida Lupino—she was great—Spring Byington, Stu Erwin, Ricky Nelson with Ozzie and Harriet right next to him. Look at Lana's angora sweater! That's the one she was discovered in. There's Huntley and Brinkley. Who's that?"

"Mayor Daley of Chicago."

"How'd you get him?"

"Just wrote. He sent a picture."

"No kidding."

"Cross my heart and hope to die."

"Some of these pictures are very old."

"With the lights on, the glossies sort of glow. They look fresh."

My movie wall's the next to catch Gloria's eye. All these pictures are large and out of the ordinary. Some have been blown up from snapshots, others are taken straight from the Broadway billboards. Bogie, Marilyn, Marlon, Joan, Sandy, Marlene, Rita, Bea, to name a few.

"Why did you put Joan and Rita together?" Gloria says.

"Don't you like Rita?"

"She doesn't have Joan's cheekbones, the architecture. Joan never posed suggestive."

"It's a very famous picture of Rita—kneeling in her nightie on the silk sheets Ali Khan gave her."

39

"Go without a bra, let your hair down, wear scanties—and the men sniff around."

"Maybe you'd like my political wall better. Everybody's well dressed. Not a girl in the bunch."

Gloria stops at my dresser. "Who's that?"

"The picture's not in my collection. It doesn't count."

"That's a beautiful upsweep."

"I got a great picture of LBJ and his scar. Someday it will be very valuable. You never see the personal side of Presidents."

"I know—it's Bonnie and Clyde."

"There was a big fuss over this picture. It was sad. Everybody's got scars—I do. I went to the penny arcade and had a picture of mine taken. I sent it to the President. Misery loves company."

"You've got underworld connections?"

"That's Mom and Uncle Mort. It was taken by a professional photographer. I was just a kid."

"He didn't even tell them to take the cigarettes out of their mouths."

"Uncle Mort paid for Mom's three Bluestreak Sixty-Five hair driers and the electric nail buffer. Mom's first job was Uncle Mort's hands."

"With your memory, you don't need a picture," says Gloria.

"Mom made me put it up. She's always asking, 'Where am I?' You've got to have an answer. The dresser's the highest spot in the room."

"You're a grown man, Benny. You don't have to do anything you don't want."

"It's in honor of the years she's worked her fingers to the bone for me."

"Notice my half-moons." Gloria holds up her hands.

"You missed a few spots with the nailbrush."

"Those are the moons, stupid. Didn't your Mom teach you anything?"

"She was very busy. The hair driers were always warm when I came home. I didn't see her much. But we had some good times—we watched TV together—walked on the boardwalk to Bradley Beach. She'd try and step on my shadow and I'd try to get hers."

40

"I'd better be going. I've got an early call."

"Just a few more minutes, okay? What do you think of my sports wall? I invented it myself."

"I don't know what to say."

"I'm flattered. I worked a long time getting the right people, whittling it down. Ty Cobb, Crazy Legs Hirsch, Jolting Joe . . ."

"But it's just names and numbers."

"That's right. That's the way it's supposed to be."

"You just painted a lot of numbers on the wall. It looks messy, if you ask me. Photos'd go with the rest of the room."

"Read the sign on the wall. I got it from Red Barber on the radio."

" 'Eternal vigilance is the price for accuracy in statistics.' "

"It helps with autographs, too."

"I still don't get it, Benny."

"If you had pictures of all these athletes, you'd only have them on one of their many good days, against one opponent. But they all had great careers. Statistics help remember them in action. Nobody can think of Willie Mays's face or Bob Feller's. They're not like movie stars, you don't see them close up. Bob Cousy looks like a businessman, Casey Stengel could be a cabdriver. What's great is how much these guys have produced. That's all in the numbers. Statistics are certified true. Look where it says DiMaggio. Under it, I've got 'fifty-six.' That was 1941, but Joe's consecutive hits are as clear as yesterday. Clearer than that. His front spike up, his elbow high, lots of space between his bat and his neck. No hitch. And then, even without wanting to think about them, the two batting championship years before that, .381 in 1939, .352 in 1940, are right on the tip of your brain. And it's all on my wall."

"I don't see it."

"You've got to concentrate. People don't just become successful overnight. That's a lot of baloney."

"Millie Perkins in *Diary of Anne Frank*. Sue Lyon in *Lolita*. Julie Andrews in *The Boyfriend* . . ."

41

"You've got to improve yourself. I developed this system. My autographs are revolutionized."

"You think a lot of yourself."

"I think a lot of my autographs."

" 'The more important the person, the more inconspicuous.' Emily Post."

"She can't be a star."

"She's an expert."

"There's a difference."

"I really have to go," says Gloria, lifting a compact from her purse and doing her lips. She takes a Kleenex and blots them. There's a print of her whole mouth. " 'Paint the Town Pink' by Revlon."

"I'm trying to show you my collection, Gloria. The files are open. You haven't even noticed. That's one of the first rules. Be alert."

I hold out my chair for her to sit down. I turn on the table lamp. The felt's as green as dollar bills.

"What's new about file cards?" she says.

"What's on them makes them new."

"New York's full of people with big ideas . . ."

"Autographs are one of the best things about New York. They're not ideas, they're for real."

"Philosophicals confuse me," Gloria says.

"There are more signatures per square block in New York than in any other city. If you were in L.A., you'd need a car. Here, everybody's outside your door, waiting to be asked."

"New York's a very tough town, Benny. If you went to more movies you'd see that. Everybody knows it. New Yorkers just pass you by."

"You sound like my mother. She said Benny stick to the linotype, collect the pension. She said stay at home, summers we can play shuffleboard. She sure tried to make it sound good. But at the *Press* I was indoors most of the day reading about all the big names. In New York, you can go up to anybody, any hour of the day. They're everywhere. I haven't had a dull moment since I checked my bags at Port Authority in 'sixty. Autographs really keep you hopping."

"Ever heard the song, 'A New Town Is a Blue Town'?"

"Don't believe it, Gloria. That was written in 1954. In 1945 they were singing 'New York, New York, It's a Helluva Town.' You should have respect for old age."

"There's too much to remember, too many autographs to get. I have my work. I couldn't organize. I couldn't keep up."

"You could do it."

"I'm too set in my ways."

"First, get rid of the *Players' Guide*. It slows you down. You can't wedge or two-pad with it. Hang out with the Horn and Hardart crowd. Their sloppy seconds are as important as most people's firsts. Read, read, read. That's my straight-from-the-shoulder advice. Actresses have to be up-to-date. They've got to know things. It's a good way."

"I'm not the mental type."

"There's nothing to it. I cut the autograph out of my book. I glue it to the white side of the index card, leaving enough room around the edges so no glue touches the ink. On the back, I list the important facts. Marriages. Divorces. Accomplishments. Awards. Any conversations. When they die, I switch them to the brown file marked DEAD."

I picked a grade-A out of the file. Gloria comes close to have a look.

BOB HOPE (Leslie Townes Hope) BORN: England, 1904. EDUCATION: High School (me too). FIRST B'WAY APPEARANCE: *Ballyhoo*, 1932. FILMS INCLUDE: *Road to Zanzibar, Road to Singapore, Road to Rio, Road to Hong Kong, Road to Utopia, Caught in the Draft, Call Me Bwana.* AWARDS: U.S. Congressional Medal, 1963. REMARKS (To me at The Homestead): "Laugh and the world laughs with you." Jan. 4, 1965. Me: "Do you have the time?" Mr. Hope: "Time to get a watch." Feb. 2, 1968.

Gloria can't take her eyes off the autograph.

"Take a card. Any card."

I turn my back and put my hands over my eyes. "I'm absolutely not looking. I'm blind as a bat. There's no way

I can see what you've picked. Don't bend the card, please."

"Okay," says Gloria.

"Now read me any fact on the back of the card. You don't have to read the first one. Begin anywhere."

" 'Membership: 1,651,240.' "

"Jimmy Hoffa."

"That's right!"

"I got him at the Copa."

"Who's he?"

"The head of the biggest union in the United States."

"How did you know who he was?"

"There's a lot of luck in this business. I thought I was getting Ernest Borgnine."

"Can I try another? Don't look."

I can hear Gloria fingering the cards for a hard one.

"Take from any file cabinet. I think I can guess from all three. I study them after work. I add conversations to the back even if I already have the autograph."

" 'Forty—nineteen—thirty-five and a half.' "

"That could be anybody."

"You'll never get this one, Benny."

"I think I've got it."

I take a pad and write an impersonation of the auto-graph. I fold it over. "The person whose card you're holding is Vera Jane Palmieri."

"Wrong. You missed it. You really flubbed this one!"

I open the piece of paper and show her my Jayne Mansfield.

"Fantastic! You were just fooling about Vera Jane."

"That was Miss Mansfield's first name."

"It's unbelievable."

"That was a tough one. I wasn't expecting someone from the dead file."

"Your mind's a trap."

"I've trained it for autographs. Sometimes I forget my own apartment number, walk right past it. But figures of the performers are gummed into my skull . . ."

Gloria wants me to do some more. I don't want to. After spending so much time with entertainers, some of their secrets sink in—get on, get your laugh, and get off.

44

As a favor, I tell her to take two cards and read me the names. David Merrick and Wayne Newton are her picks. I do the Merrick with short, broad lines. I keep the letters crammed tight together. I take my time, but try to make it look like I'm in a terrible hurry.

"Tadah! David Merrick at your service." I put my impersonation next to the real thing.

"That's interesting," she says.

"Interesting! That's a perfect imitation."

"Mr. Merrick's signature slants to the left. Yours is all the way to the right."

"You're a tough critic. My Wayne Newton will surprise you."

"I've really got to go, Benny. It's been nice making your acquaintance."

"Wayne Newton coming up. Please?"

The trick to Wayne Newton is to remember he's a singer and he's short. Like most smallies in the business, he signs very large and swirly. I use a ball-point pen for this one. The pen skates along the paper.

"Don't ask me, Benny."

"It's a dead ringer."

"Flattery gets you nowhere."

"I've been doing him for years. Let me try another."

Gloria buckles on her "Chase Me" shoes. She stands up tall as Cyd Charisse, and walks to the door. "Thank you for a nice evening."

I pull out another card. "It's not over."

"I said I'm not playing."

"I got this at the Pepsi-Cola Convention. I knew she'd be there. She's on the Board. I have triples. This one's yours."

She looks at the Joan Crawford for a long time. This is the part I hate—the happy ending. She takes my hand and holds it to her cheek.

The door clicks shut. No "thank you." Nothing.

I sit on the edge of my bed. I sniff the perfume off the back of my hand the way I used to smell glue. I'm dozy.

I lock up the collection for the night. I turn on the television. Abbott and Costello. I turn it off.

Should I curl up in the chair or take the bed? I remember Mom's letter. I'll take the bed.

Benny:
Your last two letters have been about these muscle-boy football players. There must be more news of the big city. Are you a faggot?
Keep well. All love.

                                        Francine/Mom
P.S. Good contacts are good business.

I turn out the lights. I put the shell to my ear. Soon I can hear Ocean Beach and my eyes get very heavy.

THE MORNING NEWS hasn't been the same since Jack Lescoulie retired. At 7:30—the TV's saying that it's Monday, that Hollywood's dying, that theater attendance's falling off, that the air's killing us, that the Mets lost. That's hooey. I've talked to thousands of healthy, happy people. I've got autographs to prove it. Americans take the word of one man sitting behind a desk who hasn't even seen what he's talking about with his own eyes. These young announcers think they know it all. They talk with the man in the street, not stars. The man in the street doesn't know shit, that's why he's in the street.

I cut the announcer off. I watch his head shrink to the size of a pin. I think nice thoughts. The perfume's still fresh on my hand. I go back to sleep.

At 9:00 things are looking better. The announcer says the astronauts are on their way to the moon. Five days, 263,000 miles away. Think of that.

I clock in. My name looks very big on the card. BENJAMIN S. WALSH typed in baby-blue ink. There's a special box for my card on the wall. Today, at 10:42 A.M., I slip the card into the machine, wait for the punch and the bell. I like the bell. There's a note in my box. It's written on Homestead paper—Mr. Garcia.

Morning's the nicest part of the restaurant day. Lunch is nearly two hours away. The kitchen's quiet. Light shines off the copper pots. Tiles smell sweet from mopping. Zambrozzi's taken the meat out of the freezer and laid it on the marble tabletop. It's his custom every day. He inspects his meat like John Wayne checking the troops. Lamb. Ribs. Pork. Beef. Zambrozzi walks slowly around

47

it, flops it over, pokes it, feels the grain. Meat hangs in our cellar for days. "Great food takes great care and time," according to Chef. Zambrozzi says meat has to decompose. This helps taste and tenderness. People pay up to $15 a portion.

Since Garcia put a clock over the stove, Zambrozzi's set up a table in the far corner. He sits there when he needs to rest or to think. It's a home away from home. Zambrozzi has his books between lion's head bookends: *The Philosopher in the Kitchen, Cooking in Copper, Dining at the Pavillon,* and many others. Zambrozzi's a very historical man. It's fun to hang around and hear Chef talk. He knew Tetrazzini of the chicken, his grandfather served Melba her first peach dessert. Behind his chair are two framed pictures with sayings underneath. The first is Escoffier's menu for George V's coronation at the Carlton Hotel in London, 1911. Under it is typed—"The discovery of a new dish does more for human happiness than the discovery of a new star—Brillat-Savarin, 1826." The other's a picture of Vatel, the famous seventeenth-century chef standing in what was called in those days "the galley." According to Zambrozzi, he was the king's chef and killed himself with a kitchen knife when Louis XIV's filet of sole didn't arrive on time. Zambrozzi quotes himself under this one—"No hurry, no worry—Desidario Zambrozzi, 1969."

I step into the kitchen, keeping to the dry tiles.

"Va bene?" Zambrozzi says. He never gets my name right. "Garcia stink up the place looking for your autographs. He find nothin'."

"Mad, huh?"

Zambrozzi makes a sign with his hands. Very mad.

The letter says to go to Mr. Garcia's office immediately. I show it to Zambrozzi. "You wait some minutes," he says, pointing back to his table, where Victor's just clearing a place for the soup tureen. Anthony carries the big bowl. The ladle is stuck in his belt. The kitchen crew gathers around.

"We gonna draw," Zambrozzi says. "Monday. Eleven o'clock. Every week. Every year. Rain or shine."

Zambrozzi's big on tradition. He's Catholic. In Europe,

he worked only for hotels with long-standing reputations. He brought Claridge's drinking song from London to The Homestead.

"Pool Parties," he says, "are Homestead custom." The chef decides when they will happen. He orders the wine that hasn't been drunk the day before by the customers poured into a bowl and chilled. He could call for a pouring every day, but Zambrozzi saves it for special events. He puts cut flowers on his table. He gets out his cooking medals. He takes the first sip and then calls out the name of each member of the staff, who dips in and joins him. Zambrozzi only allows the kitchen help to take part. He says waiters make too much money in tips. He considers me part of the kitchen. I don't get tips. I don't talk back, either. I listen. Standing by the big bowl, lifting his special goblet of Baccarat glass, Zambrozzi talks of restaurants long ago.

Zambrozzi reads to his staff each Monday morning. He says this makes us proud of our calling. It does. Every week he quotes a famous menu and tells another installment of his history of cooking. In less than five years he's made professionals of greenhorns.

Today, Zambrozzi says, is the two-hundredth installment of his history. He stands tall behind his desk. A book lies open on the table in front of him. *The New York Times* is at his right hand. In honor of the occasion, he says, he'll read from the *Memoirs of Carême* and try out the New Big Draw.

"Thank God," whispers Anthony. "I haven't won squat for two years."

Zambrozzi asks for quiet. "Like I say before, your clock-in time's your number. If that number matches the enemy body count *or* American casualties—you're a winner."

"You mean two people split the pot?" says Garofolo, moving closer to the table.

"Poor bastard," Anthony says to me. "Garofolo came in early this morning just to get a better number for the prize."

Zambrozzi clears his throat. "Carême, Marie-Antoine. Born 1784. From the third chapter of his memoirs trans-

49

lated by the best-selling French author, Alexandre Dumas fils . . ."

At first it was just the drinking and the song by the Big Bowl. The Draw came later. Each time we'd pick a player from a hat and pay fifty cents into the kitty. If nobody's player was leading the league in anything, the money went back into the till for Zambrozzi's next Pool Party. The New Draw is better than the Old Draw. The numbers are higher, so is the pot.

" '. . . The illustrious pastry cook Avice was then flourishing. I sought to follow without imitating him. I learned to execute every trick of the trade. But to get there, young people, how many sleepless nights.' "

"What about the Draw?" Victor pipes in.

"I no finish," says Zambrozzi, taking the book in his hand and looking at us as he speaks. " 'From behind my stoves, I contemplated the cuisines of India, China, Egypt, Greece, Turkey, Germany, and Switzerland. I felt the unworthy methods of routine crumble under my blows.' "

Chef snaps the book shut. Then, putting on his glasses, he picks up the *Times*. "Now," he says. "Everybody know their numbers?"

"Yes."

Zambrozzi studies the small print. He looks up, smiling. "A lot of money in this one."

"C'mon, Chef. How many of our boys wounded?" says Victor.

"Eight hundred and thirteen this month," says Zambrozzi.

Garofolo throws up his arms. "Great!" he says, walking around in circles, grinning, pounding his fist like a mitt. "I had a hunch. I knew it. I knew it!"

"Now the big number," says Anthony. "The enemy body count."

The room gets as quiet as the inside of the freezer. I've got butterflies in my stomach.

"The total is one thousand forty-two. The winner— Benny Walsh."

I feel like Audie Murphy and Bobby Thomson rolled into one. I'm blushing. Hands slap me on the back. The crew talks clubhouse talk to me. "How you go big fella," "The luck of the Irish," "Easy come, easy go!"

Victor puts his hairy arms around me and gives me a brotherly hug. It's embarrassing. "You done it, Benny. You split the fifty smackeroos with Garofolo."

Zambrozzi asks Garofolo and me to come forward. He gives us our money and glasses of wine as full as his. The others stand in a semicircle around us. Only the winners keep quiet. The rest of the crew, including Chef, raise their glasses and sing:

> *"Drink her down*
> *You Swazi warrior!*
> *Drink her down*
> *You Zulu chieftain*
> *Chieftain!*
> *Chieftain!*
> *Chieftain!*
> *Chieftain!"*

I can't gulp my wine as fast as Garofolo. I hold it in my cheeks. The crew keep chanting, "Chieftain, chieftain, chieftain, chieftain, chieftain" until I've swallowed the last drop.

"How do you feel hitting it right on the nose like that?" says Anthony, putting his hat on my head for a second.

"Dizzy," I say.

Everybody knows about Garcia's office. He leaves the door half open when he's out front. We've seen the picture of his three kids and the wife with hairy legs. We've touched the famous Kitchen Devil carving knifes on the wall that he says beat Henri Soulé's record for cutting a chicken in forty-eight seconds. We even know what's hidden under his desk set. When Garcia's in the office, the rule's to knock three times. Only the Boss enters without knocking.

Garcia's by the blackboard. "Walsh," he says. "We have what night school she call a *comunicación* problem."

"Communication."

Garcia turns and smiles at me. He sits down and puts

51

his boots up behind the desk. "What we gonna do?" He points to the collapsible director's chair. It's light and easy to open, but a tight fit. I take my autograph pad out of my pants pocket to squeeze in.

"Walsh, where you think I learn to carve like I do? The streets of New York—that's where. I had to defend myself."

"Really?"

"I can attack meat from any angle. I keep my knives sharp as switchblades. I slice thin. I jab and cut. I fought my way up. Carving's in my blood."

"I never knew that."

"There's much you should know." Garcia stands and walks back to the blackboard. "Look here, Walsh. This is the *organización*. The ideal the Boss and me we work out before his first stroke."

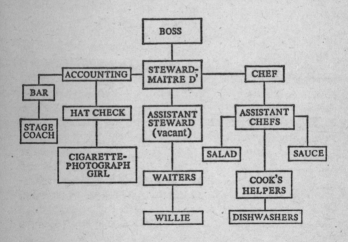

UNITY OF COMMAND

"Every autograph breaks the chain of command, Walsh. It slows down business. Speed's the big and the little brick of a great restaurant."

"Levy didn't mind."

"Levy was a lardass. A *gandul*. A clown."

"Everybody loved him. You bad-mouthed the service and the decor."

"I was deputy then. The Boss made me deputy. That was my job."

"You got him fired."

"In Puerto Rico, we've the saying, 'Los niños son sombras de sus padres.' At the Homestead, I'm parent—all those under me, the child. If the child's bad mannered, it no its fault. They blame Enrique Garcia. They write letters. The shit hit the fan."

"You meet everybody. It's easy for you."

Garcia raps the blackboard. "See, Walsh, everybody has a place. They teach this in school. 'Speedy deseminación, prompt ejecución.' "

"Zambrozzi says great cooking takes time."

"He no understand about turnover. He no study the science."

"I've never seen this chart. Who's Willie?"

"You."

"I'm Benny."

"Willie's what the textbook calls people like you."

"I'd like to be under Zambrozzi. He knows my name. He says I'm part of the kitchen."

Garcia laughs. "I'd like to be Boss. The chart's the chart."

"You made it up."

"It's The Homestead Plan. Every business has one. You got a job. You got a place. When you do the job and stay in the place, The Homestead she work like an orchestra. The kitchen she plays, the customers they sing, Garcia, he conducts. Beautiful music."

"The trouble with you, Mr. Garcia—you don't believe in people."

"A maître d's many things—actor, leader, engineer. Things gotta get done. You yell first, smile later."

"But . . ."

"Don't push me, Walsh. I'm trying the new diplomacy. In this business, it's eat or get eaten. I want Garcia to be written about like Soulé. 'The ability to never say no, saying yes when no is meant, and when all else fails appeasing with a smile.' "

53

"You're always saying no."

"*Idiota*. You make trouble. You fuck up."

"I scrape the plates. I pour the water. I bring the butter. I know my job better than any chart."

"I could pick up the phone and get ten busboys."

"Customers send you pictures. They do it in confidence. You put them in the window. Or behind the bar."

"I want to say yes, Walsh. I want to lock up each night like Soulé—without one complaint. Last night I say to my best customer, 'Mrs. Paley, how you like the dinner?' She says, 'Everything was cold except the champagne.' I got my honor, Walsh."

"A few autographs don't hurt anybody."

"People speak to me last night. They're disgusted."

"There's nothing dirty about my signatures. At least, I don't collect disgusting pictures. I've nothing to hide under my desk."

"Huh?"

"Combing the stripper's cunt at your Knights of Columbus dinner. Your name on your hat."

Garcia gets red as rhubarb. "That's it!"

"I'll say. Nobody could miss you. The scandal would ruin The Homestead."

"Walsh, I'm giving you till Friday."

"You're not firing me?"

"Yes."

"It's the new diplomacy. Yes means no."

"No," says Garcia.

"Then I'm staying?"

Garcia stands up. I try to stand, but the chair sticks to my hips. He puts on his Stetson. He goes to the blackboard. He writes—FIRED. The chalk breaks. The scratch makes my mouth taste of brass.

Garcia walks out.

"Puerto Ricans should be rounded up, put on Ellis Island, and burned! Goodbye *cuchifritos! Adiós West Side Story!* So long cha-cha-cha!"

I really give him an earful.

Zambrozzi calls me over to his table. "Garcia let you go?"

"Wrote it on the blackboard like I was part of next week's menu."

"He tell me to stop tonight's *ossobuco*. A chef's fame is in *plat du jour*."

"He's ruining the kitchen."

"In Italia, he scrub floors."

"It's America. He's got unity of command. He could fire you, too."

Zambrozzi laughs. "Don't worry about Garcia. Take today off, Benny. Get some autographs. Spend some of that money. I tell him you sick. He don't argue. I won't cook his meals."

"I keep track of things about The Homestead other people forget. I don't want to leave, Mr. Zambrozzi."

"When the boys come back, we gonna have a talk, we gonna settle this."

"I'm not in your section."

"Leave it to me."

Zambrozzi puts his arm on my shoulder and walks me toward the pantry. He hums our drinking song. He stops to watch the pasta being made. A cook's helper spreads flour in a wide circle on the table. He breaks an egg with one hand in the middle of the circle. It's beautiful—a yellow sun surrounded by white stars. Then he whips the egg with a fork. All the flour comes together in the yolk. Not a speck's left on the table. Nothing's lost. Everything sticks together in a white lump. The flour's part of the egg and the egg's part of the flour. Suddenly, the pasta's there.

"Cooking's like life," say Zambrozzi. "You have to have the right ingredients and the know-how." He thinks for a second. "Write that down," he says.

I put it in my pad, but I disagree. Cooking's not like life. If you get a bad meal, you don't have to eat it.

There are many penny arcades around Broadway, but the best are on 42nd Street. I go only on special occasions It costs more to play Fascination than the other games, but the prizes are bigger. There are movie houses on both sides of the arcades. They used to be theaters. The Earl Carroll Vanities, the George White Scandals—all those good times and great people who were in them used

55

to be right on this street. There's no theater now except a strip show on Eighth Avenue. But the names of the theaters have been preserved. That's the most important thing. VICTORY. LYRIC. LIBERTY. At night that's all you see in the sky. It's fun.

There's a fortune teller in this arcade that looks like my mother. She's old. Her fingernail polish's chipped. Her skin's rubbery and kind of yellow. You have to watch very closely to see her move. But she does move once you put your nickel in the slot. She also tells you to get comfortable, pay attention, and come again.

I put in a coin. She talks for a minute, then a card passes out at the bottom of the machine. It's the only scary part.

Say farewell to those blues you have been nursing. Get in the habit of looking at the brighter side of life. You have a temperamental nature. You lose your temper easily but regret it as fast.

The last time she said I was a sweet person.

You have a brilliant mind and enjoy reading and the fine arts.

Icing on the cake, but getting warmer. The last sentence gives me a shock. I can hear my heart.

A dark-haired person who is trying to harm you will soon disappear from your life, and you will prosper.

How could she know? Just beneath her prophecy's a note.

Drop another coin in the slot and I will tell you more. Your Lucky Numbers—56, 57, 58.

It's good to know this for Fascination. I quit while I'm ahead.

I take stool number 57. The rules to Fascination are the same as poker, except you play with five rubber balls.

56

You roll each ball down the table, aiming for the holes, which are numbered like a pack of cards. You play against the machine, and like the sign says outside the arcade—EVERYBODY'S A WINNER.

The game's tense. The prizes are on the shelves above the machine, so close you can almost touch them. Mixmasters, waffle irons, radios, golf clubs—the same prizes they have on quiz shows. Jeanette comes by your seat when you win and gives you coupons. The better the hand, the more you get. Each gift has the number of coupons under it. You know what you're working for.

A man with a microphone calls out the winners. He talks to us while we roll. "Every man a winner, not a sinner. Three aces, now you're going places. Four of a kind, rob us blind." Sometimes I know I've won even before the announcer sees. I push back my stool (you get tired from the pressure). I pretend Steve McQueen has just folded his cards. He's signing over his motorcycle to me. Tough nuggies, Steve. Straight, ace high.

"Winner on fifty-seven. Little closer to heaven."

Jeanette gives me four coupons. She smiles. Sometimes when players have been at the table a few hours and are really doing good, they give her their coupons. I don't believe in that. To the victor belongs the spoils.

The backspin's really cooking today. After each game, I rest and think about how I'll play the next. I like to remember the wins. I look around at my competition. Only ten people are playing.

Time flies when you play Fascination. There's never a dull moment. The man at the microphone names me again.

"Winner on fifty-seven. Full boat, buy your lady friend a coat."

This makes me think of Gloria. I decide to stop for a while and walk around. If you can't concentrate, you can't win.

I stop at Boothill, a gun battle in the rear of the arcade—three shots for a quarter. It'd be silly if the gunman didn't look like Garcia—yellow-brown skin, Stetson, rodeo shirt. I deposit my money, and right away a record of insults start coming from the guy—typical. "All right, you polecat, you lily-livered toad, no varmint's gonna talk to me this way. Go for your gun, whippersnapper." The gunman has the advantage. His hand's on the six-shooter. I crouch. I slap leather. I fan the gun, three shots in the dead center of the scum-sucking pig. A meter at the foot of the gunman lights up—QUICK DRAW. I pay another quarter and pull the gun far to the side. The gunman doesn't even see me. I fire a second round of hot lead into Garcia—one for Tina, one for Zambrozzi, and the last for me. He squirms. "Aaaaargh!" Self-defense.

I'm ready for the Cock Shop.

I only go into the back room when I'm feeling strong. The peep show's next door. From where I'm standing, I can hear the whispers: "Ooooh. Ooooh. That's good. Deeper." I never watch. It makes me sick.

I try not to look at the glass case filled with plastic cocks, but I'm a sucker for scientific breakthroughs. I can't get them out of my mind. "Double Dong Lesbian Type" looks like a majorette's baton with rubber nobs at both ends. "Smooth Sleeve" is an ice-cream cone, tan and rough. "The Thriller" is as pink and spiny as Mom's hair-curlers. It'd make a good backscratcher. All of these have "halters," according to the sign. Imagine wearing them! Bumping into people. Getting caught in revolving doors. You couldn't put your pants on.

Is this the normal size? Maybe for athletes. They eat special food. They have trainers.

When I take a bath, I sometimes look at myself and think of the Cock Shop. Now and then, when I'm running after a big signature, I can feel it coming back into Cock Shop shape. "Guaranteed dependable," they say—I can't count on mine. Maybe it's because of the time I lifted the chopping block at The Homestead, and strained something down there. Or maybe it's because of Prudence "The Pig" Grasso from Trade School.

They made me take her out. They gave me money for the movie show, but I had to promise to tell what happened. They told me certain words to say. We were in the balcony of the Ocean Beach Orpheum—a Red Skelton double feature. The last row.

Prudence rubbed against me. I couldn't eat my popcorn. She kept touching my hand and knocking the bag off my knee. Finally she said, "Let's do something." It's what they told me she'd say. "Okay," I said, and waited. She put her hand under my jacket and stuck it down my pants. Her fingers were sharp, and cold. I was scared to look at her. She grabbed it, just as Red Skelton was swallowing a bowl of goldfish. It was the funniest part of the movie, but I couldn't laugh. Prudence was breathing heavy. "Whadday feel? Tell me what you feel?"

I felt sick to my stomach, but I couldn't say that.

"Whaddya want me to do?"

"Beat it," I said. It's what they told me to say, I think. But it was the wrong thing to say. She yanked it from side to side—left, right, up, down. She banged it against the armrest. I was in terrible pain, nearly on my knees. I couldn't yell or the usher with her flashlight would've run up the aisle. Prudence's fingers were as strong as steel coils.

"Say what it feels like," she said. "Say . . ."

I couldn't speak. "Oooh!" I said.

She took my arm. She put it between her legs and squeezed. She wiggled for a second. And then suddenly she went all calm, and let go. Later, standing by the bus stop, she said, "I love you." They told me she'd say it. I let her go home by herself. I could hardly walk. That night, before turning out the light, I looked at it. There were scratches. It was bent.

But I know real love. You see it all the time. Fred Astaire and Audrey Hepburn in *Funny Face*, Gene Kelly and Vera-Ellen in *On the Town*. They're in love. They never say these kind of things. They dance and sing. They look into each other's eyes. No touching, just respect.

A sign on the far wall points up the staircase. I start to have a look. Then, I hear it—the jingle of spurs. My neck aches. My palms go damp. I peek up the stairwell. Garcia! What's he doing here? He's handing cheroots to Victor and Anthony! They're smiling. I have to get out!

Luckily, my sneakers don't clatter. I've got suction grip for fast starts. I back away. There's no cashier at the entrance to the peep show, only a change machine and a black velvet curtain, otherwise I'd be too embarrassed to go in. It's dark behind the curtain. But through the seam I can see Garcia coming closer.

I feel a body.

"Well, what have we here?"

"Ssssh, mister. I'm being chased."

"Oh . . . a hush puppy," The man puts his hand down my backside. "I suck cock," he whispers.

Garcia's passing by. The machine's breathing loud. "Oooh. Oooh. That's good. Deeper." He stops to listen. I freeze. The man's on my shoulder now. "Pretend I'm your fairy godmother," he says.

Garcia and the boys walk away.

"Look, my friend," he says. He's unzipped his fly. He's pulling his corporal out to show me. "The magic wand."

I push the curtains aside and run towards the staircase. My Mets cap falls off. I stop to pick it up. The man's waving me back into the dark. "Come back, darling. I'm good. I'm good."

Garcia's cigar still stinks up the stairway. The sign reads—

SCREEN FEMMES
Direct Your Own Scene
$25 an Hour

Funny Fingers won't follow me upstairs. There's no talking on the set.

Small production companies are springing up everywhere. It's all you read in *Variety*. Not many of them are as well-equipped as Screen Femmes. The heart-shaped bed. The African jungle scene. The painted backdrop of the Vatican. There's even a prop box—full of helmets, guns, ropes, coats. It's the only way—begin on a shoestring and build it into an empire.

"It'll cost ya, buddy," the receptionist says.

"Benny. Benny Walsh."

"The price's on the sign."

"I never pay for autographs. Stars don't take money from strangers."

"Morrie, there's a guy out here who wants to know if we've got any famous actresses on the set."

A Jew voice answers, the kind my mother dragged me away from on the beach. "O-sheeny-beach," she'd say. "You wanna grow up like that? A belly so big you can't see your wee-wee?"

"Tell him the guided tour starts at nine, Faye. I'm going out for a *nosh*."

"You know why Jews are smart, miss? They read a lot as kids because nobody'll play with them."

"Listen, mister, we only have starlets at this hour of the day. The stars leave early, if you know what I mean."

"I bet you didn't talk to Mr. Enrique Garcia that way."

"You know that guy?"

"We work together at The Homestead."

"He's a long hitter."

"Puerto Ricans are better at baseball than acting."

"Look, you heard the boss—I just work here."

"I'll tell you one thing, Miss Receptionist. When Screen Femmes hits it big, there'll be changes. They'll put somebody else behind the desk. Somebody who doesn't chew, who knows language and the rudiments."

"Okay," she says, swinging the wooden door open so I can pass through. "Look but don't touch."

"I know better. Camera equipment's very expensive."

"You heard of Mitzi Gaynor? Joan Crawford?"

"Of course."

"The girl in the corner's been on location with them."

"Really?"

"The blond in the long dress. With the ruffles. I'll ask her over."

"I won't take much of her time."

"Laurette, dear. Somebody wants to talk with you."

The actress doesn't answer.

"Don't bother, lady. Actresses are moody. They're concentrating on their career and their lines. Professional collectors don't push. They understand."

"Come here, Laurette."

Laurette gets up and walks slowly towards us. She's got carriage. "Hello, Benny," she says.

"You know her?" the receptionist says.

"The Late, Late Show?"

She shakes her head no.

"Dick Cavett—that's it. You and Bill Russell talking politics."

"Where's your memory?" Laurette says.

"I never forget a face. It's my business."

Laurette puts her hand on her hair and pulls off her wig.

"Gloria! Don't you say thank you?"

"I was going to ask around Shubert Alley."

"Oh, sure."

"Laurette's my stage name. For Laurette Taylor—my father's favorite actress."

"What's your last name?"

"Just Laurette. No last name."

"Like Twiggy or Verushka or Kleenex. Easy to remember."

"I owe you a present."

"Forget it."

Gloria shows me the camera and the zoom lens. She lets me look through it. The bed looks very small.

"Do you act every day?"

"When they ask for me."

"What happens when the other actresses are performing?"

"I rehearse my special material. Sometimes I hold the camera."

"You direct?"

"I hold the camera."

"They must give you a rest. People get tired under the lights. Elizabeth Taylor in *Cleopatra*. She was exhausted."

"I have lunch. I sit by the window. I read my magazines. I practice my song."

"Sing it."

"It's for tryouts."

"Go ahead."

"I hardly know you . . ."

Gloria shouldn't be shy. In this business, you need guts. "Do you have a script?"

"Sometimes they bring a script. Sometimes we make it up as we go along."

"You could use your special material."

"That's for open calls. I'm on the list."

"Don't you get nervous? I couldn't relax. I couldn't be myself."

"After a while, you hardly notice the camera."

Gloria takes my arm. She walks me around the set like it was Fifth Avenue. "Why don't you direct me, Benny?"

"I haven't gone to camera school. I don't have twenty-five dollars."

Gloria pulls out a big feathery hat to match her dress from the prop box. She also takes a cane. "Let's pretend I'm about to take a long journey to meet my lover, Lord Churchill. He's a great man. He has acres of land, and a coat of arms. He loves me very much. But my father won't let me go. He wants me to take a job as a shop girl. He says to wait until I'm sure."

"It sounds like a good story. But I'm scared, Gloria."

"You know a lot about movies."

"Not enough to make one."

"I'll take pictures of you, then."

"I don't have the money. Please?"

"There's no film in the camera. It's for free. I do it all the time when the boss goes out. I get experience this way."

Gloria stands behind the camera. I get a chair and sit in front of the black eye. I put on my Mets cap. She's bending close to the camera. I can only see the top of her head.

"You look good," she says.

"Don't I look small?"

"No. Very clear."

It's my movie debut. I feel very . . . responsible. I don't want the camera to see me being boring. I want it to see me being just right.

"That's enough."

63

"Don't be silly. Stay right there, Benny. Do something. Sing 'Blue Suede Shoes.' "

She wants me to wiggle like Elvis. What can I do? My Lone Ranger galloping sounds? No. The camera would see my tongue—the spots, the cavities. I could show my scar? Not dramatic enough. She wants me to run and jump. I can't look like Joe Namath in slow motion.

"Is it on?"

"Do something."

The camera makes me feel stupid. I can see Gloria aiming at me. "I'm turning it on!"

I hear the whirr. I hold my hands in my lap. Belly in. Chest out. Back straight. Chin up. It's what I want—very President Nixon. I hold my breath, I don't want to spoil the effect.

"A little more toward me."

Some stars have their own special cameraman. They won't be photographed by anyone else. They know what's their best side, and what the public likes to see. I don't have a best side yet.

"Benny, smile at me. Pretend I'm Joan Crawford."

I can't smile. I can't explain to Gloria while the camera's running. Just thinking Joan's on the set gives me the creeps. I should be looking at her. She should be sitting down. I won't smile. My teeth aren't so good, they've got spaces in them. I should've had braces. Mom said we needed the money to move to Rumson. At MGM they took care of these things for you. It was like a family— teeth, nose, hair, anything you needed—fixed for free.

I try to get Gloria's real eye. "Let's do the TV shows this afternoon."

I'm good at talking between my teeth. I practice with the waiters right under Garcia's nose. He can't tell what I'm saying, either.

Finally, Gloria hears me and stops the camera. My feet are prickly. She looks at me smiling. "Am I forgiven?"

"It says here on my fortune—'You have a very sympathetic nature.' "

"Give me a minute to change," she says. "One day could we go to the Passport Office and look at the pictures of some of the famous people on their first trips to Europe?"

"Who have they got?"

"Sid Caesar, Faye Emerson, Louis Nye . . ."

"Sure."

Gloria goes into a side room. It gives me time to dry off and get the feeling back in my feet.

On the way out, Faye stops Gloria. "Ten tomorrow, sweetie. Tell Louis B. Mayer there that Kim Novak might be with us in the afternoon."

We hurry down the stairs, past the breathing, and into the fresh air.

"Do I really look like Louis B. Mayer?"

Gloria turns my head to the side. "Yes," she says.

"That's the first time I ever asked somebody how I looked. It's hard to see yourself as others see you."

"Where are we going, Benny?"

"Let's start at the top—the Carson show. Joe Namath's on tonight."

Walking to Radio City, Gloria holds her purse on the outside. I'd like to run my fingers through hers. But I don't. I'm no Speedy Gonzalez.

The usher hands us the free tickets, and points to the line stretching halfway down the corridor.

"I don't understand it," Gloria says. "If it's free, it can't be good."

"Let's face it, Gloria, movies are make-believe—TV is real."

"Don't tease me."

"They call us the *live* audience, don't they?"

"At the movies, you've got privacy," says Gloria. "It's the big screen, the popcorn, and you."

"TV's more personal. You feel like you're sitting in the living room with some pretty important people. You get to know them quicker. It's good for collecting."

"On TV, the stars look so small."

"I saw Shelley Winters accuse David Susskind of breaking up her marriage. She screamed and cursed, the same as on screen, only louder and with nothing cut."

65

"I like it when you sit through twice. People kissing, having fun—nothing changes. It's the same forever. It gives you confidence."

"I was in the first row when Nick Adams told his wife he was leaving her."

"You heard that?"

"He was in New York on the show, and she was watching in California. There's a three-hour delay on the West Coast. So I actually was the first to know."

"His autograph must be a gold mine."

"You better believe it."

The ushers want you to stay in line. Most people settle for their soft soap. The trick's to get your ticket and sneak upstairs to the Green Room for autographs before the show. That way you don't worry. You can take your seat and enjoy being live.

Gloria follows me through the door marked PRIVATE. "Don't be a daredevil, Benny."

"When we get to the top of these stairs, you'll see a guard. Ask him the time. He'll turn around to look at the clock. I'll sneak past him and meet you back in the theater. Save me a seat."

"We might get in trouble."

"Show him your 'Chase Me' shoes. Sing your song . . ."

"I wasn't raised to slink around."

"Think of Crawford."

"She wouldn't be caught dead going up the back way."

"In *Grand Hotel* she worked her way up from a stenographer. She was a shop girl in *Our Blushing Brides* and with guts she landed Robert Montgomery."

"Yes," says Gloria. "But in *Mildred Pierce* she goes to jail."

I open the door. Gloria walks ahead. She goes up to the guard just like I told her. With her hand behind her back, she signals me to get going. We're a regular Dale Evans–Roy Rogers combination.

The Green Room's empty, but Makeup's crowded. If you stand behind the door, like I do, people are too busy talking to the stars to notice. I can't see who's in the chairs because Manuel and Frieda are bending over them, painting them up. On the wall there's a white cardboard

66

poster with the signatures of the people they've done. All the actors write their thanks to Manuel and Frieda. From here, I can see that Phyllis Diller called them "artists in their own right."

When Manuel and Frieda step back to look at how they're doing, I can see the mirror. It's Johnny and Joe. They sit very quietly with their eyes shut. In my mind, Johnny's always making some funny remark, saying "Oh, really?" and raising his eyebrows the way he does. And Joe—he's too much. I remember him at the Super Bowl after he'd single-handedly massacred the Baltimore Colts. He had his fist up in the air as if to tell the crowd "I told you so." He did, too. They should have listened. He's dressed very colorful. He's not wearing his white shoes, but he looks real good, anyway. The championship ring's on his finger. The ring's in the shape of a football—thirty-five diamonds and a ruby. I know what it says on the inside, the team leaked it to the *Post*—NEW YORK JETS—WORLD CHAMPIONS—1969. Richard Burton couldn't buy it for Liz. It has to be earned.

Johnny looks the same as ever—thin and handsome. He's the richest man on TV, and the most famous. Johnny's whispering, saving himself for the show. A man in a blue suit with a stopwatch around his neck bends over to listen. I think he's the producer. Other men stand behind the producer, but no one else moves closer to hear Johnny. You can tell when Johnny means something, even if you can't hear him. His hands move up and down very quick. Just seeing him makes you want to laugh. I have to bite my lip to keep quiet.

The producer acts like Garcia at a staff meeting. Everybody understands English, he doesn't have to shout. Johnny pulls him back. The producer apologizes to him. He listens. Finally, Johnny's hands stop moving. Manuel comes forward and picks up his painting where he left off. The producer turns to the others. "Johnny want us at tomorrow's meeting circa eleven."

I'd never have known Joe and Johnny needed make-up. Their faces are their trademarks, and people like them just as they are. Frieda dabs white stuff on Joe's most famous feature—the lines on his forehead which come

67

from looking for pay dirt and red dogs. The smiling lines around his mouth are gone—you'd never believe he was ever at a victory party. Manuel's putting brown lotion around Johnny's chin and mouth. When my spots wouldn't go away, Mom gave me this lotion to put on my face. She said it was skin colored, but everybody at school could see.

"*Voilà*," says Manuel.

"*Voilà*," says Frieda.

I can see my face in the mirror if I peak out from behind the door. Johnny and Joe look perfect. Their faces are smooth as satin. There are no bumps or lines or circles under their eyes. You can't see black hairs on their chin. They could've stepped off a tropical island. Somehow, when it's all over, the tan makeup makes them look natural.

"See you on the air, Joe."

Joe cocks his finger like a gun. "Not if I see you first."

Johnny gets up. I push against the wall. I don't want them to see me, especially after what I've overheard.

Once they've left, Frieda shuts the door. She sees me.

"You two did a wonderful job," I say. "You're artists in your own right."

She's flattered. She puts her hands over her mouth as if I'd said she was Queen for a Day. But Manuel doesn't know how to take a compliment. I heard the same *mierda* from him that Garcia uses at me. I run out before he's finished the sentence.

Everywhere I turn there's a bad-mouth Puerto Rican.

Gloria has saved a seat in the first row. I read her my quotes.

"Is that all they said?"

"You had to be there."

"I've never been in a TV studio," says Gloria.

"Your network debut."

"What do you mean?"

"The camera watches us at the beginning and the end of the program. If you whistle, if you have something to catch its attention—they show you coast to coast."

"Should I keep my veil up or down?"

"Let the camera get a good look at you."

She fusses with her hat. "Be honest, Benny, which way do you like best?"

"Keep it down."

Gloria powders her nose. "Will it see us from different angles?"

"The angles are for Johnny."

"I can't wait to see him."

"He looks very good tonight."

"Really?" says Gloria. "I hope he does the advertisements."

"He's the best."

"Where is he?" says Gloria. "It's show time, and I don't see him."

"You're looking at the stage. It's television, look up at the screens."

Gloria counts seven large TVs around the studio.

"Right now, all they have is that peacock. Soon, Johnny will be on all seven."

Gloria keeps watching the screens. She straightens her hair.

"Talk to me, Benny."

"What've I been doing?"

"You talk. I'll watch for when we're on."

"In the days of the old *Today* show, I used to get up early and come down here. They let us stand outside the window then, and at 7:24, just after Jack Lescoulie finished the news roundup, one camera took a picture of the crowd waving, or, in the winter, blowing hot-air hellos. People from all over the world with signs and funny sayings. I'm telling you the competition was rough. Once, when I hadn't written Mom for a while, I sent her a card and told her to watch the *Today* show. I gave her the time. She could see for herself that I was okay. Sure enough, at 7:24, there I was waving at her in Asbury Park. Mom wrote me and said she'd asked in a few of her new friends from Home-with-a-Heart. They spotted me and my sign right off.

VICTOR MATURE
SAYS 'HI MOM'

The camera stayed on me at least fifty seconds, wondering if I was really Victor Mature—actually, he's taller. If I'd have written 'Benny Walsh,' that could've been anybody. There's only one Victor Mature."

"Here he is," says Gloria, pointing to the screen.

"Victor?"

"Here's Johnny."

At the first commercial, Gloria leans over and squeezes my arm. "It's great."

"If you weren't here, if they weren't showing film clips from the League Championship, I'd be more professional. I'd be out in the alley getting a good spot by the stage door."

"You'd miss the fun."

"All you see on the TV screen is heads and shoulders."

"It's more exciting than that," says Gloria.

"In the alley, when the stars come out, you see all there is to see."

"Maybe there are things the public shouldn't know."

"You feel their clothes, smell their perfume, look at their jewelry, hear the little things that microphones can't pick up."

"They have close-ups in TV, Benny."

"It doesn't bring you close enough."

"What's happening?" says Gloria.

"Oakland Raiders. The play-off. Twenty-seven to twenty-three."

The crowd's cheering louder than I've ever heard.

Gloria says, "A penny for your thoughts."

"Third and five with two minutes to play." She doesn't know football. This is no time for chatter.

Joe's dropping back. He's in the pocket. He's got time. He hits me with a hard spiral. The crowd's screaming my union number—1-2-6-0. DON'T GO! DON'T GO!

In the huddle, Joe says, Nice catch. I say, Nice pass.

The guard doesn't treat people as nice as Johnny and Joe do. He tears my coat showing me to the exit. Gloria's waiting.

70

"You shouldn't have walked up there without permission."

"They're good guys. I got their autographs. Didn't you see?"

"Everybody saw. It was on all seven screens."

"For sure?"

"Mr. TV Star . . ."

"I don't remember . . ."

"What guts. You were prime time."

"Tell me about it."

"You could've been on the team, the way you dodged those cameramen. Everybody around me wanted to know your name."

"No kidding."

"You should've seen the look on their faces when you yelled 'We're number one.' "

"My stomach feels fuzzy."

"Let's look at the travel shops. That'll calm you."

We walk past the Golden Man at Rockefeller Plaza, past the Bronze Man holding up the world at 50th Street and Fifth. Gloria stops to look at his muscles. The man's left foot's slipping off the platform. I get nervous standing under such a big weight. This is New York, people are always dropping things.

"The 'Go Greece' window at Olympic last month was beautiful," says Gloria. "Water bluer than Lake George. Beaches pure white."

"The beaches were empty, right?"

"I rush home to catch their ad on the TV," Gloria says. "The Greek music. The dancing. It puts you at ease, gives you a taste of what's in store."

We walk past a beautiful poster of Miami Beach. I can't take my eyes off it. Neither can Gloria. A girl in a pink bikini's running hand in hand down a beach with a man as tanned as she is. Her hair's blond and floats behind her like a cloud. He's got a washboard chest. They kick up water. Underneath, the poster says:

YOU ONLY GET ONE CRACK AT LIFE.
LIVE IT UP.

"That's my motto," Gloria says. "When I've saved enough money, I'm going to have some of these guaranteed good things."

An ambulance wahoos down the street. "Fucking noise!"

"Take your hands off your ears, Benny. It's gone."

"I hate those ambulances. They don't show respect. It's Fifth Avenue."

"My father drove an ambulance."

"I'm sorry, Gloria. I still hate them."

"That driver had it on steady wail. A grade-A driver would've used the 'whooper.' It costs a hundred twenty-five dollars extra, but it's not as scary."

"You said your father was polite. Have you seen how these ambulances scream around the city—pushing people off the road, running traffic lights, making noise?"

"In Lake George it was different. He called it 'The Silver Savior.' We had some good times, Benny. I can still see us driving through the snow-cleared road to Old Forge. 'The Savior'—Omaha orange and silver—sliding around the icy curves, spinning a powdery trail behind us. Dad sat in the front seat wearing his Red Cross cap, one hand on the wheel, the other on the intercom to me in the back, lying on the multilevel rolling litter. He'd run the siren all the way to Old Forge and back."

"It sounds pretty dumb to me."

"You wouldn't talk that way if you knew Pop. We'd go over to Tulley's after the ride and sit by the fire. He'd let me sip from his Utica Club. 'Gloria,' he'd say. 'You deserve the best.'"

"Ambulance drivers were the ones afraid to kill Jerry in the war. My mother told me. She volunteered. They wouldn't let her fight, though. She had to take care of me."

"My father taught me a lot of things to help me in life. Ambulance drivers have to know how to fix fractures, control bleeding, make a cardiac arrest."

"What good does it do you?"

"An ambulance driver's trained to recognize death. One. The luster of the eye. Two. The color of the tongue—ashy blue. Three. The earlobe—cold and blue. Four. Body stiff—total lack of response."

"I take back what I said about your old man."

"Believe me, Benny, Pop had a way about him. He knew his business."

By Bergdorf Goodman, Gloria takes my arm. She does it like Kay Thompson in *Funny Face*. I feel very Fred Astaire.

"Sing me your song, Gloria."

She doesn't answer.

"I wasn't being fresh."

She keeps walking. Finally, she says, "I was thinking ... I brought you luck."

"Let's eat. I'm hungry."

"You mean to celebrate?"

"Mondays, H and H has a meatloaf platter."

Sypher holds Gloria's chair. She thanks him. He pushes the yellow seat in with his knee. "See that, Walsh? I have a way with a chair. They wanted to promote me to captain. I said no dice. Nobody's puttin' no stuffed shirt on old Louis the Lion-Hearted."

Gloria picked the fish cakes. She takes her silverware off the tray. "Let me do that!" Sypher reaches over, grinning, and puts Gloria's plate in front of her. He pulls a paper napkin out of the black holder and flicks it in the air. It unfolds like a flag. He lays it on her lap. "All these years thinkin' Walsh here was acey-deucey, and now he turns up with a lovely titbit, if you'll pardon my French. It's a great end to a great day." He squeezes Gloria's arm. "Nice," he says. "Very nice."

"I've heard a lot about you, Mr. Sypher."

"I'm number two. We try harder."

Gloria laughs. "Benny signed up Johnny Carson and Joe Namath on TV tonight. It was exciting."

"The maiden voyage is always a thrill. Right, Walsh?"

"I don't remember. . . ."

"He's teaching me. Before Benny, I never had a plan. He's showing me the ins and outs."

"I go for quantity, not quality. Two bucks a head, fifteen for a famous, twenty for an international. The money's in the turnover."

"Benny just ran up and made them sign."

"While he was getting two household names, I got fifteen. This arty-farty stuff don't pay the rent."

"Pass the salt," says Gloria.

I hand it to her. Sypher takes it back and gives her the salt and pepper together. "Waldorf style," he says. "You get better service . . ."

"It's a nice place, Benny," says Gloria.

"The twenty-five-cent minimum keeps the wineheads out," says Sypher. "You can sit down and have a good conversation, right, Walsh?"

"Right."

"I'd like to make a toast," says Sypher.

We raise our glasses. Sypher clinks ours with his. "To Louis Newbold Sypher—who just struck it rich!"

"Really?" says Gloria.

Sypher gulps down his tomato juice. "Remember Della, Benny? The frump with the hump. This afternoon I'm walkin' past The Homestead and I see her. 'What's happenin', Della?' She's slow, but she knows when they're around. She shows me her latest. 'Some old fuck,' she says. 'I didn't want him, but he was the only one I could catch.' I look at the paper and right away I iron-clad my face. I show nothin'. I whip out two of my regulars—Soupy Sales and Mary Tyler Moore. Della's blabbin' about the old days when she had all of 'em. I offer to swap. She don't think twice. I keep my hard edge. She don't suspect a thing. I walk down the street with a piece of paper as good as a C-note. Igor Eat-Your-Heart-Out Stravinsky."

"That wasn't very nice," says Gloria.

"It's winner take all, sweet one."

"You got Igor Stravinsky and you sold him?"

"Cash on the line, Benny. I don't carry no wallet. I keep the big bucks in my money clip. Fives and ones—crisp as crackers. All night I been spittin' change like John D. Rockefeller. No noise in my pockets. Nothin' weighin' me down. You see, friends, the secret's to work hard and play hard. Tonight, I'll get me a few Italian silk ties. Maybe I'll stroll over and cut a rug at the Flamingo. Buy a yard of tickets. All those good-lookers in black velvet dresses givin' you the nut rubs, strokin' the back of your neck after a hard day's work. That's what it's all about. The *joy de vive.*"

"Could I have a cup of coffee, Benny?"

"I'll get it," says Sypher.

"Gloria's with me."

"Save your money," says Sypher, slapping me on the shoulder. "You'll need it." When he comes back with the coffee, he says, "Myself, I stay anonymous. I'm slippery like a shadow. I don't like hearing about any of us getting on the air."

"You're the one who got written up in *The New York Times*, saying all those dumb things about it being a *hobby*. It sounded like *you* had the big collection."

"Just coverin' my tracks, Benny-boy. I don't want people knowing how much I make. Autographs are a good gig. If the wrong people found out, I could be in a higher tax bracket."

"I'm glad Benny doesn't do it for the money," says Gloria. "He's interested in other things."

"Pretty soon, he'll have to start eating his profits."

"I don't understand."

"You do, don't you, Benny?"

"All the time yapping, Sypher. Yap, yap, yap."

"Della told me. News travels fast. It's up and down in this business."

"What's he talking about, Benny?"

"Would you like another cup of coffee?"

"He was fired, sweet chops. Tin-canned."

Gloria stares at me. "Do they know about your collection?"

"I've got till the end of the week. Chef's trying to pull strings."

A busboy wheels his cart near us. He scrapes Gloria's plate into a can. He uses a brush, but the food sticks on his hands. His blue jeans are stained with other people's leavings. He takes a brown rag out of his back pocket and wipes the yellow tabletop. "We're not finished," says Sypher. The busboy's moving too fast to hear. He lifts up Sypher's plate and makes a few damp circles on the Formica. The bandanna around his head doesn't stop the

75

sweat. His eyes flutter with the salt sting. A few tables away, four old ladies are calling for him to hurry. One of them waves her cane. He puts his weight behind the cart and shoves it toward their table. "It's a pigpen here, mister. Food's getting cold. You see us waving?"

Our spoons ping against the china cups. Everybody's staring at the whirlpool in their coffee. Sypher looks up. "You can always work here."

"Maybe somebody'll see you on TV," says Gloria. "You never know what can happen."

"One in a million," says Sypher.

"Julius La Rosa got a record contract after the Arthur Godfrey Show. Steve and Eydie were so good with Steve Allen that the public kept asking for them. The rest's show-biz history."

"They had voices, Benny," says Louis.

"All Dr. Brothers had was the answers to the sixty-four-thousand-dollar question. I know as much about autographs as she did about boxing. Now she's an announcer."

"Can't you help him, Mr. Sypher?"

"The Waldorf's my turf."

"Benny, I have some friends who might . . ."

"Don't get me wrong, honey. Sypher's a man who likes competition. This body of mine's the product of free enterprise. I wouldn't want to be the only one around . . . I'd get lazy. My body'd go soft. It feels good bein' hungry, right, sweet Gloria?"

"Let's go, Benny."

"Think of it this way, Walsh. The Homestead's been around a long time . . . All that cowboy stuff's kinda corny . . . This may be your lucky break."

I get to Gloria's chair first. She stands up. Sypher leans back in his seat sipping his coffee. "Nobody wants to ball it up at the Flamingo?"

"We're going to see the Johnny Carson show on Benny's TV."

Sypher takes Gloria's hand and kisses it. He feels her fingers. "Very nice, Benny."

"So long, Louis."

76

"Don't do nothin' I wouldn't do, Walsh." Sypher smiles at Gloria. "Later for you, baby," he says. "Later."

"You got a camera, Benny?"
"Don't poke in the drawers. Those are my things."
"I only wanted to take your picture on TV."
"I'm gonna work on the autographs."
"Don't you want a souvenir? If I had a Polaroid Instamatic . . ."
"I've got their autographs."
"Don't you want to see yourself on TV, Benny?"
"Just tell me to break a leg."

Gloria says they save the best for last, and that's why I'm not on after the football movies. Joe and Johnny are there, but they talk as if nothing happened. We wait until 1:00.
"I guess I'm on the cutting-room floor."
The TV's showing a late-night movie. Gloria's resting on my pillow. She's snoring.
I pull out my Great Comeback section. I have quite a few signatures. Frank Sinatra, "Peg-Leg" Bates, Eddie Waitkus, Jane Froman, Ben Hogan—the people the papers call "inspirational." Even when times were tough, they kept plugging. Floyd Patterson's my most inspirational inspirational. He was the first man in the history of boxing to win back the heavyweight title. They say he ran 2,000 miles training for the Ingemar Johansson fight. He went on a special African diet of raw meat. Some people wrote he had a glass chin, but when I met him he was all muscle and bone. I talked to him.

ME: What's the secret, Floyd?
FLOYD (to me): You gotta keep moving. Keep in shape. Eat good. You gotta believe you can do it. You got to want to do it—that's very important. You can't let nothing get in your way. God's gotta be in your corner. I'd like to thank my mom, too.
ME: How did you know God was in your corner?
FLOYD: I won, didn't I?

77

It was tough getting comments out of Floyd. Stars are big on silence. Garbo, Howard Hughes, J. Edgar Hoover —they hardly ever talk. People have to guess what they're thinking. I shouldn've been more cool and collected. I should've made Johnny and Joe guess what I wanted instead of asking them outright. I should've stood there quiet as Harpo, until they signed. That would've been dramatic—Hallmark Hall of Fame stuff.

I lock the autographs away. I turn off the television. Gloria's curled up on the bed like a kitten. I lie down beside her, careful not to come too close. I don't turn out the light—that'd be sexy. I just push myself up on my elbows and watch her breathe. Looking at her makes me sleepy.

Gloria turns toward me, blinking. "What?"

"Sorry."

"I thought you said something."

"No."

"Turn out the light, Benny."

In the darkness, she says. "Benny, you can touch me."

I put my leg next to hers.

"Sweet dreams," I say, and shut my eyes.

GLORIA HANDS ME a cup of coffee. "Rise and shine." The TV's interviewing one of the astronauts. I've got him on my wall standing with the team and the wives around the model of the earth. "What's it like up there, Bill?" the announcer asks. (It's what I want to know too.) "The bluest Tuesday I've ever seen. The moon's as big as a burro's bottom." One astronaut lets his knife and fork go. They float in the air. Science is wonderful.

Gloria turns off the set.

"Hey!"

"Get a move on, Benny."

"I don't have to clock in before eleven."

"The early bird catches the worm."

"The TV said it's a nice day. How about a movie?"

"I've got to work. So do you."

"I do?"

"You've got to start looking for a job, Benny."

"Zambrozzi's fixing things. How can I look for a job when I've got a job?"

"Better safe than sorry."

"What Sypher said about The Homestead last night was bull. It's still as good as ever. With the Waldorf, everything has to be new."

"I'll sing you my song for good luck."

After I've washed, and combed my hair, Gloria makes me sit in the easy chair. She stands by the window. "Pretend this is a stage," she says, and brushes the hair off her forehead.

"In our cottage for two
Our forever rendezvous

79

We'll share rooms with a view
Of the sky.
You and I.

I'll work. You'll plant.
There's nothing we can't
Create
Me and my mate
Making our Fate . . .

"Well?" Gloria says.

"It's got a nice beat."

"Each line has a rhyme."

"Is it a tango?"

"A duet."

"They're the toughest."

"I sing both parts," says Gloria. "That way, I know they both mean it."

The pigeons are shitting on George M. Cohan. I shoo them off. They fly up and perch on his hat. Cohan would've never given his regards to Broadway if he saw how dirty they kept his statue in Duffy Square. New Yorkers walk right by. Nobody cares. I try everything— even Gloria's song—to keep those clucking mothers away. No luck. It's not a job, but it's work.

At 10:30, there's nobody to get on Broadway. None of the faces look familiar. People are still grumpy and swollen from waking up.

The Drama Book Shop on 52nd Street's the only place to find an actor before lunch. I take the elevator to the fifth floor. I sit in a chair by Show Records. No big stars need a book shop, they get all their scripts from Studio Duplicating. But I wait anyway. I feel lucky. I ask anyone who buys an acting edition to sign my pad. By work time, I have eight names.

"Is this the man?"

Garcia nods.

A policeman clears a path for me through a crew

standing around Zambrozzi's table. There's a lead pipe on the table with handkerchiefs tied to both ends.

"What's your name?"

"Benny Walsh."

"I'm sick to death of these bomb calls. Do you understand, Mr. Walsh? Pissed off. Three times this year we've been called out of headquarters on bomb threats. Three times HQ has been bombed while we've been doing our duty."

"You're batting a thousand. Any clues?"

"Walsh, I think you should know you're dealing with J. J. Burns—kin to Walter Burns, the detective who cracked the great glycerine bombings of 1910. Bombing's no way to solve a labor dispute. Between 1905 and 1910, there were eighty-three bombings of industry. They found every man and put him behind bars. Business continued as usual."

"Did you know George Metesky—the Mad Bomber?"

Detective Burns turns to the policeman beside him. "Put that down, Frelingheusen. Knew Metesky."

He picks up the pipe.

"In the 'fifties they evacuated the Paramount five times for me to go to work. I knew my way around the inside of every explosive device. The bomb squad was the Glory Boys then. Seventeen times on the front page of the *Daily News*. Now, it's dinky lead pipes or candy-ass Coke bottles filled with kerosene. No one's interested in one man's battle against illegal combustion. This bomb was found in station four."

"That's my station! I could've been hurt."

"Why weren't you at your post?"

"I gave him the night off," says Zambrozzi.

"That's your story," says Garcia, crossing his arms. "He no your responsibility."

"Have you missed a day since you joined The Homestead in 1961?"

"Up to yesterday, I was running ahead of *Hello, Dolly*."

"But yesterday you weren't here?"

"Right."

"Where were you?"

"At a film studio. Then the Johnny Carson show."

"Hah!" says Garcia. "You done it now, Walsh. The Big Lie."

"I'm telling the truth."

Fanático. I watch. I have eyes. Fuck with the bull, you get the horn." Garcia pushes past the crew and walks out the kitchen door.

"I know I was there. How could I have gotten their autographs?"

"I suppose you're going to claim this was a frame-up?"

"Yes."

Detective Burns and the patrolman look at each other. "You want to name names?"

"There's only one."

"Out with it, Walsh!" says Detective Burns. "Time's the very essence of detection."

He hands me a cigarette. I smoke it Sam Spade style, like I was kissing my fingertips. "Garcia's your man."

"Benny, you're asking for trouble," says Victor.

"We have a team here, Mr. Burns. It's the best restaurant in New York. I can show you pictures from my scrapbook. Garcia wants to break us up. He wants to wear the chain of command. Garcia'd blow us up. I bet he even left a note. He wants credit for everything."

"I didn't mention a note."

"Garcia always leaves notes."

Detective Burns hands me a piece of paper with OFF-AMERIKA typed in red. "Does this mean anything to you?"

"That's him."

"How do you know?" says Detective Burns.

"Puerto Ricans can't spell."

"I'm listening very carefully, Mr. Walsh."

"I like the police. I wanted to be one when my Uncle Jack lived with us. I'd take his hat from Mom's dresser. I'd swing his nightstick on the bed each Sunday morning until they got up."

"I think that's enough. Check out Walsh's story, Frelingheusen."

"But, Chief, I watched the Carson show all night. He wasn't on TV."

"In the old days, they begged for orders. Allow anarchy

82

in the streets, it infects the ranks. Bomb squad rule number one—follow the leader."

"Stick with me for a moment, Chief," says the patrolman, walking around the table and staring at me. "The pieces are beginning to fit together. Aren't they, Benny?"

"I love this place. If I blew it up, there'd be no more album to keep."

"Except for the newspaper photos of the charred ruins of the empire you helped to build, which you knew for so long, and suddenly, in a violent confrontation between middle management and personnel, you were forced to abandon."

"Save the Policeman's Academy stuff for the squad car, Frelingheusen."

As they start to leave, Detective Burns spins around. "Don't think because we're walking out this door, I don't have people watching each and every one of you. I'll tell you one thing, this violence is driving us crazy."

"Take it easy, Chief."

"Do you know how many assaults there were on policemen in this city in 1950? One hundred and thirty-seven."

"Calm down," says Frelingheusen. "Your angina."

Detective Burns pushes him away. "In those days a detective could walk the streets. The city had charm. Do you know how many assaults there were last year? Two thousand, eight hundred and three. A man's not safe to enforce the law."

"I thought the gun was the great equalizer."

"Belt up, Walsh," Detective Burns says. "Or I'll have your guts for garters."

The door slams behind them.

I never heard of this Manhattan Gandhi.

Zambrozzi sits me down at the table before the evening rush and shows me his book. "Benny, you a student of history. My plan is from the history book."

"Chef, *piccata* and politics don't mix. If the Boss heard of this, you'd be back at Leone's faster than I could say 'prosciutto and melon.' "

"This little pisser—look at him—he sit on the railroad track. He block the building. He bring change."

"I've seen his type. When they sat down in the middle of Times Square with candles. That burned me up. I couldn't get anywhere. No one famous would walk the streets. They'd be mauled. Stars will stop coming to The Homestead. They don't want to take sides."

"Last night, Garcia say to close the restaurant. No, I tell him, the food must go on."

"How long did Gandhi take?"

"Thirty years."

"Our customers wouldn't wait that long. They'd find other restaurants. It's the wrong publicity."

"The man was a saint. Look what he did."

Italians are crazy about saints. "What happened to him?"

"He was shot. But he was ready for death."

"I've seen too much shooting on TV. Besides, you're Italian—you're not calm enough to wait for anything."

"The boys—we talk. They know him better. We complain to Garcia. We mention you. He listen. He nod. Then look how the *cafone* talk—'Fuck with the bull, you get the horn.' Me, the only Italian chef invited to last year's Concours des Meilleurs Ouvriers d'Europe."

"Now you know how it feels."

"Today, I take my Madonna off the dashboard. I put it on the stove. Better to risk the West Side Highway than be a body buried under bricks and beef. I'm telling you, Benny, we gotta work fast."

"They try this all the time, Chef. It never works."

Zambrozzi reaches for another book. "The Pavillon, remember the Big Strike of 'forty-five? They close down the best restaurant in America, yes? And for what? Bigger tips."

"The workers at the Pavillon lost, Chef."

"They were too polite—talking to guests across picket lines, walking into the kitchen for something to eat. It was just waiters, now it's to be everybody."

"What happens when people march? What happens when the TV gets ahold of it? The Homestead becomes an incident. You'll have the blacks marching and those women's groups arm in arm with the faggot groups. And groups protesting what all of us are marching for. I don't

84

like it. We've got nice American decor. These types write over everything."

"Benny, be careful. You look for other job. Garcia could do the dirty on us."

"Can't you talk to the Boss?"

"I call Florida. He's fishing. Now actions must speak louder than language."

"You're making a mistake."

"Prepare for the worst, Benny. We try for you."

Zambrozzi closes the book. He wants to be alone.

The worst may be a good thing. Babe Ruth must've felt scared when he was traded from Boston to New York. Eisenhower didn't know he'd be President when he graduated at the bottom of his class. Cassius Clay was down in the dumps after they took away his championship belt, but he got a Broadway show. You've got to make your breaks.

In the pantry, I put five patties of butter in each dish instead of three—eight rolls to a basket instead of five. I'll work harder. If I have to go, I'll walk out like a man— a tip of the hat, eyes straight ahead like Gary Cooper in *Pride of the Yankees*. Of course, when I leave it won't be as noisy as it was for Gehrig. It won't be pleasant. I remember saying good-bye to Mom and the cats. "Bye, Mom," I said. I bent close to her. "This is all I need," she said. I touched my favorite things—the TV, Mom's autographed Gene Autry picture, the flowers by the window in the pie pans. On the bus to New York, I made myself think of them once every Howard Johnson's. It's the same with The Homestead—every spot has its memory. My first autograph—Xavier Cugat and Abbe Lane—by the wagon wheel bar. The first fight—scrappy Billy Martin and some out-of-towner who kept calling him minor-league material when he was the best second baseman the Yankees ever had. The first party in the Northwest Passage Room for the New York Critics Circle, who were so busy arguing about their constitution they didn't touch the apple pie. If I go, The Homestead and I are quits. Even if they become caterer to a major airline, even if they hold the Academy Awards in the Wounded Knee Room —well, I'll cross that bridge when I come to it.

Garcia bangs into the pantry dressed for dinner. His chaps have flowers sewn on them. The white holsters are strapped to his leg with rawhide.

"Drop the rolls, Walsh."

"The doors open in a few minutes . . ."

"There are three rules for the maître d'. One. Always smile. Two. Never be surprised. Three. The maître d' must never lose face . . ."

"If I don't get the butter on the tables, the waiters'll start screaming."

Garcia grabs my wrist. "The detective call me. Your alibi checks. But you accuse *me!*"

"That's not what I said."

"Habla!"

"I said I thought you *could* do it."

"You're on silverware—"

"But I didn't do anything, Mr. Garcia. The detective proved it. I've only got a few days. Please."

"You lie to the police of the City of New York. You drag the name of Garcia through the mud—"

"They asked my opinion."

"My credit rating's Triple-A. I bounce no check. I drive a 'fifty-six Thunderbird convertible—no violations in ten years. I go to church, with my whole family. I have a hundred-thousand-dollar Major Medical policy. Does he do that? Does he take one responsibility? No! And he call me crazy."

"Let go of my arm."

"Concha! Cabrón! Maricón!"

Garcia keeps repeating, "No brains!" All the time, I'm making sure. I'm thinking National League hitting champions. 1943, Stan Musial, .357; 1944, Dixie Walker, .357; 1945 (this is the tough one), Phil Cavarretta, .355. I get them all right after that. Garcia's still yelling. I test myself with Academy Awards. My brain's okay.

He's shouting as if I'm in another room. But I'm right here, one foot from him. I'm scared to wipe his spit-spray off my new whites. I had a shock just like this in high school. I rubbed on a girl for a long time, the way I do on sheets. Later, I went to the bathroom and there was blood on my fly. I thought it had rubbed off. I started to cry. I was afraid to look. Slowly, I unzipped my pants. It was there. I was all there, like I am now.

When I look up, Garcia has gone.

The hot water sizzles the inside of my arms when I lift the wire-mesh basket from the sink. I'm in charge of two sinks, one for rinsing and one for washing. There's nothing to see but the clock, nothing to hear but the chinking of silverware and the drumming of the fresh water filling the tubs. I can't pull any faster. My arms ache. After I dunk the basket into the clean hot water, I slide it to the side and let it cool. I load more dirty silverware into the first tub. I change the soapy water in the second tub. Then I sort. Then I wipe the sweat from my neck and eyes. Then I start again. The rubber gloves don't work—silverware keeps slipping out of my hand. By the end of the shift, my skin's speckled with pink fork pricks. My fingers are wrinkled like the apple teacher kept on our school window to show us how the world ages.

Gloria meets me at 46th Street and Broadway. From here, we can see the news spelling itself out on the Allied Chemical building and the funny cartoons showing the time on the Accutron sign. It has more than one million lights and operates twenty-four hours a day. At the bottom is the time—not ordinary time, but the hour, minute, second, and tenth of a second. Something new is happening each blink of the eye. At 10:53:3:9, a man in a straw hat knocks on a door. A woman answers and hits him over the head with a broom. WHAM is spelled out on the sign. He falls. He bounces up. She hits him again. This time his hat is banged right down around his arms. He's spinning like a top. Then she kicks him right off the screen. It's a riot, and all in twenty seconds. At 11:02:3:6, a hockey player skates for the goal. He slaps the puck with his stick, it sails past the goalie into the net.

"I wish every clock had a story."

"Benny, did the Chef make everything okay?"

"You see on the top of that building?"

"Yes."

"Yogi Berra used to be up there. He blew Camel smoke rings. Each puff the size of a pizza."

"That big?"

"A perfect circle every time."

"Did you find a job?"

"The Chef says I should look."

"You were going to look today."

"Well . . ."

"Will you look at what I brought to show you?"

Gloria hands me *Stargazer, A Guide to Tomorrow's Talent*. "It cost me fifteen dolars. It came out today."

"It's not worth it. Cheap paper. Sixty-four pages."

"You've got to improve yourself, Benny. That's what I'm trying to show you. If you look on page twenty-three you'll be very surprised."

There's a picture of Gloria and a whole page about her.

LAURETTE
(Dancer/Singer/Composer/Actress)

CONTACT: Screen Femmes
           111 W. 42nd St.   (212) 289-3533

HEIGHT: 5'3½"

WEIGHT: 119

MEASUREMENTS: On request

EYES: Blue

HAIR: Brown

AGE: Over 21

BACKGROUND: Lake George High School
              The Gaslight Club
              Viola Wolff Dance Studios

SINGING EXPERIENCE: High school choir, church choir

BAND EXPERIENCE: 4 years high school band, 2
                     years all county band

FAVORITE COMPOSERS: Sigmund Romberg,
                    Beethoven, Mozart

FAVORITE GROUPS: The Ink Spots, The Harmonicats,
               The Beatles

NO. 1 DISC HIT: "Cottage for Two" (own composition)

TASTES IN MUSIC: All types of music

"My name stays in for a whole year. Eight issues. You
never know who'll see it. It's one dollar on the stands."

"We should have this kind of magazine for restaurants."

"You've got a union. Pull some strings. That's the only
way to get ahead. Of course, if you don't have talent, no
push is going to help. But when you do, all you need is
that little extra . . ."

"I didn't get anybody tonight."

"Not one?"

"Zero."

"Are you feeling okay, Benny? You can't get depressed.
You can't let little things throw you."

"They put me on silverware."

"You've got to hold a good thought."

"I hate to think about leaving The Homestead."

"We'd better hurry."

"Where?"

"Let's try the Majestic."

At the spotlight, we look up on the second floor. Four
go-go dancers are twitching their backsides in the window.

"Do you dance, Benny?"

"No time."

"That's how I broke into show business."

"Chorus line?"

"Ballroom. My first job in New York."

"Arthur Murray or Fred Astaire?"

"No, I was uptown. Viola Wolff. Young kids. The
upper crust. They wore white gloves when we danced."

"Where did you learn?"

"Dad taught me the basic steps. We'd practice each
Friday when Mom went for Bingo. By the time I was
thirteen, I could two-step, bunny hop, Lindy. I could do
the rumba without the wiggle."

"Arthur Murray had a television show. He wore a
tuxedo. He taught famous people the latest steps."

"Joan Crawford started as a dancer. Lucille le Sueur
was her name then. She did the Black Bottom."

"Can you do that?"

"Sure. But you have to wear a shimmy dress. I don't like it."

"In dancing school?"

"Viola gave me money for a gold gown. It wasn't really gold, but it was beautiful. Wasp waist. Strapless. I wore gold shoes. Viola would stand up by the piano and click her clicker. Everybody would stop and stand in a circle. 'Gloria, would you do the Grapevine?' she'd say. 'When you're ready, Gloria!' I'd wait a second or two—the pianist always wanted to hurry. But when I was in the mood, I'd start to dance—big, swirling box steps. Around and around the room, slow at first, then faster and faster. I could see the boys' little heads shiny with hair tonic. The girls holding punch glasses with paper napkins, giggling in their pink dresses and patent leather shoes. Then the music would stop, and I'd go up to one of the young men and ask him to dance. He'd say yes, and we'd dance. I was a good teacher. I knew from experience. They liked dancing with me. They were polite. When Miss Wolff would click her clicker, they'd say, 'Thank you, Miss Franzen.' And we'd change. That way everybody got to dance with everybody else."

"Another duet?"

"The spotlight dance. I was the best, I was always in the spotlight. The kids liked watching me."

"No, what was the dance?"

"A waltz."

"Nobody waltzes. It's all jumping and twisting and shouting. Waltzes are only for big-deal celebrations."

"You don't know these kids, Benny. Some of them grow up to have seats on the Stock Exchange."

Sypher is standing on the curb by the Majestic.

"Get lost, Louis. She's ready. She's as good as any of us."

"Speak for yourself."

"I've taught her the tricks."

"I'm not conning you. Listen to Louis the Lion-Hearted, sweetheart. The Garden's a gold mine. You gotta walk before you can run. Ethel Waters, Paul Anderson, the world's strongest man, and Billy Graham—Mr. Religion himself. Got them all. The place's packed. Everywhere you turn there's another famous face. They're all kneeling. I mean they're sitting ducks."

"Benny showed me what to do. I have my pad."

"Opening night crowds are a bitch, honey cake. The first people through those doors will be the critics. They're the ones dressed in gray and running. Forget them. Next, there'll be a lot of rich types from uptown. Speak clear— they think every stranger's out to strangle them. The stars go backstage. You got to be quick."

"I'll be okay," Gloria says.

"She will, too, Louis."

The ushers swing the exit doors open and jam wooden pegs underneath to hold them in place. We can hear the applause and see the white light from the stage. Most people are standing and yelling "Bravo." For a moment, there's nobody in the lobby, then suddenly people shove through the doors, blinking in the fresh air.

"Don't just stand there, Gloria."

"I'm making a wish."

"Go right up. Remember Sardi's."

"Hey, some technique you're teaching, Walsh . . ."

> *"Star light,*
> *Star bright,*
> *First star I see tonight,*
> *I wish I may, I wish I might*
> *Have the wish I wish tonight."*

"Jes-us, Walsh!"

"What did you ask, Gloria?"

"I'm not telling. Wish me luck."

"Good luck."

"No, our way. 'Cottage for Two.' "

We move into the crowd. Autographs are like tuna fishing on the TV. The minute you snare one, you haul it in, flip it away, and go after the next. At openings, speed's important. There's no time for singing.

"Benny!" Gloria waves. "Rosemary Clooney's here . . . Hurry!"

Gloria doesn't understand that shouting spooks the stars. They want to be recognized, but quietly. She's getting excited. An usher starts to follow her.

Sypher grabs Gloria around the waist. "The number one Louis Sypher rule—I taught it to Moonstone, I'm telling it to you—rumor."

Sypher steps in front of the usher. "Apologize to Cary Grant!"

"Where?" The usher turns around.

By that time, Gloria's inside.

I wait under the marquee. After a while, Gloria appears, smiling. "I got twelve signatures, Benny. Once, I didn't even have to ask. The man just took my pen and signed. You know who? Fernando Lamas."

"I got five."

"I'm pooped."

"You have to conserve your strength, Gloria."

"Are you okay?"

"Sure."

"Did you see me with Rosemary Clooney? I yelled."

"I didn't want her."

"Are you sure you're all right?"

"Sypher left. He mumbled something about 'Yes sir, yes sir, three bags full.' I waited."

"Look at these names."

We lean against a car and stare at the marquee lights.

"You don't get your name up there easy."

"Hard work," says Gloria.

Gloria counts her autographs again. "They laughed at Lucille le Sueur. She made her own dress for a sorority dance, and they made fun of her. It gave her strength. She vowed to succeed."

"Now that you're collecting more, you're going to have to learn about other people besides Joan Crawford."

"Will that be tough?"

"The starlets are hard. After a while you'll see it."

"I will?"

"Energy."

"You mean get up and go?"

"Yeah."

"I know that already. When you become an actress, you have places to go, people to see. You have appointments."

"There are other things. Guts. Patience. It takes time. Look at The Homestead. Garcia shouldn't rush everything—the food, the service, the busboys. That's not how artists work . . ."

Gloria reaches into her purse. "You made me realize something Joan said. I've never understood it till now."

"I did?"

Gloria opens a piece of paper folded into a small square in her wallet.

" 'Then I found that incredible thing, a public. . . . From this moment on, I had a sense of audiences as warm, loving people who would care for me in direct proportion to the energy and talent I would give to a public to whom I owed a loyalty and from whom I've always received loyalty. . . .' "

"I am loyal."

"What can I do for you, Benny?"

"Nothing."

"I know somebody who might have a job . . ."

"On Broadway?"

"Near it."

"Sypher said Madison Square Garden's packed. That's more important."

Gloria takes my arm. "I never thought of myself as a public."

The Garden's so crowded that the only place we can see Mr. Graham is in his special Prayer Room. The usher shows us to the door. Inside, Mr. Graham's being broadcast on a six-foot screen behind the altar. When he asks the people to pray, they bow their heads. When he says come forward, they leave their wooden seats and kneel at the altar.

"Let's do it, Benny. Praying helps."

"The reception's terrible. You can't pray to somebody you can't see."

"It's Billy Graham, Benny. He prays with Presidents."

"I always get in trouble in church. Bad thoughts."

"My mother reached out and touched Oral Roberts during Temporary Interference. It still worked."

"We'd get up early and go to Rumson for Confession. I'd tell everything. But when I knelt down in Mass, even with Mom next to me, I'd feel the hard wood against my stomach. The perfume from the girl in front of me—always the same redhead—tickled my nose. I couldn't think holy. Bad thoughts would begin. There was nothing I could do. I'd follow her high heels up to the altar. I'd try to concentrate on the priest. But then I'd peek. Her mouth would be wide open, her eyes shut, her tongue would curl out. She really sucked the wafer, pulling it in from the tip of her tongue, scraping it between her teeth! It was embarrassing. I'd pray hard for forgiveness when I received Communion. But each time I walked back to my seat, hands folded the way Mom taught me, I'd see her. Praying in the raw. I'd get so nervous I'd chew my wafer."

"Mr. Graham has helped a lot of people. Don't be shy. He might have some job ideas."

"Let's go, Gloria."

"You're looking a gift horse in the mouth."

I walk out. She follows me past the food stands.

"Maybe I got my own idea, Gloria, and I don't know it yet. Maybe it will come to me just like that."

"That's a vision. It's very hard to have one of those."

"How do you know?"

"My mother had one, once. She kissed the bronze statue of Pope Pius XII and suddenly he spoke to her."

"What did he say?"

"He said to leave Dad and move to Fort Lauderdale."

"Did she?"

"She had to. He also said to leave me in the custody of my father. And that I'd grow up to be a very talented and successful girl."

"What does it take to have a vision?"

"Faith."

"I have faith."

"My mother said she heard music—violins, harps."

"Does buzzing mean anything?"

"No, but music's a good sign."

Outside, Gloria says, "Can I ask you a very personal question? How much money do you have in your bank account?"

"I don't have a bank account."

"What if you get sick? What if you want to make plans?"

"You can't make too many plans. You've got to be at the right place at the right time."

"Think of yoursef, Benny."

"You sound like my mother."

"There are other things to life besides signatures."

"Like what?"

"Eating well. Having a good job. Nice surroundings. Pleasant company."

"I've got all that."

"You had it."

"Don't rub it in, Gloria."

"Let's go to the Gaiety Girls. My friend's—"

"I'm not going anywhere. I'm going home. You've spoiled tonight."

"I'm trying to help."

"Why do you want to dig at me? Make a guy worry when he's having a good time."

"You've got to get another job."

"Go find Sypher. I'm not blind, you know. Letting him feel your arm, and say those things. Daredeviling under his nose. Yelling at me just to make me look like a fool."

"What's wrong with you?"

"That Waldorf wise guy. Go ahead after the bulging billfold. Fall for the dazzle on those shined shoes. Girls are suckers for amateur night."

"Stop it."

"Can't take what I'm saying about your Waldorf weasel?"

"I want to help you, Benny."

"Sure. Make me a miracle."

"If you get a job tonight, will you believe in miracles?"

"All I hear's a hum in my head."

"You've helped me."

"Don't remind me of certain things."

"My friend's the headliner at the Gaiety. The girls there are bigger than Mae West."

"Really?"

"That's how they're billed."

"On the marquee?"

"Let's go, Benny."

"Not many performers are bigger than Mae West."

A woman's voice from the wings—"And now . . . The Gaiety Girls Revue Bar . . . is proud to present . . . the Yeast from the East, the prize who makes the men rise, that sweet confection who'll be your res-*erection,* that sinner who's a winner, that quite contrary Merri with the magnificent mammaries—Miss Merri Magdalen."

It's about time. "Show's just beginning," the man outside said. That was five minutes ago. Then Gloria left to visit backstage and they sat me here in the dark. I like to be in the light, ready to move.

Miss Magdalen walks in large circles around the stage. She stops suddenly and comes right down to the edge. A man in the first row hops up and sits at her feet. She pats his head. Her voice is very confidential, but everybody can hear.

> *"What you want—take!*
> *What you need—make!*
> *What you know—fake!*
> *What you got—shake!"*

She runs her hands over her body. She nudges the man with her knee. He bites at her. She rubs up hard against him, then pushes him off the stage and into his seat. The audience likes it, even the man likes it. He raises his hands above him like he'd beaten Sugar Ray.

Miss Magdalen takes off her gold bolero and throws it in the wings. She has skin as white as lemon sherbet.

"Take me. Make me.
  Shake me. Rake me.
  I don't care
  If you forsake me . . ."

When she says "shake," her body begins to tremble.
Her skirt falls to the floor.
Her hands never touched her clothes.

"Bring the lights down, Frank," she says. The stage
gets darker. I think she has no clothes on. She walks, in
her high heels, to the front of the stage.

She has no clothes on.

She's beautiful and pink except for that one place, and
there she's golden. From the wings, she takes two majorette batons. She lights them at both ends. She starts to
twirl them. She swings them around her head, under her
legs. She takes one of them and shoves it down her throat.
She's breathing flame! A dragon.

A drum roll quiets the audience. Miss Magdalen adds
more flame to one of the sticks. It's as big and hot as the
one that put out Victor Mature's eyes in *Samson and
Delilah*. She fastens it into her ass. No matter how fast
she moves (and she's really picking up speed now) it
doesn't go out. In fact, it gets larger. I know how dangerous this is from working in a kitchen. I'm scared for Miss
Magdalen. The flame inches closer to her skin. The
audience doesn't seem worried.

Miss Magdalen is at the front of the stage, swinging
the stick into the audience. The men in the first row draw
back in their seats. The fire swishes like a horse's tail.
The man who nibbled at Miss Magdalen is now trying to
light a cigarette in the flame. He can't get near it. The
drums get louder. Miss Magdalen yanks the stick faster,
closer to her bare flesh.

Miss Magdalen spreads her legs wide apart. (I can't
watch this.) Miss Magdalen starts to draw the torch
through her legs. (I've got to watch.) The torch moves
closer to her skin. She's grinning, looking over her
shoulder at the audience, wetting her lips. The torch's
flame is as high as her shoulder. Her left hand stretches
above her head, her fingers are spread wide. Her other

97

hand holds the torch hard. Slowly, she pulls it between her legs. The heat's roasting her most private part. The flames have been sucked inside her. I can't see them. They must be gutting her stomach, charcoaling her intestines. She's quivering. There's nothing to throw my jacket on, nothing to aim at, nothing to smother. Just smoke. She's heaving back and forth. I'm ready to move.

I can't move.

The lights change. Miss Magdalen closes her legs and turns towards the audience in a hopscotch jump. She's all right. She's standing, bowing. It's a miracle!

The audience yells, "More! More!"

"Don't make her do it."

Their voices drown mine. Miss Magdalen comes back, carrying her robe on her shoulder. She touches a few hands. She starts to blow us all a kiss. Her cheeks swell up. When she opens her mouth, a flame bazookas out. She's held the fire inside her!

Gloria finds me in the bar. "Did you like Merri's act?"

"She's got nine lives."

"I don't understand, Benny."

"I never saw anything like it."

"I want you to meet her."

"Please, Gloria. Don't make me."

"What's wrong with you tonight?"

"Butterflies."

"There's nothing to be afraid of."

"She's got powers. She'll see right through me. I'm not the religious type."

"Don't be silly."

"You weren't watching from where I was. You didn't see what I saw."

Gloria leads me backstage. The music has started. Another Gaiety Girl's buttoning herself up, waiting to go on. "And now, the girl who'll rub you dry, Miss Terry Cloth . . ."

The dressing room's straight ahead. Miss Magdalen's sitting in her chair, legs crossed, stripping off her eyelashes. She's hardly got a stitch on.

"I told her about you. Go in and introduce yourself."

"Not like that!"

I close the door. I knock.

"Yeah?"

"She doesn't sound so friendly."

"Who is it?" yells Miss Magdalen.

"It's Gloria."

"Come in, sweetie."

Gloria gives me a shove. I freeze. She walks into the room and closes the door behind her. A few minutes later, Miss Magdalen's saying, "Benny Walsh, step in here and says hello to your Merri."

She sees me staring at the necklace hanging down from the corner of her mirror.

"Pure rhinestones, Benny. They used to drape it over the cash register at the Pink Panther in Miami. It was my calling card. Told the customers I was performing that night. They like seeing it on stage better than the cat."

"You worked with animals?"

"I'm all animal."

"You can be anything you want."

"Hey, he's a cute one." Miss Magdalen pinches my cheek. "Gloria says you want work at the Gaiety."

"I may need a job soon."

"He needs one right away, Merri."

"Business is off. It'll take a miracle to get a berth in this place."

"If anybody could do it, Miss Magdalen, you could."

"In the old days, maybe. When I was hotter."

"You were hot out there tonight."

"Gloria, this guy's a doll."

"I told you he was the outgoing type."

"Benny, if you weren't with my friend here, I'd kiss you."

"No!"

"Don't be frightened."

"Do many stars come to the Gaiety?"

"Jesus Christ would walk in here, honey, and nobody'd notice him. It's a watching bar, not a talking bar. Everybody minds his own business. You can't hobnob and get hot."

"You could make drinks, Benny. Keep the pad under the bar."

"It's too dark, Gloria. You can't see the faces."

"I could fire my prop man."

"Don't do that."

"Benny, the Gaiety's two blocks from Broadway. Merri's offering you a good deal."

"Tell you what, I'll ask around. Gloria says you like photographs. I've got a great one of the act at the Body Shop in L.A. I'll send it."

I shake her hand.

"What's that for?" she says.

"Thanking you in advance."

I ask Gloria back to my house. She won't say yes or no. She keeps walking. She won't even stop to look in the restaurants.

"Joan Crawford was always seeking, trying to improve herself. You could learn from her."

"I'm a man."

"What she said goes for both sexes. 'I must never allow myself to become self-satisfied. But I don't think I ever will. My ambition is too driving—too relentless to permit me to become complacent.' "

"You haven't even looked at my politicals."

"You're like Dad. You never listen. 'I want my girl to look like a million,' he'd say. 'These are the best clothes money can buy, Pop.' 'Throw them out, they look old.' But I knew what was best, what would last."

"You have a late date?"

"The Lord helps those who help themselves, Benny."

"I've got feelings, you know. I'm not just a nobody you can kick like an old shoe. I could walk away and never look back."

At the papaya stand, Gloria stares at her reflection in the mirror. "Cheer me up," she says.

"First, you're grumpy, now you want to laugh. I don't feel funny."

"You put me in a bad mood."

"I can't tell jokes. I get nervous remembering the punch-line."

"Please?"

"What did one hat say to the other hat?"

"I don't know, what?"

"You stay here, I'm going on ahead."

"Ugh."

"I'm not Bob Hope, Gloria. You want fast talking, get Sypher to tell you snappy stories."

"I was feeling good with my new autographs. I can get them just as fast as anybody."

Gloria scratches her nose.

I scratch mine.

"Stop that," she says.

"Stop that."

"I hate it." She wiggles her fingers.

"I hate it." I wiggle mine.

"Don't copy me."

"Don't copy me."

A bus door wheezes open. Gloria hops inside.

"Why'd you do that?" She doesn't hear me.

The bus whooshes out into traffic. I see her sit down. Gloria turns around. When she sees me waving, she smiles and quickly looks away.

I click on the television and get comfortable. Just before the *Late, Late Show,* an announcement crosses the bottom of the screen. It's too scary to speak out loud. The astronauts have lost contact with ground control.

The movie is *Forty-second Street,* one of my favorites. It's about the ups and downs of show business. Dick Powell plays a young singer who has his first big break in a new musical. Ruby Keeler's in the chorus. Everybody's very poor and nervous because of the Depression. Everything's riding on this show. Then, on the day of the opening, the star—Bebe Daniels—breaks her ankle and Ruby's tapped to replace her. Warner Baxter rehearses her until she's ready to drop. He's a director who works well under pressure. Ruby's very unsure of herself. But Baxter says: "You're going out there an unknown and coming back a star." Ruby's not convinced. "You've got to do it. Seventy-five actors, twenty stagehands, a half dozen ushers will be out of work if you don't." Dick kisses

Ruby good luck. She steps out onstage. The show's a smash. Everybody eats. At the end, hundreds of men and women dance down the middle of 42nd Street. The traffic stops. Everybody's rushing, but nobody's bumping. Their arms wave together like seaweed—"Naughty, bawdy, gaudy, sporty, Forty-second Street."

I sit up in bed. Garcia has refused the astronauts at The Homestead because they don't have ties. Nobody in America will feed them. It's just a dream. Even if the astronauts die, their deaths would be famous. The thought cheers me up. I put my hands above my head and sway like the chorus to the tick-tock of my alarm clock. "Naughty, bawdy, gaudy, sporty, Forty-second Street."

After that, I sleep like a baby.

ROOM 201 IS LUCKY. I got my union card here the first time I tried. The button came in the mail a week later. It means I'm professional, it tells everybody I'm on the union rolls. It's white and black. Around the outside is written United Federation of Restaurant Workers. The number in the middle is 1260, and under it is the union symbol, a crossed knife and fork. Not all the people who hang out at the Union Hall and watch the Job Board wear their buttons. Playing cards, reading the paper, listening to their pocket radios—they could be the ordinary man on the street. They don't wear anything to let people know they're special.

Nothing's changed much since I was first here. When you work at a good place like I do, the name rubs off on you. You don't drop by and showboat for the guys without jobs. You're sort of a graduate. Many famous members have sat on these wooden benches. Garten, "the busboy with the golden baton" from the Roosevelt Grill, who Sammy Kaye let lead his band three times on TV. Carpozzi of the old Stork Club, who won a lifetime supply of Morton Downey soap when he got caught on the dance floor in the Easter stampede for the Gold Balloons. If one of these fellows walked in right now, you'd hear whispers. They'd clear seats for them near the Big Board. The famous ones won't take any job. They're choosy like actors. The wrong restaurant could ruin their reputation. "Big Slice" Butterworth worked behind the counter of the Stage Delicatessen and got his nickname for the size of his corned beef portions. He decided to move to Lindy's, where they had a bigger turnover and specialized in strawberry shortcake. At Lindy's they watched him like a hawk and put him in

103

the take-out section. He had to weigh every serving. After a year and a half, Lindy's closed. Nobody calls Butterworth "Big Slice" anymore. The last I heard he was a short-order cook at Walgreen's.

"Valenti got Tavern-on-the-Green this morning."

The voice surprises me. I turn around. Lester Fein, "the Road Runner." Fein worked The Homestead when it was starting, but only lasted three weeks. He's a good waiter—polite, fast, quick with the bill. He's got his quirks. He serves on the right. If a customer spills salt and doesn't throw it over his shoulder, Fein does it for him. But Lester's real problem is he can't stay put. He loves the glamour of restaurant openings, the excitement of a new place. Once the menus have been reviewed and the customers are steady, Lester gets bored.

"Valenti'll be back, Walsh. Take it from me. It was ritzy in the 'twenties. Casino in the Park, they called it. Harry Richmond, Al Jolson, George White—they'd go there on a Saturday night. Now, it's Puerto Rican confirmations and senior proms. Who needs it? At my age, I want something classier."

"Me too, Lester. You've got to move on to move up."

"Traditional or experimental?"

"A place with a history."

In twenty years, Fein has worked almost everywhere in New York. He tells me he's waiting for number sixty-seven right this minute.

"Celebrity Burger was the pits, Walsh. The menu was embarrassing. 'Bite into a Sidney Poitier.' "

"I want some place serious."

"What about the French restaurants in the fifties? I've done every one between Fifty-first and Fifty-sixth Streets. Worked Le Mistral twice. My only repeat."

"I'm not sure about the French places. Too small."

"On a good night, you serve one hundred and fifty-five dinners. That's bustin' your chops."

"I don't think it's my type."

"How do you know unless you've tried?"

"Tables against the wall. Eyes on you. No privacy. People whispering so it's hard to hear. I don't like it. It's not for me."

"You'll be lucky to get a Chinese restaurant with the new Union Master they've brought in."

"Tough?"

"This guy's got something between his ears. He's CCNY in Hotel Administration."

"Smart?"

"Most universities take four years. He took six. Figure it out."

"Wow."

"He's a swinger, this one. The union's new look. Wears suits you see in ads. Drives a sports car with wire wheels. Has his hair done at Henri Bendel's. He's even written articles for *Management News*."

"If there was ever a strike, a guy like him could stop it quick, couldn't he?"

"Are you kidding? The minute the TV gets a load of Victor Monte-Sano, he'll be a star."

"Have you talked to him?"

"We've chewed the fat. Mr. Vic knew all about me. Said he'd read my file—it's the biggest in the New York area. I told him I was sick of wooden chairs, tablecloths, screaming over the kitchen noise. I heard of a new place with Plexiglas chairs and tables, where waiters call their orders over video cameras. That's the future, Walsh—technological restaurants. He said a fraternity brother was the contractor for the restaurant. They have secret handshakes and code words. He talked about the bonds of brotherhood. He said I could trust him. He'd go to bat for me. I'm supposed to hear today. With his connections, if there's a man-on-the-moon cafeteria, I'll be there."

"You think this Mr. Vic would help me?"

"He'll take care of you, if you take care of him."

"I've got my autographs. I take care of them."

"You still up to that?"

"It's better than jumping from restaurant to restaurant. All you've got's memories. No signatures, conversations. Nothing solid."

"Crazy bastard."

"Where can I meet him?"

"He's very busy," says Lester, pointing to the doors behind the Big Board.

"Hey, Walsh. Don't let your meat loaf."

I smile. But I don't like cooking jokes.

The letters on her ankle bracelet spell BONNI. She says, "Ssssh! Can't you see the astronauts are in trouble." She points to a TV.

"Other people have problems."

"They're taking it like men," Bonni says. "Come back after lunch."

"I've got to be at work. I want to see Mr. Vic now."

"They're having trouble breathing," she says, touching her throat. "The oxygen's leaking. Oxygen fires burn faster than Kotex. Didn't you see that Special Report on CBS after the last three went up in flames?"

"I'll only be a few minutes. It'll be worth Mr. Vic's while."

"Mister, it's history in the making."

"Who said?"

"Walter Cronkite."

"I spent the Cuban Missile Crisis with Cronkite. Everything'll be okay."

"Three years they spent building this rocket. The best money can buy."

"I've been at The Homestead eight years."

Bonni takes my name and looks through the file cabinet. "This you? You didn't do so well on the I.Q."

"They didn't ask the right questions."

"My job's to screen things. Mr. Monte-Sano's a very busy man."

"I've got my union number. I'm on the rolls. It's an emergency."

"Three men are up there risking their lives to make America great. And you want special treatment."

"I know the Union Master holds back the really big jobs from the Big Board."

"So? Everybody does. Even the President. These are for people with something special to give. It's free enterprise."

"I have my collection. It's worth a lot. Someday, he'll be proud to have it associated with the UFRW."

Bonni goes into Mr. Vic's office with my folder and a

cup of coffee. When she comes out, she says, "You just wasted ten minutes of your time, buster."

"Benny . . ."

"Bet he don't see you," says Bonni, sitting down in her chair.

The buzzer rings. "Send him in."

"He's probably heard about the collection."

Bonni doesn't look up.

Mr. Monte-Sano goes very well with his rug—dark brown alligator shoes, green pants, and a purple sports shirt. He has four telephones and a plastic runway behind his desk to swivel from one to another. A paperweight with V-M-S holds down three inches of work.

"I tell everybody I meet the first time the same thing, Walsh. I'm new. I'm young. I'm here to help. My job's a big responsibility and it needs a big man. Winning isn't a good thing, it's the only thing."

"Vince Lombardi."

"How'd you know?"

"He's signed my pad many times."

"We're like that," Mr. Vic says, crossing his fingers.

Mr. Vic takes me by the arm and strolls me around the room. His first business deal—a Mr. Softee stand on Bruckner Boulevard. His diploma from CCNY. Mr. Vic with his arm around Jenny Grossinger. "Don't think I don't know what it's like to push plates. I've been there. I know. In the Grossinger days I worked fifteen hours straight during the summer rush. We'd get our tips once a week in an envelope. If somebody didn't give me the tip I deserved, I'd spit in his food every night. I know how to hate, Walsh. Fuck 'em where they breathe, right?"

"That's why I'm here. I've been at The Homestead eight years. And Garcia's trying to cheat me."

"Enrique Garcia?"

"Yes."

"We're on the Knights of Columbus softball team. Those Puerto Ricans can pitch."

"I can't work under Garcia."

"I should tell you, Walsh, that Garcia was bellyaching

on the phone this morning. He wants you blackballed. He wants me to suspend your pin for six months."

"Everybody hates him."

"He scratches my back, Walsh. I scratch his. Understand?"

"No."

"You've had eight good years. According to *Job Descriptions of Hotels and Restaurants,* you're eligible for promotion to waiter, pantryman, cook's apprentice, head silver man, inside steward, and baker's helper."

"I like my job."

"Most of the people who go into restauranting, according to the 1965 Manpower Report, don't finish high school. Of every ten dropouts, eight reported they had no guidance. I want to change this and put my people on the right track."

"I didn't need guidance. The minute I left the composing room, I knew what to do. There are so many important people in the world and not enough time to get them."

"What are you looking for?"

"Lutèce would be the best. It draws the Impossible People—Katharine Hepburn, J. Paul Getty—people who never go out, who sign for everything."

"There's a recession on. Everybody's tightening their belts," says Mr. Vic. "Even restaurants."

"Autographs are better than ever."

"Your kind of manpower, Walsh, is easy to get."

"How many workers know the clients?"

"That's the maître d's job."

"What if the maître d's a stupid foreigner?"

"Now, Walsh. Be reasonable."

"All right. What if he's stupid?"

"Remember the motto of the UFRW—'Ours is not to reason why. Ours is just to serve with verve.' "

"Those are big words."

"You should read our rule book. I've written a new introduction."

Mr. Vic hands me a small gray paperback. I ask him to sign it. His writing's what I expected—very daring and fast.

"I like you, Walsh—there's something about you. I'm a man who plays hunches. A poker player. I love drawing to inside straights."

"I don't understand . . ."

"The Homestead's a very big restaurant to our union— high visibility. Garcia really wants to scuttle you. Whether or not this bomb thing is true, it's a blotch, Walsh. You can't deny it—a big stain. It's going to be uphill."

"Garcia knows I didn't do anything. The police cleared me."

"You know that. I know that. But in this business, you've got to keep your own counsel. You can't play favorites. You've got to please everybody."

"What can I do?"

"If this were a card game and I was dealt a hand like this—I'd double the pot."

"I don't gamble."

"You've got to bet big to win big. And this *honcho* doesn't play for less than fifty."

"What if I said sixty-five?"

"That's good for openers. Still doesn't send the salmon in me going upstream. At that price, I might fade."

"One hundred and fifty-five."

This number pleases Mr. Vic. He picks up his putter from the golf bag near the window and sits on the edge of his desk. "Remember the Stork, El Morocco, the Little Club, Quo Vadis? Those days are gone. There are very few up-and-coming restaurants. You've got to know where to cast your bait. The Yale Club. Côte Basque. Top of the Six's. They're big fish and hard to catch."

"Really?"

"But we're on the ground floor. Victor Monte-Sano— Mr. Vic to you—is making it all possible. The restaurant renaissance is coming."

"It is?"

"I'm going to be a midtown Medici, Walsh. Nothing old-fashioned. I've got style. Clout. The people behind these restaurants are CCNY graduates. They know how to credit and debit, how to retail and wholesale—everything. They owe me favors. Now what's your bid?"

"I thought we'd stopped playing?"

109

"Where's your fighting spirit?"

"How do you keep score?"

"It's all in my head. No lists."

"Should I just say any number?"

"Keep it high."

"Two hundred and ten. How's that?"

"You're falling behind the pack. Two eighty-five."

"I'm tired, Mr. Vic."

"Try again."

"It's your turn."

"Full-husky this time, Walsh."

"Three hundred and fifty!"

"Bingo!" says Mr. Vic, throwing his hands in the air. "You win."

"That was fun. You sure know how to enjoy yourself, Mr. Vic."

"There's a little more honey to the pot. House rules."

"It's my lucky day."

"A case of Homestead Scotch."

"I don't drink."

"Three hundred and fifty covers postage and telephone calls. You understand, Walsh?"

"I thought I won."

"You did. I'm in your corner at that price. I cover your bases, get you off the ropes. All it takes is a *quid pro quo.*"

"Can you buy them?"

Mr. Vic smiles and taps my sneaker with his putter. "A man with all those valuable names can afford three hundred and fifty dollars and a case of Scotch."

"I thought there were no strings. I thought this was sport."

"I'm the sport. If I don't go to bat for you, it's the Automat."

"They don't have uniforms at the Automat. No fresh tablecloths, no real silver."

"Remember, Walsh, I'm getting you into a Triple-A establishment—wine cellar, salad chef—the works. You'll keep seniority. You can get OJT—on-the-job training— if you want to move up the ladder. When you buy my services, you get your money's worth."

"But three hundred and fifty dollars. That's not fair. I said numbers, not dollars."

"You came for a favor, right?"

"Yes."

"All favors are unfair to somebody."

Mr. Vic throws three golf balls on the carpet and paces off twelve feet from his coffee mug. "Think it over for a minute," he says. "No one else'll give you the chance of a lifetime."

Mr. Vic's hair's cut straight across in back, as sharp and slick as Warren Hull's. I wish Mr. Vic's paperweight would light up like Mr. Hull's Heartline heart. Mr. Vic would drop his putter and listen to the intercom. He'd tell me to sit down to get ready for it, somebody out there in the heartland of America had heard my story and donated.

In the 'fifties it wasn't all dog eat dog. There were lots of shows where a person could get help, *This Is Your Life, Queen for a Day*. If you lived in the New York area, you could walk into a TV station (you didn't need an I.Q., just a problem). If it was big enough, they'd try and solve it. When you lived far away and wrote them, they'd send for you after checking to make sure your story was true. My story's true.

"Get me the phone book, Ben, I'm gonna tell them about Ralph."

Each time she asked, I'd say "Mom, we buried Ralph in the dog cemetery three years ago."

"Hand me the book," she'd say. "He lives in my heart."

Mom got very excited when the Heartline would start blinking and ringing and Mr. Hull would stop his questions to pick up the phone. She'd bang the coffee table with her cane. "I knew it, I just knew it. Ben, listen to your mother, at the end of a storm is a golden sky."

Warren Hull was the best and the gentlest. He never asked anything in return for his favors. He never took liberties with his hands like the man on *Queen for a Day*. He paid attention and made you want to talk. He'd tell your story in his own words, making it sound even more dramatic and getting it just right. "In twenty years, this newspaperman turned restaurateur from Ocean Beach, New Jersey, the only child of Francine Walsh, former

111

beautician, who says she can count the things that happened to her on one hand—grew up, had a kid, raised the kid, had the operation—has acquired nearly three thousand autographs. It's a truly American story—signatures to success. If we help him, he can continue his search. Is that right, Benny?"

I mention the *quid pro quo*. Then the telephone rings. Mr. Hull gets very excited. "Wait a minute . . . I think . . . the Heartline's calling . . . It's the Heartline from the heartland of America." The Heartline speaks in a deep voice. "Warren, Jack and Charlie of New York's famous '21' Club are waiting at this minute outside their spectacular statuette collection of plantation darkies to welcome Benny Walsh as a fulltime employee." I can hardly believe it. I bite my lip, but my eyes get watery. "Go ahead and cry," Mr. Hull says.

"But I'm so happy. Thank you, Mr. Hull."

"Thank *you*, Benny, for sharing your dream with us and letting us help you to *strike it rich!*" The audience's clapping. The applause meter goes to ten—as far as it can go.

"Well, what are you waiting for, Walsh?" says Mr. Vic.

"The Heartline."

"The what?"

"How'll I get this money, Mr. Vic?"

"All I know is this—I'm leaving for a little holiday upstate on Friday. I'd better have my pin money by then. You've got forty-eight hours."

"That's not a very long time."

"You're not a very important person," Mr. Vic says. Then, grinning, he puts his fists up like a shadow boxer and taps me on the shoulder. "Just joshing."

Bonni watches Mr. Vic take me to the door. "When the going gets tough," he says loudly with a wink, "the tough get going."

I get it, and wink back.

New York Trust makes an On-the-Spot Loan fun—the waterfall behind the desks, the singer who keeps banking hours at her Steinway. The TV doesn't advertise this. They only show a man walking in and whispering what he needs. The banker, who's young and whose teeth are as white as Dick Powell's, hears his problem and, with a chuckle, asks him to sign on the dotted line. The man walks out the New York Trust door with an elephant. The banker explains, "When you're thinking big, think New York Trust."

The Loan Department's the row of desks near the window with the model sailboat display.

"I just got here. I'm overheated. I'll wait a few minutes."

"Mr. Derringer's ready," the man says, patting the leather seat beside the first desk in the Loan Department.

"I'll stand until he comes."

"I'm Derringer."

"I'd like an On-the-Spot Loan. Nothing as big as an elephant."

"If I want to laugh, I'll let you know," says Mr. Derringer. "Any means of identification?" I give him my union card. He takes it and puts the info on the application sheet.

"You write fast."

"Last year I put through one thousand, three hundred, fifty-six loans. They sent me and the little lady to London. Two weeks. All expenses paid. Maybe you saw my picture in *The New York Times*—Top Fiduciary Fifty."

"I missed it."

"How much do you want?"

"Three hundred and fifty dollars."

"You'll need more than that."

"Three hundred and fifty's exactly what I need."

"Have a blast. Spend what's left over on yourself. Our Quickie–Six Hundred comes to only pennies a day. Now what's the loan for?"

The New York Trust also puts you on the spot.

"C'mon, Mr. Walsh, answer up. The recession's killing my totals. This time last year I was working on number eight hundred and forty-five—a home repair loan. They're taking this year's winners to Honolulu."

"I'm moving from The Homestead."

"To?"

"Can't say."

"No chitchat, Mr. Walsh. You get to be East Coast champion by actions, not words."

"A Triple-A restaurant. I don't want to say any more."

"You mean you don't live at The Homestead?"

"I work there."

"That's an expensive move."

"A busboy collects a lot of things after eight years of loyal service. Favorite trays. Champagne bottles from famous guests. We've got a lot of traditions, too. When you move on, the custom's to give a little something to the chef and waiters. It's a great restaurant. You can't leave looking cheap. Tiffany ashtrays, pen and pencil sets, bottles of rare wine. It adds up."

"Any layoff between jobs? We need a three-week guarantee."

"No."

"I've never made a restaurant moving loan, but . . ." Mr. Derringer takes out a Bible-black book. He flicks the pages. He studies it carefully. "That'sa boy, Big D," he says. "You've got it, big fella. We'll work a little time-margin variable on them."

"What's that?"

"It's like stealing third base, Mr. Walsh. The same thrill. You need a good jump, a sharp eye. It's in the rules—but it's a risk, a gamble. When you're behind, you take chances. If you're caught, you're out. That's what makes ball games. But Big D's fast. Hold on a minute, Mr. Walsh."

Businessmen like Mr. Vic and Mr. Derringer aren't the only ones who can talk baseball. I know about stealing, too. I can still see the green Coca-Cola stand behind home plate the day I pinch-hit against the Pioneers. Coach Fasolino put his arm around me and said not to swing no matter what. In the eighth inning with no runs and Peter Parella pitching the game of his life, a walk was as good as a hit.

The Pioneer catcher kept insulting me. He called me four eyes and no hit and rubber duck. He tried to make me mental. The coach yelled at me to remember the instructions. Our signal was hand on hat.

Parella's pitches whistled. I didn't see the first two, but

114

I heard them. Strikes. The next pitch hit me in the toe. I was the first Trade player to get on base.

Coach Fasolino was the third-base coach. He ran all the way to first to talk to me. Coach whispered to keep my foot on the base, to tag up on the fly, and to watch Parella at all times. Parella's next pitch went over the catcher's head. Everybody on the bench shouted to run. But coach hadn't given me the sign—hand on cap. Finally, I saw him throw his hat on the ground. I ran as fast as I could. I slid into second base. The catcher hadn't even found the ball. The cheerleaders yelled—

> *"Big dog, little dog,*
> *Fluffy-eared pup—*
> *C'mon, Benny,*
> *Chew 'em up!"*

I couldn't hear myself breathe. I felt like I'd been mugged.

"Watch me! Watch me!" Mr. Fasolino kept screaming. I couldn't keep my eyes on the pitcher and the coach. After Parella's next pitch, coach yelled, "Walsh, you missed the steal. Come down here on the next pitch, goddammit!" I started for third as Parella went into his windup —but halfway there, I saw the third baseman already had the ball in his glove. He was coming toward me. Mr. Fasolino was on his knees, slapping the ground. "Hit it, Walsh. Hit it!" I did my slide. But the third baseman tagged me between my legs just as I was doing my hook. "Where'd they get you, kid?" Fasolino said, standing over me. My place ached. I couldn't talk. I stared at Mr. Fasolino. I was the winning run. I remember Bobby Thomson's homer, the "shot heard 'round the world," I remember Jackie Robinson stealing home against the Yankees in the World Series, but with all these sports thrills, the clearest thing in my mind's my slide. That was no thrill. That hurt.

"But you're all right now, Mr. Walsh? I can put down you have no physical disabilities?"

"Who said I wasn't?"

"Formalities. We're hanging in there. I think I've found

115

a ruling for a case like.yours. One quick call to your boss and we've got them by the short hairs."

"The Boss doesn't know me. We've never been introduced."

"Who's your supervisor? All I need's a guarantee of your term of employment up to the date of transferral."

"Mr. Enrique Garcia. You won't get much from him. He's Puerto Rican. He can't talk good."

"We've got a lot of triple threats at Trust. I can talk Spanish, French, and English." Mr. Derringer swivels his chair close to mine. *"Me pregunto un amigo/lo que era celos/no sabe el bien que tiene/con no saberlo./De buena gana/trocaria mi cìencia/por su ignorancia.* Can I speak Spanish or can I speak Spanish? The bank doesn't know there's dynamite in the Loan Department."

Mr. Derringer picks up the phone and holds it to his ear with his shoulder and neck. He laughs to himself. "D, you're too much. Sit down, Mr. Walsh. This'll only take a minute."

"Maybe I should come back later."

"Big D always gets his man."

"Garcia's hard to pin down."

"Slippery, huh?"

"I'd say greasy."

Mr. Derringer puts his hand over the phone. "It's ringing now."

"This man's very touchy, Mr. Derringer."

Mr. Derringer asks for Garcia. He has a pencil already sharpened. His pad's right in front of him. On top of the paper it says BULLET BOB DERRINGER, and underneath, like an ad for a Broadway play, it says "The Banker Who Throws No Curves."

"Hello, Mr. Garcia . . . This is Bob Derringer of the New York Trust . . . I want some verification on Benny S. Walsh."

Mr. Derringer turns to me very surprised. "He says he has no comment."

"That's because of the bombing . . ."

"Mr. Benny S. Walsh's right here beside me, Mr. Garcia . . ." Mr. Derringer holds the phone away from his ear. "What do you mean, 'bombing'?"

116

Mr. Derringer turns up a speaker by the telephone. We can both talk to Garcia and both listen to him. "It's very important, Mr. Garcia. Could you check your files to make sure this is the right man?"

"We no keep files," says Garcia. "If we did, I never tell the *Post*."

"The *Trust*, Mr. Garcia. The New York Trust. This is Robert Derringer, senior officer in charge of loans. Mr. Walsh is here with me."

"Put Walsh on the phone."

"What about the bombing, Mr. Garcia. I want to know about the bombing?"

"Tell Walsh that's a bridge under the water."

"Sir, at New York Trust bombing's a serious business. Mr. Walsh has applied for an On-the-Spot Moving Loan. He told us everything about himself. If there's anything you can add . . ."

"I no talk."

"You've got to talk for Walsh to get his moving loan."

"Don't believe him. He no move. He ours. We need him at The Homestead."

"I can hear every word you're saying, Mr. Garcia. You've howled wolf-wolf for the last time."

"Benny?"

"I'm right here."

"Benny—you come home."

"I'm moving to Lutèce, where a busboy's treated like a busboy."

"I no yell, Benny. I'm saying from the heart. There's big problems in the kitchen, Benny. I don't speak on the phone."

"I want one thing cleared up, Mr. Garcia. Does Benny S. Walsh have anything to do with your crisis at The Homestead? Yes or no."

"Yes *and* no."

"Mr. Garcia, you're talking to an officer."

"Yes and no, sir!" Garcia squawks more Spanish through the speaker.

"Mr. Garcia, we here *habla* three languages. Spanish was my major at college. So watch it."

"You don't know how dirty he can talk, Mr. Derringer.

That's not school Spanish, that's street Spanish. See why I want to move?"

"Benny, please. I put you on station four. I make the last three days happy days. I pay big overtime."

"Can I eat with the kitchen staff?"

"*Sí.*"

"Can I keep my autograph pad in my pocket?"

"I look the other way."

"Excuse me, Mr. Garcia. Did I understand you to say Benny S. Walsh has only three more days of employment?"

"Uh-huh."

"Thank you for cooperating, Mr. Garcia. Good-bye."

Mr. Derringer hands me the application. "Read the fine print, Walsh."

" 'I represent, warrant, and affirm that all of the statements made by me in this application are true and correct and have been made by me to induce you to grant credit to me with knowledge that you will rely thereon. . . .' "

"What do you think about that?"

"It's clear English?"

"The clearest."

"He's wasted Big D's time. He sits here while Big D hustles a loophole in the bank bylaws. He lies like a rug. He's out of a job in three days and he tells me three weeks."

"You said three weeks."

"With twenty-one days we could've parlayed it. Erlanger in our uptown branch probably got three While-You-Waits in the time I've been on the phone. Now Big D's been insulted by a maître d', and almost conned by a bomb-throwing busboy."

"I had nothing to do with it. The police know that. They checked with Johnny Carson."

"The typing pool's going to be yokking it up for weeks. If this gets out, I'll be eating alone in the Officers' Dining Room. Big D. Steady fella. Hang loose."

"Mr. Derringer—it says outside 'No wait. No red tape.' We've been here twenty minutes. You're a Trust officer, aren't you? I trust you."

"I have my superiors to account to."

"I didn't mean to fib. At least, I didn't tell you about the *quid pro quo*."

"Mr. Walsh, I really must ask you to take your business elsewhere."

"But the New York Trust's the friendliest and the best."

"And should be treated with more respect."

"Don't I get my On-the-Spot? I answered all your questions. You've got me excited. Pay up!"

"Guard," says Mr. Derringer.

The *Post* has two important stories on the front page, a picture of the astronauts in their capsule and a headline that makes me dizzy—TOM SEAVER LIFE THREAT. The Mets' front office has received a note from a member of the Chicago Bleacher Bums.

I'd have let you live if you'd kept your won-lost record below 15 games. You're getting too good. You've gone too far. I'll shoot you in the sixth inning when you start against the Cubs, Friday. The Cubs for first. The Cubs forever.

DETERMINED FAN

The spacemen are having trouble breathing near the moon. But it's not easy down here, either.

"Eeeeeeeeeeeh!"

The scream spins me around. My heart's skipping. An old lady pushing her way along the building wall, standing on a subway grate. At first I want to slap her a good one with my *Post*. But I might rip the story.

"Eeeeeeeeeeeh!"

"There's nothing there, lady. Stop it!"

I don't want to see her. She's got white hairs on her chin like Mom. Her stockings are rolled up to her knees. Her ankles are black with dirt.

"Eeeeeeeeeeeh!" Her fists tighten.

"What did you do that for?"

She smiles at me, like if I were shouting, not her.

The Homestead stagecoach pulls up to the stoplight on 44th Street and Broadway. The horses are shiny with

119

sweat, so is George Rumsey, the driver, who's a dead ringer for Gabby Hayes and who used to break in horses on the back lot of MGM. Rumsey's in street clothes—no bandanna, no boots, no hat with real bullet holes that kids can stick their fingers through. Usually, the horses are brought out after sundown to get the customers, who pay $40 or more, to the theater on time. The Homestead stagecoach is one of the sights of the city. It's higher than your ordinary car and says THE HOMESTEAD across the luggage rack. The Homestead horses are authentic Western types, none of these phony English kind with their tails pointing in the air like pinkies.

"You shouldn't drive the stagecoach during the day, Rumsey. People are too busy to notice."

"Nine o'clock this mornin' Garcia calls. He's beggin' for me to come down to the restaurant. The wife gets really pissed. 'Reb,' she says, 'I may look good, I may give the impression of health, but I'm a very sick woman. I can't take emergencies. Tell him to fuck off.'"

"You shoulda heard me talk back to Garcia. He was on his hands and knees asking me to come back."

"I had a hard time hushin' her up. The wife don't like me ridin' the streets of New York in an open carriage and cowboy suit. She thinks some crazy'll mistake me for a plainclothesman and drill me."

"Garcia's paying me overtime. It's a grubstake."

"Don't get me wrong, Walsh. I ain't afraid of rushing. The Rumseys rushed all over this fuckin' country. Hightailed it to California in the Gold Rush around eighteen fifty-four. Back to Kansas in the Land Grab of 'sixty-two. That didn't work out, either. So Gramps up and came to Hollywood in the boom of 'nineteen. Things got tough for cowboys when they brought in those stunt men, so the family moved out to Colorado near the oil fields."

"I like staying in one place."

"You gotta pick up stakes to raise the stakes. Don't this beat all? A grown man who's rode with Andy Devine and Randolph Scott deliverin' groceries and sendin' ten-dollar telegrams to the Boss in Palm Beach. No time to even put on my outfit. 'Guests and food must go through.' You'd think Garcia was the Pony Express."

"Did you hear about my move? I'd like to stay at The Homestead, but I got an offer that's too good to turn down."

"That's the spirit, kid. Keep movin'. Don't look back. The wife was talkin' to her dead daddy at the spiritualist the night before last. The old man said to go back to the Tucson Trailer Park on account of her heart. 'Molly,' I says, when she sprung it on me, 'you don't have no heart problem.' She looks at me all angry. 'Dad means my asthma.'"

"It's not easy leaving. The Homestead, I was there from the first. Sort of a pioneer."

"Shit, boy, who wasn't? It'll really raise your dander to see it today."

"What's happening?"

"Garcia says not to quote him, but Chef's flipped out."

"Did Garcia talk about me?"

The light changes. Rumsey slaps the reins against the stagecoach seat. "Giddyap."

The Homestead looks like it's being attacked. Most of the staff's outside waving their hands at the restaurant from behind the gray and black barricades. They walk in circles like Garcia when he's mad.

I've dreamed of being many things, but not a protester. You don't see quality on the hoof.

The line's a real melting pot. Waiters are marching with dishwashers who are marching with cook's helpers who are being led by Jan the cashier at the bar. Their signs say THE HOMESTEAD IS UNFAIR TO EMPLOYEES. "Pass it by. Pass it by," they yell. They don't really mean it. The Homestead's a brand name. When The Homestead does good, it rubs off on them.

The policeman starts to ask me to leave the area. "He's with us," shouts Jan. She tosses a cardboard sign over my head and hands me a piece of paper with writing on it.

"Welcome to the wildcat strike, Benny. Thanks to Desi, we've done it. Thanks to Desi, we're organized. If

121

they want rolled butter, let them pay for rolled butter! If they want to alienate labor, that costs extra!"

Jan's working her way through secretarial school. School's where she gets her lefty ideas. She starts to sing "Solidarity Forever."

"What's this paper about?"

"It's what we're striking for, Benny. We've got a twelve-point program. I just touch-typed it up. There are four categories. You're one of our nonnegotiable demands."

"I'm on that piece of paper?"

"You're number twelve."

"Who gave you permission to use my name?"

"Desi."

The minute she mentions Zambrozzi, somebody hollers, "Say it loud, say it proud." The veins in Jan's neck swell up. *Desi! Desi! Desi!* she screams.

Zambrozzi's a great chef. He shouldn't allow his name to be used like this in public. It's all right if it's a food label like Fanny Farmer or Chef Boyardee, but this waters down his by-line.

"Desi wrote the draft," Jan says. "He's a student of Gandhi."

"That guy was nonviolent. This is a stab in the back."

"We want you reinstated, Benny. Can you dig it? We're prepared to go to the NLRB."

"How long will that take?"

"We could have a decision in three months."

"That's too long. I need money now."

"If we close the place down, there's a strike fund. Forty-two fifty-five a week."

"The Homestead can't close. We stayed open even after the assassinations as a tribute to America."

"We've got to get it together. Don't you understand?" says Jan. "We've got to get it on."

I agree. The Homestead's got to get on with business. Jan marches me around in the line and calls me "brother." I don't get it, she hasn't said more than one hundred words to me in the last year. She must want one of the autographs from my collection—a gold digger of 1969.

* * *

A cab pulls up to The Homestead. The marchers push against the street-side barricade. "Pass it by!" "Freeze 'em out!" "Keep going!" Jan starts making a speech about bringing The Homestead to its knees. David and Goliath and things like that.

Inside the cab, I can see that it's a lady. Short blond hair. Charm bracelet. She pays the cabbie and waits for her change.

Who could miss the smile? The straight teeth? The cheeks? The red lips that always look wet? It's Mary Martin—my world record for second acts. I snuck in twelve times to watch her in *I Do, I Do*. I couldn't walk past the theater without getting me the Martin itch. I had to have her smile and hear that Texas drawl. Just seeing her—one of the great, all-time money makers of the Broadway stage—makes you happy. It's like thinking nice things before going to sleep, only you're awake. She's always sunny. Of course, it was no use trying to get her autograph then. People crowded in her dressing room until the late hours. Miss Martin's a star from the old school—well-dressed, neat, proper, perky. That's not the style these days. Jane Fonda, Mia Farrow, Vanessa Redgrave—they're all kinky. They wear sandals and swear. They get political and pregnant. Of course, they're still famous and fun to watch, but there's something about the old-timers. They don't pretend they don't give a damn. They don't slouch. All their colors match. What's the sense of hiding you're a star like Dustin Hoffman or Robert Redford or Steve McQueen when you are one?

Miss Martin looks beautiful stepping out of the car. She smiles and tries to pass by. Garofolo and Jan link arms. "Try another restaurant, lady!"

"Get out of the way," I shout. "Let her pass." I push myself in front of them—a human shield.

"Don't do it, Benny!" says Garofolo. "United we stand."

"Jerk. That's Mary Martin."

When they hear that, the protesters back away.

Miss Martin's grateful. As I get her to the door, she opens her purse and gives me a dollar.

"I don't want the money, Miss Martin. Just your signature."

"What's your name?"

"Put 'Benny.' "

She laughs and draws ☺ beside her name. That's Mary—bright as a daisy.

"Tell me about your first Broadway smash in *Leave It to Me*. Gene Kelly in the chorus. A show-stopping song. Cole Porter said he loved writing for you and Ethel Merman best."

"Merman didn't have my innocence."

"And there was a struggle, right? The hard but good times."

"I was a kid from Weatherford, Texas. I always had faith. When it finally happened, it was just the way it was supposed to be."

"Me, too. With The Homestead. I won't let my autographs go to my head, either."

"Remember what I said in 'Climb Every Mountain.' "

"I know it by heart."

"It's the climb that's the thrill. The unattainable . . . I don't know."

"People gave you a push up that mountain. A helping hand."

"Sometimes."

"Speak to Mr. Garcia. Mention your South American ranch. Tell him I'm a good guy, that you want me to stay here. Tell him to cut the crap."

"Enrique!" Miss Martin says, turning toward the front door and holding out her hands for Garcia the way she did for Ezio Pinza.

"Madame." Garcia hurries to her and kisses her rings. When he clicks his heels, the spurs rattle. Some nerve.

"This young man here nearly saved my life."

"Homestead hospitality, Mr. Garcia."

"Drinks are being served as usual, Miss Martin. I apologize for this confusion."

"We live in troubled times, Enrique." Miss Martin takes Garcia's arm. I start to walk in behind them. Garcia's looking at Miss Martin and smiling. Behind his back he motions for me to stay where I am.

When he comes out, it's not the usual "Mr. Ricardo Montalban" Garcia.

The pickets are yelling—"Two, four, six, eight. Garcia's second-rate."

"All day. This! Can you believe it?"

"I wasn't with them, Mr. Garcia."

"Then why you wear a sign?"

"Don't believe everything you read. I came as quick as I could. No hard feelings."

"Listen to them. The waiters, they call in sick. The hatcheck girl, she slow down in sympathy. Zambrozzi only want to talk, no cook."

"The restaurant's still running?"

"Skeleton crew."

I take off my sign.

"I don't beat the bush around, Walsh. You know I hate your guts." When Garcia talks quietly, everything makes sense. "They talkin' a lot about you."

"I'm only number twelve. I feel so bad I could die."

"If I could only believe that . . ."

Garcia puts his arm around me. The kind of man-to-man get-together that Joe and Weeb have, pacing up and down the sidelines.

"I give you three-fifty an hour. That's a big bankroll."

"Could you make it ten dollars an hour?"

"The bartender, he don't get ten dollars an hour."

"People can go without drinks, but who's going to clear away their plates?"

"You got me by the *frijoles*, Walsh. Seven-fifty. Three days only. Take it or let it go."

"Miss Martin put in a good word, didn't she?"

"We need manpower, Walsh. If Zambrozzi, he don't get what he's askin', The Homestead's gonna be hurting. He might leave. We'd lose our Michelin stars."

"I'll work hard my last three days, Mr. Garcia."

"You better."

"The money's great."

"A jackpot for a jackass."

The kitchen's a ghost town. There's nobody behind the pasta machine. The faces standing over the plate racks

125

are all new. A few of the regular waiters are showing hired help how to lay a table Homestead style. Zambrozzi's standing over the stove, stirring the soup himself. When he sees Garcia, he puts down the ladle and meets him by the chopping block. He waits for Garcia to speak.

"Walsh, he say he work for the Boss tonight."

"You've got the right *not* to work, Benny."

"I want the right *to* work."

"But you're one of the nonnegotiable demands. If you work, you gotta be dropped from the cause."

"I need money."

"They gyp you. They pay you off. They try and frame you. You still want to work here without changing things? *Marrone,* you need awareness!"

"He got the right to do what he wants."

Zambrozzi turns his back and starts to put on his apron.

"Sorry," says Garcia. "The maître d' must be a diplomat."

"We talk at the table," says Zambrozzi, pointing to his corner.

Zambrozzi speaks first. "I got only one question, Benny. What you want most?"

"I want to get autographs."

"Can you get autographs now?"

"Not many if I work in the kitchen."

"We're like brothers. I want to cook, but I can't cook the way I want here."

"Bullshit. You ask for *piccata,* I get you *piccata* from the Boss."

Zambrozzi's eyes get wide. For a few minutes he says nothing. He's looking beyond us. Garcia even turns and looks behind him. Nothing's there. "I have a dream." We pull our chairs nearer and listen closely. Zambrozzi's looking into the future! "Every day I have dozens of food ideas. I wake up thinking the new recipes. Even before I come to America—in Como—I have the ideas, revolutionary ideas. At the Villa d'Este, the chef kept the bouillabaisse simmering on the back of the stove. I told him keep the bouillon and boil fresh fish with each order. You know what the old dog did? He handed me an Italian cookbook and told me to study it. 'There are ten thousand recipes in here, Zambrozzi, and only one way to prepare them!' The next day I left the hotel. I come to America where things are free and modern, where somebody with ideas gets ahead."

"And you made a great success—the Capri, Mamma Leone's, The Homestead."

"No, Benny, that's just popularity. I want the history books to know what I've done. I want to be the Escoffier of Italian foods. I'm as ingenious as Albert Stockli of the Four Seasons. I take bigger risks than Mario of the Century Club."

"You're mentioned in all the guide books and the reviews."

"I want to create. Look at Stockli. I want menu power."

"The chef's on my right hand, the accountant on my left. It's like a stairway. Only one can approach the Boss," says Garcia. "That's me."

From his table drawer, Zambrozzi takes out *Esquire* magazine. He shows us the pictures.

"Look at that! Sparkling Coconut Snowball. Apple Messalina. Fiddler Crab Lump à la Nero. Boneless Columba, a Bird of Rome, Stuffed with a Delicate Mousse Trimalchio. Stockli's boss gave him the green light. He send him to Italy—my native land—and he discovers one hundred and sixty-nine dishes. I know these dishes. My father used to sit me on his knee and talk about them. But who can do them in a kitchen like this?"

"But, Mr. Zambrozzi, just this year *The New York Times* said—wait a minute, I'll read you the exact words —they said you were 'one of the highlights of the New York culinary establishment.' "

"But, Benny, don't you see? I don't want to be established. I want to be memorable. I want to be—how you say?—*avant-garde.*"

"Everybody knows you're a great cook, Mr. Zambrozzi."

"Tell somebody you cook Italian, they think you make pizza! With a say in management, I create a menu that stands the Cordon Bleu on its head. The things I could do with aubergine and fresh fish! Nothing frozen. Real flavors."

"The Boss, he always give you what you want."

"The Boss gives me cans. I ask for tomatoes, I get number-ten cans. I ask for pineapple, I get number-six cans. Could Michelangelo do the Sistine Chapel without paint? Can I cook without real food? The Boss is *stupido*. He's Cornell Restaurant School—he no from the hillsides of Como. He no grow up with zucchini and melons and wild game. If Zambrozzi plans the menu, the restaurant makes money like never before. They come to me like Baron Rothschild and Talleyrand to Carême. I need freedom to cash in."

"The Boss, he say the wine list's yours." Garcia's shoulders sag.

Zambrozzi scribbles on his memo pad. Without signaling, the cook's helper is by his side. Zambrozzi tells him to take the message to Jan. "Our first step to radical change."

"The chef no supposed to choose the wines. Even Mario of the Century no choose the wine. They do it by committee."

"Committees never work. Zambrozzi knows his wine."

"For five years, an afternoon a month in the backroom of Louis Sherry. All the maître d's from the grade-A restaurants. We scientific. Pad and pencil. Twenty-four numbered glasses at each setting. First we taste. Then we talk. We get good buys."

"Your Chianti spoils my *farinacci*."

"What you think of the Moselle?"

"Piss."

"Those Moselle afternoons were fun," Garcia says, quietly. "The people no complain."

"Americans don't know shit about wines. Change or die."

I think Mr. Zambrozzi's going too far. If he doesn't like America, he can leave. But I'm nonnegotiable, and Zambrozzi's negotiating. I keep quiet.

"Wine's the maître d's department!"

"If you choose the wines, Garcia, I go. I take Victor and Anthony with me."

"I quit!" says Garcia.

"Good."

"You'd let me go?"

"You sneak out most of the time anyway," says Zambrozzi.

"All work and no play make Enrique a dull *hombre*. The customers like me."

"I watch from the kitchen window, Garcia. Kiss-kiss. Squeeze-squeeze. A maître d's supposed to have the class. He supposed to act like a king, not Sammy Davis, Jr."

"I get big tips."

"Zambrozzi gets hard work and no thanks. It's time for a change."

"Like it or lump it, Chef, Mr. Garcia's a drawing card. Look at the pictures in the window."

"Shut up, Benny! You gotta earn the right to speak. I need more space to cook great. We move the wine cellar. I want a fresh- and a salt-water tank down there. No more frozen fish. No more sending to the docks in the middle of the day. I want them alive, right under our roof. We don't lose tenderness or time."

"Won't that be dangerous? Fish bite."

"Quiet, Benny! There'll be a fish chart. Everything organized. I want a humidity-controlled greenhouse down there. It's possible. Italian foods need lots of herbs and the right earth. We fly soil from the hillsides of Bellagio. The iron, the lizards, the olive humus will be there. The herbs will be *bellissimo*, and right from our own garden. Magazines will photograph. In the afternoons, when things are quiet, the Boss can give the guided tour. We can make a pamphlet. Sell it for a dollar on the history of the Zambrozzi kitchen."

I wish Zambrozzi'd watched *The Price Is Right*. He'd know to quit while he's ahead.

"Where the Boss raise the money?"

"The Zambrozzi kitchen's the price of one vacation to Palm Beach."

"The Boss, he a good man. He want to help, but you ask too much."

"That's not all we want. Look at number eleven. I want the right of first refusal!"

129

"What?"

"I don't want you coming back here asking me to ruin my cuisine because the customer wants something special."

"I never do this," says Garcia.

"What about Tina Turner?"

"That was special."

Zambrozzi pulls out his pocket diary. "On September 1, 1968, you scream at me to brown my dover sole under the grill, I sent the *plat* out under a covered dish to hide my shame. I don't want no more out-of-towners pouring *crème vichyssoise* on their strawberries. *Gesù Cristo*—the humiliation."

"Look, Mr. Zambrozzi, I no tell the Boss I give you everythin'. He won't think I bargain. I tell him about the equipment, the menu. He be very mad. He swear at me. I say to him I'm repeating your words. I no tell him about first refusal. You must speak for yourself."

"Unless this settles within twenty-four hours, Zambrozzi leave. No gourmet chef will work here again."

"We got a good thing, Zambrozzi. Don't mess it up."

"Twenty-four hours."

"Don't tell the Boss that. You know his heart. Without you, we no have a chance."

"Then the Boss meets our demands."

"You said this was a bargaining table."

"It is."

"Where's the bargain? What do *we* get?"

"You get *me*. You get the old experienced crew and a new improved restaurant. You get more profits."

"But that's for the future. The Boss, he want to know what I won for him, how I hold down the fort. You tell him I busted balls, okay? You say Enrique Garcia's a mean *honcho,* okay?"

"Sure."

"Then I must win something to prove it."

Zambrozzi's silent. He writes a note and gives it to the cook's helper. "I want a hand vote."

The messenger returns. Garcia reads the note and puts it in his pocket. "All right. Tell Boss you won number twelve."

130

"That's me, Mr. Zambrozzi. I'm number twelve. You can't give up number twelve."

"You broke the picket line, Benny."

"I need the money."

"You let me down."

"I want to be part of this new restaurant."

"Then why you scab?"

"What about our drinking song? The Big Draw? You're pulling a Garcia."

"Watch it, Walsh!"

"He's right, Benny. Gandhi says—'The future depends on what we do in the present.' It's now or never."

"You and I were buddies, Mr. Zambrozzi. We swapped stories about the great customers you'd cooked for, remember? I wrote them down and filed them. I consider you an autograph."

"Will you picket until we win?"

"That could be months. I can't wait."

"That's all I want to know."

"But, Mr. Zambrozzi ... Chef ..."

Zambrozzi takes his hat and puts it on. The meeting's over. They whisper together. There's no use pretending I'm not here. Garcia finally turns to me. "Walsh, take pots and pans."

"What about my old station? You promised."

"You want overtime?"

The pans have been lying dirty for hours. They're hard to clean. You need nails for scraping the corners. Steel wool pricks your fingers. Steam—thick as cotton candy —tickles my nose. Suds swoosh against the inside and mark it like waves sneaking up on the sand.

On hot days, I'd run into the ocean with my goggles. My toes and fingers sank into the sand. I was solid as a clam. The waves couldn't budge me. The others swam to the raft with the diving board. You could hear them laughing and see them pushing each other off. I'd take a deep breath and duck underwater. There was a nice silence. Everything floated in slow motion together. When I came up for air, the beach looked new.

The others called me "Flounder" and dared me to go

131

into deep water. I didn't even look their way. I'd slide up on the sand and let the sun bake me. When the yelling got loud and I got bored from sitting, I'd go under the waves again and lie quiet in my special place by the shore. Sometimes, the goggles left marks on my forehead. When I came home Mom would try to rub the red lines away with her thumb. "You weren't looking at beach pussy, were you?" She said God would paralyze my face for doing those things. But there was nothing bad in my swimming. I remember it when I want to pass the time. I'm loyal to my good memories.

The pans pile up. No matter how hard you wash, somebody's always shoving more by the sink. If I daydream, I get behind. If I look across at the other washer—McDougal—I see those two black holes, like a bowling ball, in the middle of his face.

"Think this is a bitch, huh? It's better'n seein' the ass end of the Statue of Liberty every four months on that freighter. I'm fuckin' stayin' away from freighters. Mister, let me tell you—stay away from freighters."

I put more powder in the sink. I rub the dish covers until I can see my T-shirt in them. There's only one trouble with temporary help—they don't concentrate.

"I've got a story to tell, man. The Department of Health, Education, and Welfare should send me on tour. The Jimmy McDougal Story—the Syph Saga. I'd do the dockyards, the off-limits bars, the Merchant Marines. Nobody'd prod bar snatch after they heard what I've got to tell 'em."

I try to think of the summer. And then I think of trees. And that starts me remembering station four with the weeping willows and the shrubs that divide the tables. I've dusted those plants since they were first installed. They listen to me. Mom says the secret to caring for plants is talk—there's no use having them if you're not prepared to give them conversation. She's right. Only a few of mine have melted, but that's because they bent too close to the indirect lighting.

"Don't want to talk, huh, kid? Want to see me French-inhale a cigarette? Want to sing?

> *"A hundred bottles of beer on the wall*
> *A hundred bottles of beer.*
> *If one of those bottles should happen to fall*
> *Ninety-nine bottles of beer on the wall.*

"C'mon, kid, sing along! It's good for you. You learn this song, junior, you can stay in the saddle an hour without shootin' your wad. I once fucked a broad in Charleston—that greaser couldn't sit for a week."

I sing my own songs to myself—"Over the Rainbow," "Everything's Coming Up Roses," "He's Got the Whole World in His Hands."

McDougal's splashing the water while he sings. He doesn't care if he soaks me. He's down to sixty-nine bottles of beer on the wall. He sings the chorus again.

"Sixty-nine bottles of beer, kid. Don't you get it?"

"No."

"Not eighty-two bottles, not seventy-five, but sixty-nine. The daily double.'"

"Is your water cold?"

"Hot as a pistol. Sixty fucking nine, kid! Cheez."

"I can't get the grease off without hot water."

"Don't talk to me about hot. Spent three weeks at a time in the boiler room. Grease like you never seen. You could fry an egg on the floor. Drank three hundred and ninety-four bottles of beer in the run from Charleston to Panama City. Drunk for thirteen days straight. James Michael McDougal of Eugene, Oregon, was drunk and dirty . . . Oooooooheeeee!

> *"Fifty-five bottles of beer on the wall*
> *Fifty-five bottles of beer.*
> *If one of those bottles should happen to fall*
> *Fifty-four bottles of beer on the wall. . . ."*

"You missed a few bottles of beer on the wall."

"I did not."

"You were in the sixties, now you're nearly in the forties."

"You're crazy."

"I've been listening . . ."

133

"You callin' me a liar? If you don't know what sixty-nine bottles of beer on the wall means, how do you know I missed any? Want a piece of advice, kid? Don't ship out. Stay off the poop deck. On board, dumb-dumbs like you could be killed for less. Once the chef called the bosun a faggot. The next day they found half a chef stuffed through the porthole."

"I'm sorry. I can't talk and wash. I'm getting overtime."

"You think I took this job for money? Buddy, you got another think comin'. I signed on to bust some Commie chops. If enough of us work cheap, those protestin' pinkos will be out on their ass. We'll take over the joint."

"I've worked here eight years."

"You're not temporary?"

"I've got two days to go."

"So, you're temporary."

"The Homestead's really going to be better once this strike's settled."

"It's rotten with the pink, man. Once they get their hands on it—they'll share the profits. No tips. Nothin'. I'm telling you this place's washed up."

"Restaurants are a good living."

"Are you kidding? A man of my experience? I got seniority. I could be stashin' it away. If I could find somebody to write my story, I'd make a million. You don't write, do you?"

"I collect signatures."

"Forgery?"

"Autographs."

"Ever try anything longer?"

"Sometimes."

"I got a story, kid—murder, rape, pure love, laughter. Cinemascope's too small for what's happened to me. I'm forty-two, and I look sixty-five. That comes from fast livin', kid. My story's just catchin' up with me. It keeps gettin' bigger every day. Yesterday, this college punk at Temporary (I could tell he'd never worked a day in his life—his hands were smooth, his shoes weren't scuffed) asks me what kind of a job do I want. He says to me, 'Mr. McDougal, what kind of a job do you want?' And you know what I said—right off the top of my head—I says,

'Give me a nose job.' The punk blushed—candy-ass. A knee-slapper, huh? I wrote it down, somethin' funny between the dramatic parts. Imagine the suspense. The doctors versus Jimmy McDougal. For twelve years (we'd show this with a calendar and the pages of each year being ripped away) the doctors watch my nose drop off. Each year it gets a little less. But this don't stop me from a career of crime and wanton lust. They never used to notice me. I had to wait days for medical treatment in the hospitals before my nose started to disappear. Then, everybody at the clinic wanted to see me. I was the main event. I can scare the shit out of people, now. That's how the movie ends."

"That's it? That's the end? Who goes to movies to be depressed?"

"It's got everything, man. It's arty, too. The meaning's left up to the audience, know what I mean? Do I get my face fixed or what? You have to guess."

Little Richard used to be a dishwasher in Macon, Georgia. He invented "wop-bop-aloo-bam-balap-bam-boom" to stop guys like McDougal from bugging him. But after standing over The Homestead sink, who has the energy? Only Little Richard.

The replacements should be here by 10:00. I'm too tired to talk. Eyes burn. Pants stained with soapy water. McDougal at twenty-four bottles for the fifth time. Anything I hum sounds like his song. I think I've forgotten how to think. Zambrozzi walks over to McDougal.

"Hey, Chief, whadda they call Italian singing?"

"Tell your friend a Miss Gloria call the kitchen. She says she waiting at the same place. Tell him from now on, no more calls."

"You didn't answer the riddle, Chief."

"I don't know."

"Wopera! Get it?"

Zambrozzi passes me. The silent treatment. My ears are hot.

McDougal laughs. I have to look at him. "Here's something to sing under the girl friend's balcony, hot lips—

135

> *"Take it to your mouth Mrs. Murphy*
> *It only weighs a quarter of a pound*
> *It's got hair on its head like a turkey*
> *And it spits when you shake it up and down."*

There's vomit in my throat. McDougal makes me sick. I *am* loyal.

At this hour, Saint Malachy's—the actors' church—is the only place on Broadway where you can sit and talk quietly without a cover charge. Gloria has nothing to wear on her head. I give her my Mets cap.

Gloria sits back in the pew. "Say you're sorry for last night."

"What did I do?"

"Don't make fun of me."

"I didn't."

I'm bushed. My hands still sting from the soap.

"Say something, Benny."

"I did."

"You know I don't like it when it's quiet."

"A guy has to relax, you know."

"I hate it when it's quiet. My mind starts thinking."

"It's peaceful."

"I imagine things. They scare me."

"Nightmares?"

"No, good things."

"What's scary about that?"

"I stop myself. Read a magazine. Turn on the TV."

"I worked pots and pans tonight."

"If you don't expect anything, you're not disappointed."

"I wasn't expecting pots and pans, but I was disappointed."

"I want to light a candle."

"Why?"

"I don't mind if my mind thinks about other people."

She kneels down. Instead of taking the missal in the rack beside her, Gloria reads *Screen* magazine. She bows her head. When she looks up, she's crying.

"What's wrong?"

136

"Carol Burnett." Gloria hands me the magazine. "Page four," she says. "Where it says 'The Operation Carol Must Have.'"

I hurry to the last paragraph. "Pray for Carol" it says. "What's wrong with her? What happened?"

"Didn't you read it?"

"That takes too long. What is it?"

"They say Carol has the Big C."

This takes the wind out of my sails. "Are you sure?"

"I pulled her through the Emmy Award. It was between Carol and Lucille Ball. I love Lucy, but she's had the brass ring. When Carol accepted, she said somebody must be watching over her. And I was. I feel responsible. You know—'in sickness and in health.'"

"You can't always believe what *Screen* says. They wrote Sinatra had only six months to live. That was three years ago."

"I got her through once. I can do it again."

"You're stupid to get mixed up with comediennes. How much work can they get? They all end up in Las Vegas."

"You can't explain these things, Benny. It's chemistry."

"Go ahead. Light your candle."

"Come with me, Benny."

"I'm not going up there. Things always happen to me."

"You've been here before?"

"I took Communion here my first week in New York."

"How was it?"

"Delicious."

Gloria's heels click on the marble. Her coin drops in the box. I remember Saint Malachy's that first week and signing all the actors after Mass. Everybody signed, some of them twice. When the priest came out, I asked him, too. He smiled, put clips on his trousers, and got on his bicycle. I watched him pedal away. A box, strapped to the back of his bike, fell off. Communion wafers flew up in the air and scattered like pigeons. The priest ran after them. Communion never tasted the same after that.

"I feel better now," Gloria says, sliding back in her seat. "Let's talk about something else."

137

"You hear anything more about the astronauts?"

Gloria takes a pocket radio and plugs the earphone into her ear.

"What's happening?"

"Ssssh!" she says. "It's a church."

"I'm sorry."

"Ground control says the oxygen's at the danger level."

"Are they dead?"

"They may have enough to make it back to earth. It's touch and go."

Gloria unplugs herself. "How much overtime did you earn?"

"Fifty-four."

"That's half a week's pay in one day."

"Zambrozzi said, 'In revolutionary times, the stakes are higher.'"

"It's so much money, Benny."

"I could make a down payment on a color TV."

"A washer-drier."

"A Ford Mustang."

"A dinette set with Portuguese tile inlays."

"A Japanese tape-cassette console."

"Isn't that too expensive, Benny?"

"The Japs work cheap."

"Oh, Benny, it feels like Christmas. You'll have one hundred and eight dollars in two days. This Mr. Vic you were talking about, how much does he get?"

"Three hundred and fifty plus a case of Scotch by Friday."

"Today's Wednesday."

"I get a three-star restaurant."

"Why'd you promise something you can't deliver? Why didn't you think, Benny? Where can you raise the rest of the money?"

"Overtime."

"That's not enough money."

"It isn't?"

"Don't you know how to plan for the future?"

"I had to make up my mind there and then. Mary Martin was inside. I though it'd be enough. It's more

138

than I've ever made. Maybe The Homestead'll give me a bonus."

My ears are warm again.

"Let's try and think," says Gloria. "You need three hundred and fifty dollars plus the Scotch. How are you getting the Scotch?"

"The Homestead's giving it to me as a going-away present."

"At least that's settled. Now, Benny, I know a place where they buy autographs."

"I'm not listening."

"I'm trying to help, Benny. Beggars can't be choosers."

"I got my collection by myself. I'll get the money by myself."

"They give thirty dollars a book."

"Highway robbery."

"Don't be stubborn."

"She knows about ambulances. But autographs—forget it."

"You get me mad."

"I didn't do anything to you. You're a beginner. I've been around a long time. I've a reputation."

"It always happens like this. Somebody makes you happy, then they make you sad."

My chest aches. Gloria's face is all twisted with worry. If she'd only been with me when I got the big ones, she'd understand. If she could shut her eyes and see what I see. Buster Keaton as close to me as Gloria. He's carrying his ukulele. I yank the rope, the bus door opens. I run after Buster. I twist my ankle, but it doesn't hurt. I catch him at a newspaper stand. He signs my pad. He tips his pie-pan hat like in the movies. I tip mine. We laugh together. The pew's as hard as the upper mezzanine at the Polo Grounds. Willie's at bat. He fouls one up above the Chesterfield sign on the third-base side. I have my first baseman's mitt. I'm leaning far over the railing. I'm being pushed by the crowd. "Get it! Get it! Hands. Shoving. The ball sails above us. I spear it. In the clubhouse beside his locker, Willie signs the ball and gives me an autographed picture. His sweat smells sweet. His stomach's as stiff as frozen meat. He's wearing a Saint Christopher medal, so am I. "Say hey, baby. We're twins." Willie smiles his home run smile at me.

"Are you listening? You've got to sell something. And the autographs are the most valuable things you own."

"You don't understand, Gloria. They're not just pieces of paper."

"Sell your doubles."

"I need my doubles."

"For what?"

"I need them. For special occasions. For trading. For security in case something happens to my number-one autograph."

"You gave me Joan Crawford."

"That was a special occasion."

"The autograph's worth at least thirty dollars."

"It's worth more than that."

"I could get thirty tomorrow."

"You'd sell my Crawford?"

"You gave it to me."

"You said you loved Joan Crawford."

"There's more where that came from."

"Don't be so sure."

"You're pigheaded sometimes, Benny."

"The first person I've ever given any part of my collection to. And she'd sell it at a drop of a hat."

"Benny, I'm doing it for you."

"That Joan Crawford's probably worth five hundred, for your information. I got it right in front of the Pepsi headquarters. I gave it to you because you were nice, because you made me feel nice, too."

"Oh, Benny, I love that autograph."

"Enough to peddle it? To somebody who buys other people's hard work?"

"Believe me, Benny. It's the nicest present a man ever gave me."

"You've had others?"

"That's not the point. I want to help."

"If that's help, I don't want it."

I give her the silent treatment. After a few minutes she stands up and throws my hat on the floor. I hear her walk up the aisle. "I wasn't making fun," I yell as she genuflects. "You bent my peak!"

In church, all the prayers are by the book. I always prayed best by myself. "God bless America, Ma, Uncle Jack, Uncle Bill, Ralph, and Mrs. Ryan (in case Ma needs help and can't reach the doctor)." I said it fast because it's wrong to ask God for too much. Prayers should be special. When the players prayed for a Trade win, we'd put our hands in the middle, kneel down, ask God for victory, and end with a cheer. Trade was undefeated.

It's hard to pray in New York. There's too much to do, too much action. Last year, I went to Confession. "Forgive me, father, for I have sinned. It's been eight years since my last Confession." The priest asked me to repeat the number. I walked out. I felt so old, and full of sin.

My head feels like a soufflé pushing out of its pan. I've got to get organized. Three hundred and fifty dollars. It's not for me, God, remember that. It's for the collection.

The face on the crucifix is familiar. He's dressed in black except for his chest and hands, which are white as meringue. His arms are raised high. His head's tilted. His feet point down and are gracefully crossed. Long face, straight hair . . .

It's Fred Astaire.

The Apostles curve around the altar to watch him. They're dressed in gold. Blonds, with hair to their shoulders, blue eyes, pink cheeks, and ruby lips—they look like Ginger Rogers without breasts.

Fred hears me. He's doing a number for my benefit. His head rolls, his arms float above him. The chorus picks up his beat. An Apostle holds out his right hand. His finger's the baton. He's conducting my favorite film—Shall We Dance. The altar's their revolving stage.

Fred's doing his famous soft-shoe. He slides his patent leather feet in a circle on the marble altar. He gets both sounds at once—a tap and a swoosh, just right for "They Can't Take That Away from Me." I'm laughing because

141

Fred's laughing and belting out "They All Laughed." Fred forgives everybody. He was the first to sing about "reaching for the moon," and now the astronauts are on their way. The altar's whirling. The novena candles bend with it. But Fred keeps his balance. The Apostles spin above him. They're singing to me—

> *"They all said we'd never get together*
> *Benny, let's take a bow.*
> *'Cause ho-ho-ho,*
> *Who's got the last laugh now."*

I feel great. Everybody's having a ball. The Apostles are dancing. Gloria's up there. So am I. Fred leads us through the confusion. Nobody stumbles.

"We're closing, mister." The voice sounds far away, but the face comes close to mine. An old man. Slow. Black fuzz in his ears. He doesn't have the beat. He's not smiling. He's trespassing.

"Ssssh! We're not finished."

The music gets faster, so do the people. I can only see Fred's feet. His taps spark as they hit the stone floor. Everyone else is lost in the light.

"Mister, if you want to sing, there's a High Mass tomorrow at eight."

"I'm not singing. I'm dancing. Leave me alone."

"Mister, it's a house of God, no Roseland."

"God's dancing."

"Sure."

"He is."

"Mister, do I have to call Father Donahue or do you leave peaceful-like?"

Fred reaches out and catches Gloria. Nothing ugly or sexy. He sweeps her off the ground. The white spots have shrunk from balloons to snowflakes. Fred has Gloria in his arms. She's wearing a long gold dress. I can hear it crinkle as she does the Grapevine. I've never seen Gloria so happy. Her laugh's sudden and sharp like tinkling glass. She's waving. "C'mon, Benny, Fred wants you, too," she says.

"Mister? . . ."

142

"He's going to hold me."

"We're closing."

"Wait. Just a second, please."

I can feel a hand on my coat.

"Can you wait a few minutes?"

"Okay. A minute."

When I turn back, Fred's danced away. Everything's silent. I feel cold. I hear a tap, but it's only the old man's fingers on his watchman's clock.

"You finished?"

"I'm finished."

"This your radio, mister?"

"It belongs to the lady who's with me."

"Happy pecans and merry almonds," he says, shaking his head.

I walk out. There's no time to genuflect.

On the Broadway bus uptown, I hook up the transistor radio's earplug. Things are quieter this way. Sophia Loren's just been robbed of $100,000 in jewelry while walking up Fifth Avenue. Is nothing sacred?

THURSDAY BEGINS like every morning. I wake up, pull the shade, open the grate and then the window, stick my head out as far as I can into the alley, and look up at the sky. Sunny and blue—a nice day.

My head's full of voices. At this hour I should be hearing fire engines, airplanes, car horns, babies crying. Mrs. Berado's not out on the stoop playing her cha-cha records and yelling for Leroy, her dog, to stop barking. The tuberculosis truck and the Mr. Tastee don't pull up to the playground until ten.

I lie back in bed. I put the pillow on my forehead to stop the sound and shut out the light. The sound won't stop. "If you can hear my voice, you can help mankind as well as yourself. Your body—be it blood, eyes, kidneys, or heart—can help someone else to live. Your donations mean dollars and dignity. Be a Good Samaritan today, invest yourself in science. The dividends will pay off in the future of mankind. Call 822-3344 or write Our Lady of Victory Donation Centre, New York 10001. Remember —giving is the best part of living. This has been a public service announcement."

Transistors are wonderful, you can sleep on them and they don't break. Sometimes, like now, they give you ideas.

A letter from Mom in my mailbox—

Dear Benny,
Madge is typing cause I feel bad. They're giving me an enema this morning and I got to be ready.

Benny, after all the money I spent on your educa-

144

tion, you could put a few quarters in the pay phone to call your mother, couldn't you?

Love,
Francine/Mom

P.S. Contacts. Don't forget.

Mrs. Berado's looking out the window with Leroy when I walk out the door.

"Walsh. There y'are. I got a letta for ya."

"I'll pick it up tomorrow, Mrs. Berado. I'm—"

"Walsh, it was twelve cents postage due. I don't take no packages and no lettas. I did yuz a fava. The letta's been sittin' hea since yesterday mornin'. If I was a bank, I'd be collectin' interest . . ."

"I've got a busy day."

"Wash, I think ya better read it."

"Is it from Johnny Carson?"

"The Asbury Park Hospital."

Getting into Mrs. Berado's apartment's very hard. First, there's the police lock. Then there's the accordion grate to protect people from the dog. Then there's the dog.

"Leroy, be quiet!" Mrs. Berado hits him on the snout with her slipper. Leroy stops growling.

"S-I-T." Mrs. Berado's voice goes hard and deep. Leroy lies down.

"Sit," she says, talking to me now. She points to the living room. The chairs are filled with boxes of clothes. Her husband, Val, is asleep on the sofa.

"Don't mind him," she says. "He's in maintenance. Works early, sleeps late."

The only place to sit is on the window sill with Mrs. Berado's collection of flags.

"I got 'em all. Irish, Chinese, Jew, Italian, Greek, P.R. You gotta show you're a good neighbor. It pays off. The building's only been robbed five times in the last year— that's a block record."

"Mrs. Berado, I've got business . . ."

"I know I got it. Wait a minute," she says, looking in her drawer. "The letta was very big with special delivery purple, and stamps like Vatican City only with Presidents.

145

I tried to steam them off for Val's collection. Well, why not? I paid for 'em. The letta came undone. Here it is . . ."

It's the fattest letter I've ever gotten. I open it quickly. There's a note and a long, Xeroxed report called "History." On top, it says—

WALSH, MARGARET F.,   HOUSEWIFE   CAUCASIAN
72   FEMALE   HUSBAND—UNKNOWN

That's Mom.

"Well, she had a good life, Walsh."

"I heard from her this morning. She wasn't feeling so good."

"No use cryin' over spilt milk."

"I'll call her tomorrow when things are settled down."

"Wanna talk about it?"

"There's a note. Maybe it's from Mom."

"I tried to get ya three times yesterday, Walsh. You know how it is leavin' things in these corridors. Read it. Go ahead. Read it out loud if it helps."

" 'Dear Mr. Walsh. Unable to reach you in time for the termination at four forty-four A.M., this Tuesday. We are enclosing the final report. Yours truly, George Bromberg, M.D., and Phyllis McGuire, M.D., Consultant.' "

"I thought I wuz doin' a fava, Walsh. You know I don't take no packages for nobody. It's a rule."

"The history's very long."

"Yeah?"

"Impressive."

"Wanna read it?"

"No time."

I read down the first page quick like a menu.

1. Duodenal ulcer, peptic with hemorrhage 651–951
2. Bone metastatic carcinoma   360–951
3. Lung tumor emboli   234–951
4. Kidney, nephrosclerosis (arteriolar)   710–517
5. Heart, left ventricular hypertrophy   400–533

The report goes on for pages. It has footnotes like a book. Mom always said she was a rare specimen.

"I don't do favas easy."

The letter fits inside the secret pocket of my windbreaker. Leroy growls at me as I go to the door.

"S . . . I . . . T!"

"Here's your twelve cents, Mrs. Berado. Thanks."

"Walsh, did she give y'anythin'?"

"I really can't talk about it now, Mrs. Berado."

Mrs. Berado walks me to the door. Leroy's ahead of her on the leash. He nearly yanks her down the steps.

"Fucking dogs," she says. "They should all be dead."

"See you tomorrow, Mrs. Berado."

"Walsh, can I ask you one question?"

"Okay."

"Did y'inherit anythin'?"

"I think Mom left me her body."

This must be the place. The billboard has a newspaper story blown up the size of a door.

THE MAN WITH GOLD IN HIS VEINS

Mr. Joe Thomas, of Detroit, is about to start receiving $12,000 a year as legitimate blood money. Mr. Thomas, a 34-year-old assembly belt worker in a car factory, is a blood donor. Thomas was found to possess blood containing a remarkably high concentration of a rare antibody called anti-lues B. The discovery is the medical equivalent of a gold strike or an oil strike in Texas. Scientists knew there was gold in those veins. Now, after a fiercely competitive auction, involving five biological supply companies, Mr. Thomas' blood has been valued at $1,500 a quart. Mr. Thomas is amazed at his good luck. "It's hard to believe, but I've signed the contract. So I guess it's true."

"It could be you," says a man from the window of the trailer parked next to the Donation Centre. "I been watching you from the window. You're the first today."

"I gave blood on Forty-second Street. I fainted."

"That's chump change. Here, you get twenty dollars in two minutes."

"I've got a plan. How many pints for three hundred and fifty?"

"Seventeen plus."

"Could you take eighteen right away?"

"Will you settle for two? You won't feel a thing. I'm a fast syringe. They don't call me 'Quick Draw' Scarpino for nothing."

"It's eighteen or nothing."

"Mister, if I took eighteen I'd have to send you to the morgue. Blood's not the big money, man. Try Scientific Research. Ask the girl at the Information Desk inside. Her name's Anne. Tell her Quick Draw said to stick 'em up."

"Thanks."

"Hey, next time come back and see us. Blood money's better'n no money."

Anne stands up behind the desk. Her breasts point straight at me. They're too large for her dress. You couldn't describe them as "knockers" or "boobs," which sounds like there are two. Hers are like one wedge of Cheddar cheese. She could donate a breast to science herself, and not miss a thing. I don't want to think dirty thoughts in a Catholic hospital. I keep my eyes on her eyes—blue, with green mascara and eyelashes all around like Twiggy.

"Yeah?" she saids. "Deliveries around the corner."

"Quick Draw says to stick 'em up."

"You can tell Quick Draw to go fuck himself and all his funny friends."

I'm shocked. That's no way to talk to a scientific gift. Maybe I'm the cure for cancer, the missing link, the Nobel Prize. "I heard an announcement on the radio."

"So Quick Draw sent you in here?"

"Yes."

"Wasn't blood good enough for you?"

"I wanted to make a bigger gift."

"Glory boy, huh?"

"The announcement said I'd be helping mankind and making money."

"Whaddya want to be—a guinea pig or a gift?"

"Which pays more?"

"Let's see . . ." She pulls out a file card index and licks her fingers to flip through them. Her tongue's as smooth as pink velvet. Her nails are polished red. "I've got something in Dream Research. Dr. Rogers—the guy written up in the *Post*."

"What's that about?"

"They watch you sleep."

"I don't sleep much."

"They're studying the REM cycle—that's rapid eye movement."

"I sleep with my eyes shut. I don't dream."

"I'd go up there and try it myself, but you've got to sleep alone."

"I once had a dream."

"Tell it to the doctor. You want this or don't you? They put wires on your head. It's fifty dollars a day, controlled conditions. They've got everything up there—air-conditioning, Muzak, the magazines."

"No television?"

"How can you sleep if the tube's on?"

"But how do you know what's happening outside?"

"That's the point. You don't. It's like one long Sunday morning—walk, talk, eat, read. You're guaranteed a week's work."

"Got anything else?"

"There's the Sperm Bank—one hundred and fifty dollars a yank."

"I don't understand."

"Listen, I'm doing you a favor. We don't advertise this one. People don't know about it. How many times do you have a chance to get your rocks off and get paid? Artificial insemination. You know—test-tube babies. First we get the pill. Now we're getting rid of pregnancy."

"We are? That's against the Church, isn't it?"

"Ever heard of the Immaculate Conception? Now our hands'll be clean, too."

"I'm surprised Our Lady of Victory allows it."

"Don't lecture me, mister. I only work here. The Sperm Bank's the latest thing."

"Really?"

"Soon there won't even be survival of the fittest. Everybody'll be fit as a fiddle. They'll mix up the chemicals before birth. No more weaklings. Everybody'll be normal."

"Who discovered it?"

"I'm only in reception, but even I know Darwin and his beagles. That's one of the first things they teach you in biology at the convent."

"You mean stars won't be born, they'll be made?"

"Yeah."

"I don't believe it."

"You can't argue with science. That's not scientific."

"It wouldn't be good if everybody was a star. If everybody was equal that wouldn't be American."

"Dr. Rudd? It's reception. I have a man here who'd like to make a donation . . . I don't know . . . I'll ask."

Anne puts the phone in her neck like Mr. Vic and talks to me.

"Did you go to college?"

"No."

"Did you finish high school?"

"No."

"Did your parents have a history of diseases?"

"I don't think so. But I've got Mom's history with me."

"It's 'no' across the board, Doctor. Sorry to bother you."

"What if I donated two bodies?"

"You and your shadow?"

"Would you take me? Could I get the money fast?"

"It's the same with everybody—rush, rush, rush. In science things take time. There's no joke about giving something to science. It's bigger than marriage. It's forever. You can always donate your whole body to the hospital. They give you five hundred dollars and a tattoo. But they only pay you for yourself."

"I'll take it."

"Think about it. It's a big step. Once they give you a contract, that's it."

"Like an audition?"

"Yeah, but it's a show you can't quit."

"Quitting wouldn't be professional."

* * *
150

The nurse in room 753 tells me to relax.

I'm not sweating. I'm not talking loud. I don't look nervous. She makes me fill out a form.

"For the purposes of our files, Mr. Walsh, what inspired the decision?"

"Money."

The nurse smiles and waits. "Many people joke when they give their body to us. I wrote a paper on the phenomenon for my psychology class at Hunter. Anguish has many existential outlets."

"That's it. I wanted an outlet."

"That's very interesting," she says, clicking her ballpoint pen. "For what, Mr. Walsh?"

"An outlet for money."

"There must be some conviction—let's not call it religious at the moment, Mr. Walsh—for you to want to give your body to the city of New York. These things are important for us to know."

"I guess if I could pin it down to one person . . ."

"Yes? . . ."

"It'd be Vince Lombardi."

"I don't know him. What did he write?"

"He said—'Quitters never win. And winners never quit.' "

"I'm sure the medical attendants will understand all this," she says. "Have a seat."

All around me are pictures called GREAT MOMENTS IN MEDICAL HISTORY. These are paintings with details so real they could be photographs. The people look as if they were alive now. "Benjamin Rush—Physician, Pedant, and Patriot." "Suskruta—Surgeon of Old India." "Hippocrates —Medicine Becomes a Science." The patients who made history don't look as healthy as I do. They've got no color, no business to keep them interested in things. And the settings are very simple for such important moments. Everybody's lying on the floor. If they paint my picture, I'm having it in the contract that it's done in my apartment. I'll be surrounded by interesting photos of Marilyn, Bogie, the Babe. It's for them that I'm donating my body, and they should get some of the credit when the doctors discover the cure in me. My caption could read—"Modern

151

Medicine Discovers Cure for the Big C." "C" could stand for cancer, cardiac, cataract, or just common cold. Maybe Mom could be in the paintings, too. They'd paint her in her house, sitting in her chair holding the TV remote control switch. We'd be known as the Walshes— The Flying Wallendas of medicine. But our deaths wouldn't be entertainment. Our stories would be in textbooks. Our faces in paintings.

Donating your body's a great way to start the day. It gives a guy a boost. Our Lady of Victory should mention it in their advertising. What the doctors don't use of me, they could give to other people. I've seen headlines— BOY GETS KIDNEYS, MAN GETS GIRL'S HEART. I'll make a list. If they want my religious preferences, they'll take my personal preferences, too. The top ten. Joe gets my ligaments. They're strong from standing most of the day and making short sprints for autographs at night. Frankie can have my stomach, it's used to Italian-American cuisine. Dean Martin can have first dibs on my liver. I don't know who'd want my eyes. They're not much to look at or to see through. I'll leave that one up to the hospital. I'm as worried about my brain as Mom used to be. Zambrozzi could make it look beautiful. By then he'll have his new kitchen. He'd invent a special sauce with liqueurs that flame when you light them. I'll only allow it if Zambrozzi agrees to serve the dish to someone he considers famous. They say brains are the most nourishing food in the world. Wouldn't it be great if some part of Benny Walsh was swallowed by one of the greats? And then to be a recipe! Better than ashes to ashes.

"I didn't expect two doctors."

"When you get Crane," says Dr. Crane, "you get Farber."

"And when you get Farber," says Dr. Farber, "you get Crane."

"You're a team?"

"We're a one-two combination," says Dr. Crane, chuckling.

"When do I know if I pass?"

Dr. Farber tugs on his stethoscope. "That depends on how we feel."

"How do you feel?"

"If we've had a bad breakfast and slept fitfully, we usually don't feel too good. If it's a nice day and nobody bugs us, then we're inclined to be happy."

"I hope everything works out."

"Dr. Farber's the gambler. He plays the long odds. He'd run on fourth and four, if you know what I mean," says Dr. Crane. "In college, he did his thesis on probability and risk."

"I'm no risk. You can count on me."

"I'm more conservative. Three yards and a cloud of dust. I've been with Dr. Farber ever since he chose me from the graduating interns. Don't get me wrong. I'm no yes-man. I'm a choice, not an echo."

Dr. Farber sits down beside me. "Any body marks? Scars? Tattoos? Skin diseases?"

"No."

"That's good. The hospital doesn't accept anyone with external markings of any kind."

"Mom used to say my skin was as soft as a duck's backside."

"Your old lady doesn't have medical credentials."

"Sure she does, Dr. Farber." I hand him Mom's history. "If you take me, I'd like to donate her. Two for the price of one."

"We only deal with the living."

"Look how many doctors inspected her. There must be eight people who wrote her up. Long paragraphs. See how many categories she had—medulla, sacral nerve, skeletal muscles."

"Let's punt, Dan," says Dr. Crane.

"This is a donation center. What's crazy about donating a gift?"

Crane whispers loud enough to hear. They're not as polite as Dr. Kildare.

"What's wrong with me? I'm an American. The report's for real. I thought you'd be interested . . . sir."

153

"We need bodies for medical research, Mr. Walsh. Not bits and pieces. Now drink this barium solution."

"I'm in good shape."

"We'll be the judge of that," says Dr. Crane, tapping his clipboard with a pencil.

I don't like taking my shirt off in public, even for the fluoroscope. On other people, skin looks all right. It's a pleasure to see people like Harry Belafonte without their undershirt. Their skin stretches tight as plastic. Light bounces off them. Their bodies shine. My skin sags. In the summer when I took my vacation from the composing room, Mom used to beg me to take off my shirt and go outside. "Be a man, Ben," she'd say, rapping her cane at my feet, trying to shoo me out on the porch. "Let the skin breathe. Skin is God's undershirt." Mom liked my chest, and to keep her happy I'd take off my shirt and walk around. Sometimes she made me walk to the mailbox with nothing up top. I tried to act casual and take my time. If I rushed, she'd make me do it again. I'd flex my muscles like Charles Atlas. "Look at my big Benny, Mr. Universe. Some tits you got." Mom used to poke my body with her cane the way the medics are doing with their fingers now. Mom said I looked the same at eight as I did at twenty-eight. She said she had pictures to prove it. But we never found any.

Since I left home for New York, my stomach has puffed out. My chest has dropped. I tried jogging when it first came out. When I run, I can feel my body just behind me. My skin's flopping up and down, but I'm always ahead of it, going forward. I can't control the bouncing. Autograph collecting's better exercise than the jog. I run in sprints. My mind's always on the personality I'm trying to get. Then I'm sweating without even trying. I have that pain in my side. I can feel my heart beating in my throat. I head back toward Horn & Hardart. I walk a few yards, then jog a few so my muscles don't get tight. That's what the professionals do. Mom always worried about my health. She sent me clippings about football leagues in Central Park where you joined and worked out every day to get tough. She never understood. Autographs are a contact sport.

Dr. Farber and Dr. Crane are pressing a black window up against my chest. The glass is cold. My skin goes bumpy like a plucked turkey.

"All right, Mr. Walsh, breathe regularly when the lights go out."

"What's going to happen? You're not leaving me here in the dark alone?"

"It's a very simple process, Mr. Walsh. We do it to hundreds of people. Essentially, we'll be taking a look at your insides."

"It wouldn't hurt, will it? If I get hurt you won't want my body."

"How do we know we want you until we get a good look at your insides?"

"Can't you take my word? I'm healthy."

"That wouldn't be scientific."

"Can you keep the lights on?"

"No."

"Can I have the negative? I mean, if things look good, will you send me a copy?"

"It's a fluoroscope. There's no photograph."

"When the Rockefellers give a building or Jerry Lewis writes a check for cerebral palsy, there's always a picture."

The light from the fluoroscope shines on Dr. Farber and Dr. Crane.

"Valve orifices competent."

"Check." Crane makes a note on his clipboard.

"Pyloric channel is patent. No calcification on wall or plaque formations."

"I want you guys to know I'm turning over all my bodily patents to you."

"Keep quiet, Mr. Walsh."

I try and peek over the top of the picture. Farber pushes me back in place.

"It's touch and go, Mr. Walsh. Now keep still."

"I live a clean life. No smoking. Three baths a week. Never touch the stuff. I'm not insulted if you find a few faults. I don't need the five hundred dollars."

"Stomach. Evidence of ulceration." Crane makes a note.

"We've got a borderline on our hands," says Dr. Farber.

"I'll take three hundred and fifty. That's fair for a borderline body."

I passed! After dressing and sitting in the Great Moments lobby under a picture of "Galen—Famous Healer of the Middle Ages," Dr. Farber walks out of the conference room and hands me some forms.

"Sign the first line. After Benstedt in room seven fifty-six puts 'Property of Our Lady of Victory Hospital' on your foot, come back here with the signed document. The nurse will take care of you."

"Does it hurt?"

"The tattoo? Some find it excruciating."

"Does that mean good or bad?"

"It depends on what you like." Dr. Farber smiles at me.

"I like things to be painless."

The tattooist doesn't hear me. He's standing by the radio, humming "The Trolley Song" and holding his electric needle. He's a little man. Bald. Sixtyish. He has two colorful arms—one mostly blue, the other a rainbow of black, blue, and red. He's touching up the blue one. He turns around with a start.

"I've come for a tattoo, Mr. Benstedt."

"You know me from the Boardwalk?"

"Leo Benstedt—Death before Dishonor."

"Did I do you before, kid?"

"Your shirt's open. I can read your chest."

He looks down and laughs. "My first tattoo. Amsterdam, 1920. I was a kid. Those were the days. Clipperships for three guilders. Snakes. Mermaids. There was an old man on the docks who did dragons as good as Chyo of Japan. He used ivory needles. It was an art then. Look at my schooner. The cut of the jib, the luff of the sail. You don't see that around these days."

"The hospital just bought me. I've come for the tattoo . . ."

"I just showed you my arm, kid. Don't say 'tattoo.'"

"But that's what . . ."

"I know what *they* say. It's body engraving."

"Mine has to last a lifetime."

"There's nothing to it. No stencil, no three-tone work. All I do is spitball for fifteen minutes, and you're through. Forty-eight years behind the needle, thirty-five of them on Atlantic City's busiest pier, and now I'm stuck in room seven fifty-six with my radio and my memories."

"Why aren't you still on the Boardwalk?"

"Hospital is the only place you can work in this state since we was outlawed. I'm too old to be a renegade. What else could I do? Not one of my clients got the yellows. I got thank-you letters from all over the world. I was famous. Now, it's nine to five, one hundred and thirty-five dollars a week plus benefits. I was full of the piss and the vinegar in those days. 'Death before Dishonor.' I meant it. I say to myself now, 'Leo, erase it.' But I don't. I want to remember. I'd do five full designs in a day. I was fast, maybe the fastest. I had a flair for colors. Even as an apprentice, I made designs that had never been worn. An art professor came to take pictures."

"I collect autographs. They're memories, too."

"Chickenshit. It don't count unless there's pain. Then it means something."

"What makes you happy can't hurt. You should have a system like me. My collection's famous, too."

"Yeah?"

"They didn't pay me full price for nothing. My body's going to the people in my collection. It's only fair. They've asked for me."

"Did you ever get your picture in *The New York Times?*"

"No."

"Did people come to the city to find you?"

"No."

"Do they ask you to sign your work?"

"No."

"Do you turn people down?"

"No."

"Then don't stand there and tell me you're famous!"

Bendstedt pounds the palm of his left hand with his fist. He shakes his head. "What's got into me? I snap at everybody. People come in, sit down. I bathe their foot. They don't even look at me. I'm not even allowed to put my designs on the wall. Nobody knows."

"You were really famous?"

"Ever hear of Great Omi, the zebra man? That job took five hundred and fifteen million pinpricks. Covered him from head to toe with a black stripe design. One hundred and fifty hours. My longest job. Omi made headlines all over Europe. Look at these hands. Straight as a board. No shaking. I've got great designs still in me. But who can I work on? In the old days, I got calls from plutocrats. I had a card with my name on it. Women begged for a king cobra like Lady Churchill's. Men offered stock for a gremlin like King Frederick's of Denmark."

"You mean you spent time with your people?"

"You're the first one I've ever told this. I'd sit with them for two days, and they'd talk to me. Their most secret secrets. I wouldn't do it unless they told me the truth. Loneliness, Love, Adventure, Violence—the whole thing. I got a feeling for them. The first day I'd work on atmosphere. The second, on color. The third, I'd begin. When I finished, their memory—whatever and wherever they wanted—was alive! I didn't even know the power in these hands."

"Could I have your autograph for my collection?"

"Kid, if it was legal I'd write my name on your shoulder. Today, your hippies and models—they walk around with their faces and legs painted. I hate it. It's all throwaway. That's what they call modern. Not for me, mister. I did tableaux. I worked from art books. They didn't call me Benstedt the Beautifier for nothing!"

Mr. Benstedt sits me down and tells me to take off my right sock. He puts alcohol in a pan. I soak my foot. It tingles. I won't go and see the guys at The Homestead after I make my move, they'll come and see me. I don't know which restaurant I'll get, but it'll be blue chip. Some place that's been around a long time and that's staying right where it is.

"See this." Mr. Benstedt holds up an inky blue jar.

"One color. That's what they give me. And they call this the Land of Plenty. It's a mockery."

He puts his ear close to the radio. "Listen to that voice. Garland could sing. She's been a real influence. I've done dozens of rainbows. And the other side of the rainbow, too—the bluebirds, mountains, lemon drops, everything."

"She made a comeback, so can you."

"The public don't deserve me. Nobody wants the old symbols. The snake was wisdom and truth, the tiger was strength and courage. And who believes in love and constancy these days, so the rose is out. I'd rather stay in retirement and highlight the memorials on my own body. A thousand years from now I'll be preserved like an Egyptian tomb. Archaeologists'll have a field day."

"You mean your body tells story?"

"Details you'd never get in photographs, kid. I made up great designs, but I saved history for myself. The Bonus March. The Bombing of Hiroshima. Joe McCarthy and Roy Cohn. It's all on my stomach. The main events from 1924 to 1965. I made a few mistakes, but after a while you get to know the difference between a publicity stunt and a real catastrophe."

"Could you call my tattoo . . . engraving . . . history?"

"It's only history when you kick the bucket. Your name isn't there, just the hospital's. It's words, not pictures. I'm not even allowed to jazz it up."

Mr. Benstedt pulls up a stool and lifts my foot out of the alcohol bath. It feels cool and light.

"Can you take pain?" says Mr. Benstedt. The machine's buzzing in his hand.

"I'd rather not."

"Hold onto the bottom of your chair. Think of something nice."

The first bite hurts terrible. The needle moves so quick. I can't keep up with my pain. My leg pulls back automatically. Mr. Benstedt holds my ankle tight. For an old man, he's got a strong grip. "Think hard!" he says. "Think big!"

You need peace and quiet to think of the stars. I'm dripping with sweat. "Stop, Mr. Benstedt! Stop, for chrissake!"

159

His machine clicks off. I open my eyes. Mr. Benstedt's not smiling. "I'm not even up to the 'e' in property."

"Turn up the music. Maybe that'll help."

Mr. Benstedt goes to the radio and makes it louder. Still Judy. When he takes his seat gain, there's blood on his blue arm.

"Mr. Benstedt, you're bleeding."

"I did it for her." He nods his head toward the radio. "Before you came in."

"For Judy?"

"She's my only modern since 1965."

"It's her slippers from *The Wizard of Oz.*"

"I had to do them in blue. That's all I've got."

"They're ruby like she wore."

"That's 'cause of the blood. The engraving's fresh. Blue and red make ruby."

"The blood's in the shape of her slippers. It doesn't drip. It's right in place. Shining."

"That's craft."

"It's magic."

Mr. Benstedt turns on the machine. "She was the greatest singer in America. She gave me a lot of pleasure."

"Was?"

"Dead. They just flew her in special from London. If I didn't have this nine-to-fiver, I'd be up at Frank E. Campbell's paying my respects."

Mr. Benstedt says nobody's ever walked out while he's working. I tell him to turn off the machine. He says my foot might get infected in my sock. Too bad. I'm going to see Judy. I'll be back.

It's the way Mom would've liked it. Crowds three blocks long. Flower trucks backed up and honking, filled with every kind of fresh flower in every possible design. Mom was here—81st Street and Madison Avenue—when Valentino passed on. He got headlines like Judy, but he wasn't as big. He was only a sex symbol, you couldn't hum his work. Judy means more than the physical stuff. She's the voice of America. Mom came all the way from Ocean Beach for the Valentino Vigil. She stayed up half

160

the night. She said there were 100,000 fans waiting to say good-bye to Rudy. They held pictures and souvenirs like this crowd. Mom was only allowed a few seconds with him. She said that was enough, the black hair, the smooth complexion, the gorgeous head lying on silk sheets in Frank E. Campbell's. She kept the front page of the *Daily News* in a frame on her dresser. It's brown and shredding, but you can still see Rudy's head and chest, and the guards standing at attention to protect him. Mom said it was one of the greatest moments in her life. "After that," she said every Sunday when we walked home from Mass, "Death will always be beautiful."

Mom would like the way the fans are behaving themselves. She got mad at the women who tried to crawl into Rudy's coffin. She broke the spruce cane I bought her telling me about the two girls who committed suicide the day Rudy died. She thought they were after publicity. "They didn't even stand on line." Mom got into one of her red furies. "They didn't own him. He wasn't their property. What did they do for him!" Mom showed me the letters she wrote on Valentino's behalf—in the early days when all her fingers could move at once. She wrote to every magazine and newspaper that called him a "pink powder puff." It took months, but Mom did it. "Benny, I swear to you, Rudy was no pink powder puff. He was all man. I saw the movies. I saw him. Believe your mother!" I believed her, but she never stopped telling me.

We loved Judy. She was the first star to make Mom forget Rudy. Sure, Judy had her ups and downs— marriages, suicide attempts, drinking. But that's all part of being a star. Judy came through it. Her fans stuck by her. Mom and I never missed her on TV. When she played New York, I'd always hang around the Westbury, where she stayed. Rudy was a big seducer, people fell for his looks. Judy went right to the heart.

Flashbulbs are popping near the front of the line. It's Good News Probst and his Instamatic. He's photographing the kids squatting down on the pavement playing Garland on their portables. He's with the rest of the Horn & Hardart crowd—Sypher, Macready, Moonstone, and Gloria. He waves me over. "Trigger was dead and stuffed

161

two months before Roy Rogers told us. There was no time to mourn."

I duck under the barricade.

"The nearest and dearest are always the last to know," says Gloria, touching my arm as if we hadn't been fighting and were friends again. "She was making such a good comeback in London at The Talk of the Town."

"What comeback?" says Sypher. "They were throwing food at her."

"How do you know, Louis?" says Gloria.

"I heard it from one of our international entertainers."

"I bet it was roses," says Gloria.

"It was food."

"Hey, man, cut this food jive. I feel sick." Moonstone closes his eyes after he speaks. He's hugging himself like a baby.

"What's with him?"

"When he heard about Garland," says Sypher, "he went to Walgreen's and bought bottles of Darvon, aspirin, and Seconal. He took two of each."

"Three," says Moonstone.

I whisper to Gloria. "I got five hundred dollars."

She throws her arms around me and kisses me.

"Cut it out, Gloria."

"He got it! He got it!"

"Got what?" says Macready.

"Benny got the money to move to another restaurant. He's going to have the biggest collection in the world."

"*That's* good news," says Probst.

"Where you moving?" says Sypher.

"I'm not sure. Maybe Lutèce, or the Basque Coast."

"Frog food."

"Louis, they're very good restaurants," says Gloria.

"Do they have entertainment?"

"No."

"Then what's the big deal?"

"Benny's getting a three-star restaurant. Put that in your pipe, Mr. Waldorf Towers, and puff it."

"Is that nice talk for a guy who helped you out at the Majestic?"

"I forgot," says Gloria.

"Wanna get married, sweetheart?" Sypher says. "You're like my first wife. Everything I asked, she forgot."

"Can't you see she's embarrassed, Louis?"

"Slam it, moneybags. Where'd you get the coin?"

"Sold an heirloom."

"An heirloom? I didn't know you went that far."

"Judy had such a nice family," Gloria says. "They were helping her with her comeback, giving her strength and backbone. After long hours on the nightclub floor, she'd sit with them by the open fire. Have tea. Joke. Judy'd pick up some old sheet music and sing a favorite. They were so nice together—a team. They were so scrubbed, so talented. Liza the singer, Joey the drummer, and little Lorna."

"Don't cry, Gloria."

"You wouldn't feel bad, lady, if you kept away from newspapers," Probst says. "I don't read them. I feel great."

"How do you keep up?"

"Read the almanac. You get all the facts, but a year late. It's too bad about Judy, but look at it this way—in 1968, over four million Americans established two point one million new families, over ninety-two percent of all Americans live in families. You don't read about that in those scare headlines. It gives you a boost to think of all those happy people—praying together, bowling together, probably listening to Judy's songs together."

"You're full of shit, Good News," says Moonstone.

"Facts keep you on the sunny side of the street. You can't worry too much about one suicide when you know Judy's only one of six thousand, one hundred thirty-eight this year," says Probst. "I've been through serious crises before—the Battle of the Bulge, the Berlin Airlift, the Dodgers leaving Ebbets Field. The almanac's got it all. In small print, things aren't so horrible."

"Pills, man. Dig it."

"That's just temporary, Moonstone."

"Whaddya mean?" says Moonstone. "Sometimes it lasts for days."

"Moonstone knows what he's talkin' about," says Macready. "When JFK got killed, he musta swallowed half a bottle of Seconals. He was out like a light."

"I had the hungers. Slept for three days."

"That was a coma," laughs Macready. "The police took you to the hospital and gave your stomach a pumping. You had yourself one big coma, jim."

"What's the difference? My eyes were shut, weren't they?"

"You took half a bottle of Seconal? They say that's what Judy took," says Gloria.

"Five—I took five Seconals and washed them back with a dozen aspirin and Coke. The blinkers slammed like iron gates, or somethin'. I was flying."

"How come you didn't take the same for Judy?" says Gloria.

"She was great, but not that great."

"You're too young, Moonstone," says Gloria. "Your hearing's bad from all those rock bands. You don't remember Judy riding in Andy Hardy's jalopy up Main Street. Or the excitement when we thought Glenn Ford was going to marry her and take her away from all her trouble. You never saw the yellow brick road that the crew painted out of respect in front of her air-conditioned dressing room. I wish I could go to sleep and wake up in a month when this is over."

"A month?" says Moonstone, swaying. "You know about Sodium Amytal?"

"No."

"Two with a glass of Gallo. It's a wipeout."

"I'm afraid to take those things. I might dream of Judy. I always do, standing with the Wizard, getting into the balloon to come back to black and white."

"No dreaming with Sodium Amytal. Days and days of dead time."

"Then I could pretend this never happened. I was never here. I could listen to Judy. I could watch her films. It'd be like she hadn't gone away."

"She hasn't," says Probst. "With cable television, cassettes, tapes, there's going to be more Judy Garland than ever before."

"I never thought of that," says Gloria.

"That tramp routine with her teeth blacked?" says Moonstone. "Corny, man."

"She made ten thousand dollars a night when she played the Palace," I say. "She sang in E-flat. Her records on Decca sold millions."

A girl listening to Judy's records on the pavement pushes up beside me. She's wearing a lumberman's shirt and blue jeans, with a black armband that says "33,000" and the word JUDY pinned over it. Her glasses are the wire ones. "I want to say something. If you're not going to speak up for Judy's soul, I will. Have you ever heard Edith Piaf? Helen Morgan? Marlene Dietrich?"

"Sure."

"Well, Judy was greater! All her life she wanted to be free, to fly over the rainbow. Understand? Drugs helped, but she had a bad karma. Death was the great leap. She was free of her husbands, the networks, the star system. She was *free* because she chose *freely*. In that act, that last moment, Judy showed us how great she was, and how brave. She was liberated! No more pig capitalism, no more sexist guilt . . ."

A Rolls Royce pulls up to the front of Frank E. Campbell's. The sun shines off it. Television reporters, their hats tipped over their eyes from the glare, rush toward the car with their cameras.

The girl keeps talking. I don't have time to answer.

"She was free. No more exploitation. No more media freaking. Now she can do her thing . . ."

"Who is it, Benny? Can you see?"

"I think that's Judy's Silver Cloud. It was custom designed for her."

"No kidding?"

"See the running board. I rode three blocks when *I Could Go on Singing* premiered."

"You could've been hurt," says Gloria.

"The windows are bulletproof and electronically controlled. They have to be closed most of the time for the air-conditioning and hi-fi. Acoustics are very important to Judy. I had to push my pad through the side vent. Judy signed it."

"You really rode with her?" says Moonstone, opening his eyes. "Wow!"

"Judy and I were friends. I talked with her many

165

times. The car cost forty-eight thousand dollars. The bucket seats are made of kangaroo, the softest and rarest leather in the world."

"We got peacock leather at the Waldorf."

"Peacocks don't have pouches. This was made from the kangaroo's pouch where they keep the baby. Extra soft."

A lot of people are listening to me. "It's a home away from home. A singer's on the road a lot. The car's got banked mahogany panels, twenty coats of paint, a television, a radio with tapes, a bar, a refrigerator that folds out of the arm rest, and an electric clock that chimes 'Come Rain or Come Shine' on the hour."

"That's poetry," says Gloria.

"Is it stick or automatic?" says Macready.

"This is a funeral, not an auto show!" the girl with wire glasses butts in.

"I'd love to own that mother," says Macready. "One big bet. That's all I'd need. How do you think these rich guys do it? They don't bet tens and twenties. They bet a bundle. When they hit, it's a real jackpot."

"It'd cost a fortune."

"Whadda you know, Walsh?" says Macready. "Maybe I'd get lucky and hit the daily double."

"That's a great human interest story," says Probst. "I'm gonna take a picture of that car."

The girl shoves her face up to mine. I can smell her toothpaste. "Judy's dead! Don't you see? She's dead!"

"Amateurs don't understand, miss. When a person becomes a legend, everything about him counts. James Dean's cigarettes—they called him the 'human ashtray.' Joe Namath's alpaca carpet. Hugh Hefner's round bed."

"You don't know squat about history!" the girl screams.

"Judy spent some of the best times of her life in that car. That's a historical fact. I watched her grow. She's as great after a performance as during it. The time I leaped on the running board, I could see her mouth moving. She was singing her heart out. When the window come down, I said, Judy, I've seen you six times in six nights. She smiled and pushed my pad (and pen) back. 'Only see me once,' she said. Do you get it? Once. I went to the show again.

Nothing happened to me. She was better than ever. I passed the test."

"You don't care!"

"Don't say that, ma'am."

"You don't care!"

"I'm waiting on line like you."

"Were you a member of her fan club?"

"No."

"Do you own any of her records?"

"No."

"Did you send a telegram of condolence to the family?"

"No."

"Creeps! You don't have any respect for the dead!"

A man pulls the girl back into the crowd. I take out my pad and show my pages. "See how people write to me. 'To Benny With Love,' 'To Benny Yours Truly,' 'To Benny the Best,' 'To Benny.'"

"You think they'll make us leave the line?" Gloria says, in a whisper.

The crowd quiets down. "She's a friend of mine, too. She's a good woman. She's a performer's performer."

The people look away. They wouldn't if Judy were right here signing my pad and wisecracking like the old days. People remember the times they've seen her. You've got it in your brain when you need it. She's small, but somehow very large. I'd be in their dreams, too, next to Judy's right hand, standing quiet until she gave me back my pen.

Sypher's saying, "These people really take Garland serious. You're no legend unless you cash in on it. Tyrone Power—the Golden Shower, know what I mean? Garland never grossed as much as Connie Francis at the Empire Room. She never even got one commercial. The minute they do a TV spot, the autograph price skyrockets. She lost a lot of big opportunities. She could've grabbed the rainbow, but she blew it."

"Will you two stop it!" says Gloria. "You're missing the poppies they're unloading."

"The Boy Scouts of America recently planted thirty thousand flowers on the most deserted land in America," says Probst. "It was part of the government's beautification program."

"Poppies are for veterans," says Sypher.

"Judy *was* a veteran," says Gloria.

Miss Helen Hayes hurries past us with her son, James MacArthur. On stage she moves fast, too.

I slip under the barricade and go after her. "Excuse me, Miss Hayes."

"Oh!" she says, and jumps back, shaking as if I'd hit her. I rush back to the line.

I hate quick movements.

The doormat says—

FRANK E. CAMPBELL
"The Funeral Chapel"

It's no chapel. It's a hotel. High ceilings. Chairs with velvet covers, smelling dusty and perfumed. Tall men with slick black hair and pleated pants stand guard by the sign-in book on either side of the entrance. "Straight ahead and watch your step."

The voice sounds familiar. I ask if he's in show business.

"Straight ahead and watch your step."

I can see Judy's coffin. It's propped open like her concert piano. I thought I'd want to say good-bye to Judy, but I can't. Some people kneel, others stand and gaze. I always think of Judy moving, I don't want to see her still.

"I wish I had a flower to throw," says Gloria. "Aren't you coming?"

"I'll wait here."

Gloria walks ahead on tiptoes. My last chance, but my feet won't move. There's a weight on my chest as if Mom's cats had been sleeping on it all night.

From here, all I can see is Judy's nose. It shocks me. If other people are looking at what I am, they should shut the coffin right away. The nose isn't a nose. It's a man's ding-a-ling. Tears are in my eyes. People probably think I'm sad, but I'm laughing. People praying to a

168

cock's a scream. I got the giggles like this once before at Saint Luke's kindergarten, when my thing got caught in my fly. Sister Angelica came into the bathroom and crossed herself. She slapped my hand for playing with it. "It got stuck." She slapped my face. We walked three flights down to the Matron's office. Sister Angelica tried to shade me with her big brown dress. She wouldn't look behind her, and I was afraid to tell her to go slow. All the kids saw it. They came out of finger painting to look. The girls giggled. The boys giggled. I laughed, too, but then the pain hit me and shriveled me up.

Sister Teresa finally got me free. It took her a long time because her crucifix kept dangling in the way. She said I should be ashamed of myself, and to use my will power. The next day at school, they caught George Sage and Mary Louise Rizzo kissing, and the class giggled about them. What's so funny about a kiss?

Gloria's eyes are puffed and pink from crying. "They only gave me thirty seconds with Judy. The women in front got hysterical. The ushers grabbed them and took them away."

"You'd never raise your voice to Judy."

"I didn't make a sound. All the time I was in front of the coffin, I was thinking the three Cs of ambulance emergency. Stay Cool, Calm, and Collected." Gloria folds up her handkerchief smudged with lipstick and puts it back in her purse. "Cotton tastes terrible."

"Was her nose strange?"

"Everything seemed strange, Benny."

"What did she look like?"

"Her face was very round and rosy."

"But Judy was pale and skinny from suffering."

"Remember Judy's cheekbones? Next to Joan's, Judy had the best cheekbones. I used to try and Scotch-tape mine to look like hers. She looked different lying down. Her cheeks were baggy like anybody else's."

"Was her hair short and swept back like brown duck feathers?"

"It was reddish orange."

"That's too loud for Judy. You must be wrong."

"If you don't believe me, look for yourself."

"I'll take your word."

"Her skin was very smooth, Benny."

"No wrinkles from squinting out over the footlights?"

"None of that."

"Gloria, are you sure that was Judy?"

"Other people were with me. They thought it was Judy. But she always carried roses at her finale. The coffin was filled with gardenias. It was all wrong."

"Maybe it's another Marilyn Monroe trick."

"What's that?"

"Me and my big mouth! You're not supposed to know."

"We're friends, aren't we?"

"Marilyn Monroe's living in Bolivia—her death was a publicity stunt to get out of a bad contract with Twentieth Century-Fox."

"You're crazy. I saw pictures of her husband—the ballplayer—at the funeral. He was crying."

"That's just it. You don't know Joe DiMaggio. He didn't even cry the day they retired number five from the Yankees."

"I think it's our duty to inform the proper authorities."

"Don't make waves, Gloria."

"It's in the public interest."

Gloria and I walk to the main entrance. We go quietly like nothing was the matter. The usher's standing there.

"Straight ahead and watch your step, sir."

"That's not Judy in the coffin. Judy wouldn't go to heaven looking like Corinne Calvet."

"All arrangements are made by the deceased's family. Step this way."

"They freeze people now, like meat. They stay fresh. I read where a Japanese scientist kept his dead wife looking like new for twelve years."

"Katsaburo Miyamoto," says the usher. "He crystallizes blood, which keeps the body pores open."

"I don't understand science. It's too complicated."

"We keep up with the latest trends."

"Judy deserved the best."

"Frank E. Campbell is the best."

"You could've preserved her. 'Better living through

chemistry.' How about it? Plastic hearts and lungs. You could've saved all these people from crying."

"Monday morning quarterbacks. Step this way, please."

"Save your breath, Benny," says Gloria. "His mind's made up."

Outside Gloria takes my arm. We lean against each other, not talking. I know how she feels.

Sunlight surprises me. So do the voices.

"BENNY!" "GLORIA!"

We only see arms waving from the curb. We push, but it's hard to move this crowd. Nobody wants to leave Judy, and nobody wants to stay inside, either. People walk away slowly with their heads down. Only our friends are making noise. It turns out to be Macready and Good News. Moonstone's taking a nap on the hood of a hearse.

"I'm glad you guys waited," says Gloria.

"Where's Sypher?" says Macready.

"He was with you," says Gloria. "We haven't seen him."

"Let's split," says Moonstone, without raising his head. "Louis's foxy enough to find us. Anyway, he doesn't give a shit about Judy."

"We've got to stick together. Nobody remembers her the way we do."

"Benny's right," says Gloria.

"My flash attachment worked like a charm," says Probst.

"You took pictures?" says Gloria.

"It's color film. Did you get a load of the tulips and azaleas? Stand by the Cadillac. I'll take a group picture."

"It's not like the time we jammed the ballot box for the Miss Rheingold contest and our girl won, Probst. It's a setback, not a victory."

"We're alive, ain't we, Walsh?" says Macready. "You win some, you lose some. Tomorrow's another day."

"I say stick tight. Remember the last assassination. There weren't as many people around for a loss as a win. That's why it's important to have your own crowd."

"So Garland kicks, so what?" says Macready. "There's Streisand waiting. She's young. She don't mainline. She

171

hits the high notes. She makes people just as happy. She's a winner. You whisper her name to people—a little joke or somethin'—they cough up some jingle. Whisper Garland after today and it's a guaranteed goose egg. People forget. Take it from a guy who puts the touch on hundreds of people a day."

"You're wrong. Judy's no ordinary loss."

"Walsh, you remember the touchdowns, not the fumbles."

"Don't pay attention to Macready," Gloria says. "I don't want to go back to my room either. Good memories should be shared."

There's shouting in the middle of the crowd. "It's hot! It's hot! Watch out!"

Sypher elbows his way out of the crowd. "Hey, where were you guys? I was talkin' to Otto Preminger, the producer. He wants to make me an extra. I think I can kiss you douche bags in on the deal."

"We'd be downtown already," says Probst. "But Benny said to wait."

"Hey, that's great, Walsh. A fraternity."

"See, Macready? Sypher feels the same way."

"Fuck off with this Boy Scout shit, Walsh."

The funeral has done Sypher good. He puts his arms around Macready and me. Probst takes our picture. "Get me in my street clothes," Sypher says. "Autographed pictures in my peasant outfit later."

"What are you talking about?" says Gloria.

"Preminger's making the life story of the Pope. It's called *Pope*. They're filming in Spain. Catholics are cheaper there. In technicolor. Thousands of pilgrims. Otto said I could be a pilgrim."

"That's how it happens," says Gloria. "You never know where or when. Somebody discovers you. You make new friends. You move up. You have to start low like Louis, so you can rise high."

"Who cares about stardom," says Sypher. "If they give me a contract, I'd rather have the money than the publicity. I won't forget you guys."

"See, Louis struck it rich at this funeral," says Probst. "Right under our noses."

172

"How'd you go up to a guy like that?"

"It happened so quick, Walsh, I can't hardly believe it. I heard him talking about Judy, saying how great she was. We struck up a little repartee."

"What balls," says Moonstone.

"You know I've been thinking," says Sypher. "People who need people are the luckiest people in the world."

"That's a very nice thought, Louis," says Gloria.

Good News snaps Sypher's picture again.

"Am I right, Benny-boy?"

"Did you get Preminger's autograph?"

"My mouth should be washed with soap for what I said about Judy. I make myself sick. She's worth a lot. Mr. Preminger wouldn't lie."

"Judy was always touching people, always friendly with everyone. Seeing her must have rubbed off on you."

"You got to like people, Walsh. You've got to give them the shirt off your back," says Sypher. "I promised Mr. Preminger one of my Garland autographs."

"You don't have any."

"I told him my name was Benny Walsh. If I land the part, I'll say Sypher's my stage name. You've got four Garlands. He's waiting inside. You don't want to cross a big man like that—he could blackball us in the industry."

"But they're my autographs."

"All for one and one for all, remember?"

"My autographs are from different times in Judy's career. They say 'To Benny.' They're mine."

"We're a fraternity, right?"

"But—"

"Then loan me one autograph. It's my big chance, Benny."

"I can't do it, Louis. Anyway, I wouldn't carry Judy on me."

"Look, Benny, it's how you get ahead in America. Beg, borrow, or steal. You gotta give to get. All the big shots do it. They come into our restaurants, right. They tip for better service. You give something extra, you get something extra. That's democracy. I bet I can get this movie if I grease his palm with a Judy Garland."

173

"You said you had the part."

"Give me the worst one. It doesn't matter to Otto."

"I thought you were a friend."

"I am. Who else can you trust in an emergency?"

"I can't."

"All right, I'll make a deal. I'll give you twenty grade-A autographs. Big stars for one Judy Garland."

"You don't collect the types I need."

"How'd you like Lena Horne, Katharine Hepburn, Jack Benny, Harold Arlen, Peggy Lee, José Ferrer, Helen Hayes, Glenn Ford, James MacArthur, plus ten mystery stars including Mitch Miller and Mel 'Velvet Fog' Torme."

"Those are good names."

"I know quality."

"I don't believe you."

"See for yourself."

Louis reaches into his coat pocket and pulls out a piece of paper. All the famous names are on it, and more. "How about it, Walsh? You're in fat city. I'm willing to give you these for free. Don't look a gift horse in the mouth. No money. One signature."

"Well . . ."

"Where'd you get all those names, Louis?" says Gloria.

"My private collection."

"The paper's ripped," says Gloria.

"Sypher fuckin' pinched the fuckin' names out of the fuckin' sign-in book," Macready laughs. "In broad fuckin' daylight."

"I found it on the floor."

"Louis Sypher, you go right back into Frank E. Campbell's and give those names to the Garland family. Those are their only record of who's here. They're not yours."

"Possession's nine-tenths of the law."

"You're a professional, Louis. We've been collecting together more than seven years. It's against the rules. You're disgracing Judy and the Waldorf."

"I bet Otto Preminger doesn't use extras," says Gloria.

"I'm tired of penny ante," says Sypher. "I want the big money. Judy's an expensive signature. There's no rules in this business but success."

I grab Gloria's arm and walk across the street. Judy's voice is still in the air.

"She's a great singer."

"Thanks, Gloria. She's the best."

We turn the corner and walk to the subway. "Where are we going?" says Gloria.

"I'm going to collect my money. At '21' or Lutèce, they won't have jerks like Sypher."

There's a new nurse in the reception room. She tells me to pick up my sock and take my bare foot off the desk.

"If you'd just look at my foot."

"It's bleeding. You should see a doctor. Emergency Services in room one-oh-one."

"That's from Benstedt's blue ink."

"He's out to lunch. And, in case you're interested, it's Berendt."

"It's Benstedt. Before he came here, he was a famous man. Ever hear of the Great Omi?"

"I only work here. The name's Berendt."

"Well, it was Mr. Benstedt who said he'd finish my tattoo so I could get my five hundred dollars. His name's tattooed on his chest. He wouldn't lie on his own skin."

"Berendt."

"Have you ever seen his chest?"

"I beg your pardon."

"Then believe me—it's Benstedt."

"It's Horst Berendt, or my name isn't Joan Piri, S.R.N."

"I swear Mr. B. has my file. He was just putting the finishing touches on my foot when I had to leave."

"We have no record that you were here, Mr. Welch."

"Walsh."

"We can't do anything without the proper authorization."

"I can prove I was here. The picture in the corner says 'Hippocrates—Medicine Becomes a Science.' "

"A woman takes up nursing because she wants to help people. I'd like to help you. If I could, I'd pass every applicant, okay their physicals, stand in the door and hand

175

out five-hundred-dollar bills like John D. Rockefeller. But I've got supervisors. They watch me like hawks."

"What am I going to do, Miss Piri?"

"You're going to take this foot and put it in your shoe. You're going to place your cap on your head. You are going to put one foot in front of the other and walk out of here."

"I can't leave without my money."

"You're sick."

"I'm a donor, not a patient."

"If you were a donor, it'd say 'Property of Our Lady of Victory Hospital.' All I see on your foot is 'Prop.' "

"I had an emergency."

" 'Prop' tells me nothing, Mr. Walsh. There are five hospitals in the Metropolitan area who offer this service. How do I know you're not a reject? You could've done this yourself. It doesn't look very professional."

"If you don't know the Great Omi, you don't know professional."

"What do you think this badge means?"

"Benstedt didn't reject me. I left on account of a sudden death."

"With Piri, you get a complete overhaul."

"Can we start again?"

"We could, but the lesion on your food disqualifies you."

"It comes from your hospital."

"As far as my records show, you never existed."

"This blood's real, isn't it?"

"Wear white socks. Your foot won't get infected."

"I'll wait for Mr. B. He'll sign the papers like he said. I'll get my money. Everything'll be all right."

"I'm afraid he won't be able to help you until we get a ruling on your foot. It's a very unorthodox situation. It may take a few days."

"Couldn't you look the other way?"

"Mr. Walsh, I'm *registered*."

"They already ruled me a gift."

"It's the first case of malpractice I've ever been involved with."

"You're not involved. I'm involved."

"The higher-ups will have to deal with this."

"I know some important people, too."

"You better get on the phone."

"What's wrong?"

"Could've died. And if you do belong to us, we would've lost our rights."

"But I gave myself to the hospital."

"For all we know, it's a swindle. Berendt signs the HD-one-oh-three, gives you a fake tattoo. You split the money, and you still retain the rights to your own body."

"I'm telling the truth."

"It's too late for the truth, Mr. Walsh."

Gloria's standing by the magazine rack reading *Good Housekeeping*. "Look at this, Benny. How to turn your apartment into a mountain hideaway for twelve dollars a week."

"Didn't I say Our Lady of Victory Hospital to you in the subway?"

"You can save on drapes and upholstery if you know how to sew. They show you where to buy the material. I sew."

"Our Lady of Victory?"

"That's what it says on the door."

"I had the money an hour ago. Now there's a lady upstairs who says there's no record of me."

"What happened up there, Benny?"

"I don't want to talk about it."

"How can you have the money one minute, and lose it the next?"

"I don't think I can remember."

"You feel okay?"

"I don't feel anything."

"That's good."

"I learned something today, Gloria. There are people in this city—some of them in very powerful positions—who are nuts."

"Really?"

"It makes you sick to your stomach. All you want to

177

do is leave. When you give your body to science, they make sure there are no loopholes. They don't take everybody. I gave them my address. There's going to be a ruling."

"You said you sold an heirloom."

"Did I say that?"

"If you sold a certain something, you could've got more money than selling your body."

"This way I can donate my signatures to the Library and myself to science."

"Time's running out, Benny. What are you going to do?"

"I got a plan, Gloria. I thought of it in the elevator."

"Why not sell some you-know-whats, Benny? At least, some of your doubles?"

"Then I'd only have one. What if they get stolen? You've got to have security."

"Security's what I'm talking about."

"N-O."

"Benny, I know a place. Very classy. They pay the highest prices."

"Walk me home, Gloria."

"What are you going to do?"

"I told Miss Piri I knew famous people. She told me to get on the phone."

Gloria is very quiet waiting by the bus stop. I've got nothing to say, so I listen to my body.

I puff my cheeks and tap them. I grab my hands and push the palms together until air farts out. I pat my stomach. Everything has a nice, hollow sound.

Gloria stares at the long yellow line painted on the curb. "Know what that is?" she says.

"What?"

"The yellow brick road."

"We're off to see the Wizard."

She laughs.

"There was something I wanted to ask you, Gloria."

"What?"

"Tell me about Judy's funeral."

"You know. You were there."

"Tell me again."

I roll the easy chair to the window and sit Gloria down with her transistor radio. "You collect the stars, but you don't learn from them," she says.

"Turn the radio up loud. Get comfortable."

"Joan didn't waste her time. She knew what she had to do. And she did it. In *Photoplay* she admitted, 'I knew I had to work, and work hard. I kept setting the goal higher and higher.' Sometimes, Benny, I think all you're interested in is sitting at the desk and playing with the collection."

"I'll be right back."

"Where are you going?"

"I'm calling Big John."

"That's the spirit! Wayne or Rockefeller?"

"I know what to do."

On the stairway, I remember John's number crystal clear. That's lucky. His last name begins with "G," and most of the telephone book's been torn up.

I've never meet Big John Getz, but it's as though he lived next door. I know he came to New York in 1957 from Minneapolis. Drove here in his Ford V-8. He has three children—Louis, Larry, and Lester. His wife, Nora, cooks mainly French, has a good sense of humor, and shoots under 100 in golf. Big John (he's six-four and has a full head of hair) flies his own plane. He wears the newest clothes. He's rich now. They don't have slums in Minneapolis—they have lakes. He came from the wrong side of the lake. He's popular. He gives you advice. Sometimes he even helps. He's the "Wonder Boy on the Wonderful World of WQLM Radio."

I try the number once without the dime so I get used to dialing. I don't want to lose my dime. If it's busy, I keep dialing until nighttime if I have to.

The phone's ringing. A deep voice says, "Hello, Big John. You're on the air."

"I'd like to speak to Big John Getz."

"Speaking."

"Big John? Hi."

"Welcome to the Wonderful World of WQLM Radio. 'All information, all the time.' "

"I've been listening to you for nearly ten years. It's my first call."

"The welcome wagon's open. What's your name?"

"Benny Walsh."

"What's on your mind, Benny? We're talking about the astronauts landing safely."

"They made it?"

"You betcha, Red Rider. They're going to get a hero's welcome. The President's declared a national holiday. He says it's a triumph."

"That's wonderful."

"You always get the wonderful news first on the Wonderful World of WQLM."

"The astronauts are really down?"

"That's what we've been saying. Back from their big, limitless adventure. There was three hundred fifty million dollars of hardware floating up there with them. It was a call for help heard 'round the world."

"That takes a load off my mind. I forgot what I was going to say."

"We're on the air."

"Oh, yeah. Big John, I'd like to ask a favor."

"Shoot."

"Would you lend me three hundred and fifty dollars?"

"I don't know you."

"You didn't know the man you saved from burning himself on account of the war, either."

"You got to admit I get some weird requests."

"You made headline news."

"We gave the call to the WQLM Community Action Center. They went right to work. They're almost as fast as NASA. That's a big joke from Big John."

"That's what I want you to do for me."

"We were talking about the astronauts, Benny. Do you have any feelings about them?"

"I'm only thirty blocks away from you on 102nd Street and Broadway."

"It was really something to see those parachutes billowing down to earth. I used the phrase 'like the canvas of covered wagons.' Our space pioneers were coming back from the valley of death."

"Big John, you wouldn't just be saving me, you'd be saving the finest collection of autographs in New York City."

"Would you like to go to the moon, Benny?"

"I've got a TV."

"Well, it's been nice talking to you."

"But I'm not finished. I need the money. If you could put in a good word for me at the Community Action Center."

"That's only for emergencies."

"This is an emergency."

"The astronauts were an emergency. Stranded in space. The whole world watching. You've got a problem. They came through with flying colors. So will you."

"Big John, I'm sorry about asking for the money."

"Forget it."

"Instead could you speak to Miss Piri at Our Lady of Victory, room seven fifty-three? You're the best there is on the phone."

"I don't know her."

"You're a big name. She'll listen to you. Say I'm a good guy. Reliable."

"Call back after the show."

"I'd just like to say . . . I'd like to say . . . I'm sorry about missing the astronauts. But you see Judy Garland died . . ."

"That's old news. We're up to the minute on the Wonderful World of WQLM Radio, ninety-nine point three on your dial. All information, all the time. Seven days a week."

"If I told you that it wasn't Judy in the coffin, what would you say?"

"This is the Big John Getz show moving along on this trailblazing day. There's no boundary these boys can't break, nothing they can't make our machinery do."

"Big John?"

"Yes."

"Give my best to Nora and the boys."

"Will do."

"I read you're living on Central Park West in the same building with Lauren Bacall. Maybe some afternoon I could drop over and get your signature."

"Call before you come."

I don't mind waiting for Community Action Center to get on the line. If they'll tell me when they'll have the money, I can pick it up. Big John's got to be careful, otherwise he'd have every nut in the neighborhood bugging him for favors. I think I hear somebody speaking— no words, but a kind of whisper. Maybe they don't realize I'm still here, standing by.

"Benny Walsh. Community Action?" Another click. Then a hum. We've been disconnected, but they heard.

I hope I wasn't too pushy.

The door to my room's open. Gloria has moved from the window to my autograph table. The radio's on the window sill. Big John's voice's loud and clear. Gloria's looking through the file reading the names, smiling. She deals out some of my signatures like cards. They slide across the green felt, lying in clumps around the table. A few of the cards drop on the floor. You don't treat people that way. It might be Jean Seberg or Gale Sondergaard. They'll be smudged. Gloria shouldn't take liberties.

"Gloria?"

She applauds me. "Mr. Radio *and* Television Personality. You should have your own autograph in here."

"What are you doing?"

"Getting a head start."

"How was it?"

"It's easy. Some of them are very valuable, Benny. They go back ten years."

"I mean the radio. How did my plan go?"

"You spoke right up. You sound very real on radio."

"Did I make a good impression on Big John?"

"You two talked long enough."

"A dime's worth."

"It seemed longer."

"Friends can cram a lot into a few minutes."

"Well, let's start sorting out some autographs, Benny."

"What for?"

"We don't have all day."

"Big John's going to help me out."

"I didn't hear him say that."

"You weren't listening."

"I was."

"I set the dial. I tell you to keep your ears glued. You were looking through my autographs. Who gave you permission anyway?"

"Big John was talking about astronauts."

"That's not all. He was talking about lending me the three hundred and fifty himself. He asked me if I need more than that. I'm not greedy, I said. A friend in need's a friend indeed. This moved him. He switched my call to Community Action Center."

"Then I'd have heard it."

"Hasn't it been on the air yet?"

"Not yet . . . You promised Mr. Vic three hundred and fifty dollars by Friday. It's already Thursday. You can't put all your eggs in one basket, Benny. You've got to be as good as your word."

"What did I say?"

"Don't you remember?"

"It's the details I forget."

"They're important."

"I work around the clock. I don't sit behind a desk. I don't make the big money. But I'm in business. I move around. You have to be on time. Except for signatures, one day's like any other."

"Benny, maybe you should have a rest."

"Not in my line. There are too many important people these days. You've only got so many good years. I get nervous thinking about it. We should be out on the street. Why are we waiting around?"

"You called Big John Getz."

"Did he call back?"

"You don't have a phone, Benny."

"Then we'll wait for the radio announcement."

"First things first."

"I remember my first Ann Miller movie. My first Mickey Mantle home run. The first time I saw Marilyn on

Fifth Avenue. They'll always be first. Nothing can take their place."

"You'll have time for your autographs, Benny. Business before pleasure."

"All I have to do is pick up these triples—and everything comes back. Vera-Ellen. Sundown. 1964. Vera-Ellen. Hot and humid. Corner of Forty-ninth and Seventh Avenue, 1965. Vera-Ellen . . ."

"What are you doing?"

"See. I know the time of day I got them, and the weather. I can tell you where, too. It's all up here in my head."

"You want to be a messenger walking all over New York, checking with the boss after every delivery? You want to park cars?"

"I can't drive."

"You need a good location."

"I'm not selling, Gloria. Big John'll come through."

"Suppose he doesn't?"

"All you think about's money. What do you care? I'm only another guy."

"Benny, you're crazy."

"I'm not crazy, Miss Sell-All-You've-Got. I'll go to Hollywood."

"How?"

"Judy's got fan clubs all over the country. They'll help. I'll work in a cabana. I'll distribute *Variety* to the famous homes in Coldwater Canyon. No throwing, hand delivered."

"Benny, after tomorrow you've got no job. You don't have enough to ship your magazines and autographs to the West Coast."

"I can always get something in Brooklyn. Nobody'll know my real job. On weekends I'll sneak away and take the subway to Broadway and hang out. I'll save my money. I'll buy my way back into the big time. It's only a matter of years."

"All you think about is Benny Walsh. Other people have careers, you know."

"I'm thinking about my collection."

Gloria's crying. Black lines, like dirty fingers, point

down from her eyes. She pushes away from the table and stands in the corner by W. C. Fields. He's holding a hand of cards close to his chest. He wears a high, funny top hat. Gloria's turned towards him, not me. He's saying what I would if I could. "Don't worry, my little chickadee." He talks out of the side of his mouth. Gloria should be smiling, but she doesn't even look up at him.

"What's wrong, Gloria?"

She won't look at me either.

"I'm crying for myself."

"What?"

"I'm sorry, Benny. It's private. Haven't you ever had something . . . I don't know . . . secret."

"My life's an open book."

"Something personal."

"You mean like private conversations with public personalities? Sure."

"Deeper than that, Benny."

"I don't know what you mean."

"Your own secret."

"I guess I haven't had one."

"It's not supposed to be this way. People are happy at the end. Where's the background music?"

"The radio's on."

She's shaking now. I'm afraid to go near her. "If something hurts, leave it alone." Mom was right.

"There were so many times—and promises. At Lake George, he said he'd take my picture by the fort. He never came. I waited two afternoons. Another time, when I was working at Screen Femmes, he said he needed money. I was just up and coming, but I gave it to him. He had a Leslie Howard look about him. I stayed in bed a lot that winter. I read the magazines. I watched the old films on television. They didn't treat women that way, then. He could be so nice. He said he would take me away from my film career. He bought me drapes for my window. He knew the best furniture. He said I had taste. He said I had an eye, and that he liked me. Then, after a while of liking, I'd cry like this. He disappeared."

"Who was 'he'?"

"They're all the same."

"Nobody's ever cried in front of my collection."

"You didn't see me cry."

"Three thousand signatures and still growing."

"Don't say you're going to work for a Triple-A restaurant, if you're not. Don't say you're staying, if you're leaving. Don't talk about being best, if you're giving up."

"Why did you believe those guys?"

"You believe Big John."

"There's a difference."

"What?"

"He's famous."

"Well, your collection will be famous."

Gloria goes quiet. The worst is over. I ask her a few questions, but she's statue still. Then, as if W.C. slapped her, Gloria's head snaps back. Her hands grab at her forehead.

"What's wrong now, Gloria?"

"A wave."

"Look at me."

"My head won't stop. Oh! Stop!" She says "stop" three times. After each scream, she slaps her skull.

"Don't come near me, Benny. Stay away."

What am I, a sex fiend? Do I smell? I hate loud noises. What's gotten into her? She's a maniac. "I'll have to call Mrs. Berado."

"Nobody can help me when I'm like this."

"You've got to stop it, Gloria. Big John's calling. We've got to be ready to act fast. Think of Joan."

"Three months. Four months. I almost think I'm free. Then it comes back. Why me?"

"This is a happy home. Groucho, Marilyn, Mr. Fields, Bogie." It's an insult. She won't listen to anyone, even them. They say cool it. "Stop crying, Gloria—please. Look, I'm doing my Uncle Miltie imitation. Stop crying or I'w kiw you a miwion times. I'll show you my Montgomery Clift, Gloria." She won't stop. She's a weirdo. "I'll sell some of my autographs."

Gloria turns around. Her cheeks are wet with tears. "I'm the happiest girl in the world."

186

"No Academy Award winners. No retired first-stringers. No top grossers."

"Nothing you don't want, Benny."

On Third Avenue, businessmen hurry by—eyes straight ahead, clean shirts, big briefcases, shoes kicking back the sunlight. They step like Gil Hodges to the mound. They know where they're going.

I ask Gloria to slow down. But she takes my arm and pulls me faster—past shoppers, in between the taxis that honk at us. People might bump me. My autographs might spill out of the paper bag and get run over.

My sneakers flap on the cement. I'm walking, but it doesn't feel that way. Nothing stands still.

"You okay?" says Gloria.

"I get lost easy."

"We're almost there."

It's the big time. I can tell by the leather. Leather chairs that wheeze when you sit in them. Leather desk tops. Leather signs branded with gold words.

TOP CASH PAID FOR LETTERS AND DOCUMENTS OF FAMOUS MEN AND WOMEN & Interesting Old Letters & Pioneer Journals & Whaling Logs & Old Broadsides & Poster & Books Signed By Famous Persons

Pictures of famous people are framed with their signatures. They hang around the room. Most of the signatures are from another time. I can tell because they are scratchy. But, without TV, how could a person really be famous?

The shop sounds like a library. The floor creaks. You hear footsteps. Even Springer, who owns the place and looks as old as some of the faces on the wall, whispers on the phone.

"Speak up," Gloria says. She thinks I'm nervous because I'm breathing heavy.

Springer wears a green shade on his forehead. He also has glasses. It's hard to see his eyes. He's from Vienna, he says. I explain I'm from The Homestead. He's anxious to see what's in the paper bag.

187

First I show him some of my collector's believe-it-or-not, the really hard ones—Wernher Von Braun, Edward R. Murrow, Mark Van Doren, Christine Jorgensen, Alger Hiss, Satchel Paige, Ernie Kovacs.

"Very interesting," says Mr. Springer. "You have letters from these people?"

"Autographs are letters."

"Well . . ."

"Look at the one you have in your hand. 'To Benny, Who found me on the twelfth floor of the Plaza. You win. Best regards, Howard Hughes.' There's a whole story there. What else's a letter? With autographs, they write you before your eyes. No waiting. No postage due."

Mr. Springer tilts his head right, then left. "Maybe."

Mr. Springer's a buyer, not a doer. He doesn't understand how hard it was to get these people. Mr. Springer holds each autograph close to his eyes. He flips them over gently. Each name's a picture in my head. Hands. Smiles. Doors shutting. Elevators opening. There aren't twenty people in New York who have these kind of signatures.

Mr. Springer talks slowly. It's hard to listen, but I open my eyes wide and nod back like at school. "Historians, biographers, libraries find them of great value. There's a market." Gloria squeezes my arm. "For letters," Mr. Springer says.

"Some of these people are dead. The live ones are on the move—working, training, going from place to place. It's hard to keep up with them except on TV or the magazines. They don't have time to write."

"Ah," says Mr. Springer, and picks up my second category, The Great Achievements—Wilt "The Stilt" Chamberlain (most points scored in one game), Joe Namath (most yards gained passing), Alfred Drake (most consecutive performances in a Broadway musical comedy), Raquel Welch (biggest bust).

"These have a great value to you, Mr. Walsh?"

"They certainly do. I'd say the collection comes to between fifty and a hundred thousand dollars."

"But to me, you see, individually, they are not worth much. They have no enduring literary value."

"Joe Namath and Johnny Carson wrote books."

"Yes, but nothing has been written about these people."

"Thousands of articles."

"In my business, Mr. Walsh, you have to be careful. You can't invest everywhere."

"How about Buster Keaton? The Alka-Seltzer commercial, remember?"

"They're very interesting, Mr. Walsh. But Mischa Springer only buys historical. A president, a writer, an inventor or explorer. Now if you had Bonaparte, Luther, Disraeli, Einstein, I could give maybe five hundred dollars for one autograph. I pay the best prices. I'm well known for it."

"You want Jews? I have Jews in here—famous Jews. Of course, they've changed their names. They're Americans now."

"I buy people who have made their mark."

"That's what I'm telling you. Look at the back of each card, Mr. Springer. Living history. Their exact words. Two centuries from now, people will be able to know what they said while they signed their names. It's preserved."

"Bismark, Lenin, Picasso, Marx, Tolstoy—those are big names. I pay a lot for them. To be frank, I can mount them with a nice engraving, like my Andrew Jackson over there. A wonderful Christmas gift idea."

"Do they come to New York?"

"They're dead. Anyway, they were Europeans."

"My people are great Americans. There's a new President every four years. There's only one Frank or Joe or Wilt. They put America on the map."

"I give you fifty dollars for the Keaton, one hundred if you throw me in Murrow, Garland, and Wernher Von Braun."

"Now wait a minute! I thought this was a high-class place. You're not taking Buster any fifty dollars."

"The offer stands. You want to think it over, I'm here six days a week, nine to five."

"This isn't Andrew Jackson. It's Buster Keaton—the funniest man in the world."

189

Mr. Springer asks me not to yell. I'm not yelling. I wasn't even talking to him, I was talking to Gloria and looking at him. On his desk is an old *Who's Who in America*. I open it to Keaton.

"Mr. Walsh, I know the man."

"Look, Mr. Springer, Keaton has at least four inches of history."

"What are you doing?" says Mr. Springer. "Put that ruler down!"

"Now let's measure Andrew Jackson."

"Andrew Jackson's not in *Who's Who*."

"He's not in the top four thousand."

"He's in the almanac." Mr. Springer takes another book from his desk. We all lean close to it. I read.

" 'Andrew Jackson, seventh President of the United States (1829–1837), was born on March 15, 1767, in Waxhaw, South Carolina, the son of a linen weaver who, upon migrating to the U.S. from Ireland, became a farmer.' "

"What does that prove, Mr. Walsh?"

"Keaton has four inches of history, Jackson has one inch. Keaton's got a bigger history and you want to steal him away from me for fifty dollars while Andrew Jackson's on your wall for six hundred."

"It depends on what you call history."

"History is what happens to you when you're alive. And more has happened to my Americans than any mick."

"Benny!" Gloria says. "Hush!"

"Andrew Jackson was a great man," Mr. Springer says.

"How do you know? You weren't around to see him."

"I'm a professional."

"So am I."

"That's a matter of opinion."

"You're trying to jew me down."

"Benny!"

"Shut up, Gloria. No kike's getting my collection for a song."

"Benny, control yourself."

"He knows what they're worth. Jews are shrewd. He knows."

"Mr. Springer's an expert. He gives the best prices."

"What does he know? Andrew Jackson's family was foreign like him. He's trying to boost the price of his own kind. I've been here all my life. I know what's valuable."

"Benny? Take the money. Apologize to Mr. Springer."

"My blood's pure. My body has been sold to a major American hospital. I came from pioneer stock. He should kiss my ass!"

"Benny!"

"Jews are cowards. History proves it. So do the movies."

"Let's get out of here."

Springer picks up my autographs and stuffs them back in the paper bag. It isn't the A & P. He can't treat my signatures like soup. I grab them and put them back on his desk. So what if Springer turns away from us. Springer's got ears—big ones. He can hear.

"He wants me to sell. He wants me to get out. He wants me to give up. Just like a Jew. I'm no quitter, Springer. Ask Big John. I'm an American."

"Out! Out!"

Gloria pick up the autographs and pulls me outside. Springer locks the door behind us, and stares out from behind the glass. He can't scare me. I'm looking at him. I've caught him doing the dirty.

"Wahoo! Wahoo! Jew!"

"Benny? Put your hat on."

"I'm scaring him."

"He's not moving."

"He's terrified."

"Benny, he's seen the autographs. He's in business. Those are the facts."

"He wants to split my collection."

"I feel a wave, Benny."

Springer's taking cover. He pulls the shade down over the window. I can see my reflection, and his cheap shoes at the bottom of the glass. Only the laundress'll know how scared he is.

"I'm talkin' to you, Springer. You scum-suckin' pig. You autograph rustler. Slap leather!"

"Benny, there's electricity all over me."

"I'm fighting mad, Gloria. I gave him a chance to make a good offer. He can't push me around. Hear that, Springer!"

"It doesn't matter any more, Benny. We lost."

"He wouldn't have tried the swindle unless the collection was a gold mine. If you could see what I see. It's so simple."

"But Springer said . . ."

"What does he know? He doesn't even pray to the same God. When he lies in bed at night, I bet he dreams European."

A pencil tips open the mail slot. A voice says, "Go away! Or I call the police!"

"I had a dream, Springer! You're not going to shaft us out of this one, Mister Big-Time-Loser."

This close-range yelling's better than a ball game. My voice sounds deeper, my body tingles. I cross the street with Gloria. I slap the taillights of the taxis.

"What did you see in the dream?"

"How things would be. Comfortable and warm. Very blossomy. The best money can buy. People happy together forever. Peace and quiet."

"Did you hear music?"

"A hum. There were words, too."

"A message?"

" 'Take what you can get. It's a free country.' "

"That was some message," says Gloria. "What's going to happen?"

"Meet me at The Homestead after work. I'll have some results. I swear it."

"Sing 'Cottage for Two' with me. For luck."

"I can't sing."

"A barbershop duet. I'll sing, you repeat the words you like. *In our cottage for two . . .*"

"Cottage for two."

"Our forever rendezvous."

"Our rendezvous."

"We'll share rooms with a view of the sky . . ."

"Of the sky."

192

"You and I."

"This is silly, Gloria. The songs come later."

Why can't people keep their bodies and their breath to themselves? All the way to The Homestead on the subway, they rub me with their knees, their shoulders, their backs. They try and spin me off course. But I'm on the scent. Nothing can stop me. Not Springer with his denture breath. Not Rumsey, who smells like his horses and won't let go of my arm. I tell him the barricades are down, everything's back to normal. He pulls me inside the stagecoach and rolls up the window. Boxes are on the floor.

"I held down the fort, right? You saw me, Walsh?"

"I've got an emergency."

"I'm not payin' no never mind to any emergencies. No tip. No thanks. No day off. You bust your balls, and nobody remembers. They plan a party for Chef's birthday tomorrow—a big blowout. They lean on you for contributions for the entertainment. But do you think I get an invite? I wouldn't go if they had a gorilla high-steppin' out of a cake. I'm tellin' you, Walsh, things have changed."

"Things can't change that quick."

"Would you believe they're talkin' of phasin' me out, scrappin' Blackey and Spot? We led the Macy's Parade two years runnin'."

"You're kidding?"

"Nope. They're gettin' up a new menu. They put a suggestion box in the pantry. There's talk of a contest to rename the restaurant. Zambrozzi's handin' out typed memos left and right. It's a new world."

"I'm going to a restaurant where there are no sudden changes."

"Everything changes, kid."

"Not if you're rich and successful."

"I told 'em I wouldn't come in this mornin' after workin' fourteen hours yesterday. 'If you don't hitch up today, don't hitch up tomorrow.' I'm not wearin' street clothes on this rig for the rest of my life. I'm a driver, not a delivery boy."

"I need help."

"So do I. We're in this together. Their best busboy out on the street. And then me workin' from the inside to topple 'em. When we're finished, only shitheels'll work for them."

"I need money."

"Let's bleed 'em. The Rumseys know about revenge. Sent smallpox in with blankets to avenge the late, great General George Custer. Dammed up a river on our Colorado territory to keep the sheep farmers off our grazin' land. The Rumseys know how to hate."

"I want a case of Scotch and three hundred and fifty dollars."

"You got it."

"I don't."

"Walsh, the Scotch is yours. What do you think I been pickin' up all day, daisies? Look in that box?"

Rumsey's laughing, slapping his side. "Watch me now, Grandpa. The Homestead's gonna be my Wounded Knee." He takes out a piece of paper, wets the tip of a pencil with his tongue, and writes. "Changin' numbers is easier'n spittin' in a skillet. I'll put a case under the seat."

"I still have to do some fancy footwork."

"Help me unload the rest. When you're ready to make tracks, give a yell."

"I've got to float like a butterfly, sting like a bee."

"Well, you won the first round, Benny."

"Benny Walsh is still in there punching."

"Hot dog!" says Rumsey.

Nobody says anything to us as we stack the boxes in the pantry. Liquor's very heavy. Rumsey puts his arm around me walking back to the stagecoach. "There was a whole side of the Rumsey family that did this. Desperadoes. Stole from the rich to give to the poor."

"You mean like Errol Flynn?"

"No," says Rumsey, lifting out the last case. "Like the Lone Ranger."

The phone booth stinks of piss. "Mr. Monte-Sano, please."

"He's in a meeting. Can I help you? This is his assistant, Bonni DeGregorio."

"Tell him the game's not over till the last out."

"What?"

"Can't you take a message?"

"Who is this?"

"Tell him Benny S. Walsh gets results."

They let me punch in. They let me put on my whites. They wait till I'm excited about getting back to station 4 and making a last-ditch stab at big-money contacts. Then they hit me below the belt.

Zambrozzi's the hatchet man, even after I waved hello and asked him to sign my book. Now he tells me I'm not going out there today.

"To the victor belongs the spoils, Chef. But I'm no spoil."

I try to talk to Zambrozzi as one Catholic to another. "The first day of our all-Italian menu. You miss the first shift, Benny. I got to be practical."

Zambrozzi's no Catholic, he's a Jew.

McDougal's on station 4. He's not even union. Zambrozzi says it's not hard to get a card. (It's not easy, either.) McDougal's got personal problems. He's got sex on the brain. The Homestead's respectable. You can't chew your food and listen to that filth. He'll be bad for tips. Guests'll see McDougal's two holes. Zambrozzi doesn't know what it's like out there. You're on show.

Victor sits me on a stool. I can see through the swinging doors into the main room. The crowd's wandering in. Victor makes me watch him carefully. He takes an egg and holds it in his right hand. He grips it tight with his thumb, middle finger and pinky. He snaps his wrist. The shell splits right up the middle. The egg drops into the steel bowl, the yolk isn't even broken.

"I need four dozen eggs right away, Benny."

"For who?"

"Break the eggs."

Nobody tells you anything back here.

I open each egg with both hands. It's very messy. Sometimes the egg shell falls into the pot. I pick it out.

The egg whites suck my hand like quicksand. My wrist gets slimy. The ooze makes my skin feel like mud. I wiggle my fingers in the pot. They move like snakes— slow, skinny, curved. I can't tell where my fingers stop and the snakes begin. I'm scared. I yank my hands. Some of the waiters come over to say hello. I don't want them to see my hands.

Victor wants more eggs. He says I'm wasting egg white by spooning the shells out of the pot. I'm not sticking my hand back in there. He says to watch what I'm doing. I know my aim's bad, but I don't want to look in the pot. He stands over me. I have to look.

The yolks are yellow eyes.

Nobody'll miss the Scotch.

"Hello, lover boy," says McDougal, showing off his Homestead whites. "While the mouse's away, the cat will play." He stands right by the stool. He gives me the finger.

"You've got your work cut out. Station four's very busy now."

"Didn't I tell you I was gonna bust some Commie chops? I'm on the inside. That's what they teach you at spy school—how to kiss ass and strike while the iron's hot. You got to be at the right place at the right time."

"I never missed a day in eight years. Lou Gehrig has nothing on me."

"Junior, it's a new ball game. I'm making notes on everything. Who talks to who. Who looks suspicious. In a few months I go state's evidence—sing like the most beautiful fuckin' canary you ever heard. Get wise, Walsh. This place is a Mafia-Commie front. All you got to do is see the decor, and you know it's a nest."

"Everything's on the up and up at The Homestead."

"Don't play dumb with me, Walsh. Everybody's on the take. I could put the whole bunch of you pretty boys in the slammer."

"Not me."

"I bet you got something stashed."

"You don't have any evidence."

"I hold my cards close to the chest. When I'm ready to play my aces, you'll hear about it."

"You got no respect for a place, McDougal. You sail from port to port. You love 'em and leave 'em. You don't know what it's like to care for something."

"The day I clinch this case, I'm celebratin' by droppin' some salt cellars under the table. I'm doin' a little high-class muff-divin.'"

"How much is it worth to you to keep this from Zambrozzi and the Boss?"

"Who's gonna tell him?"

"For three hundred and fifty dollars I'll forget everything you said."

"Are you kiddin', Walsh? You think blackmail's gonna stop a great spy? Temporary didn't send me in here by chance. I wasn't the luck of the draw. There's a whole fuckin' network—people I ain't even seen yet—that know me by my number. We got a code."

"There's a code of decency, too. You don't just take another guy's job."

"You were late. They said you were bein' retired anyway . . ."

"Retire at my age? You get kicked upstairs. I'm getting another position at '21.'"

"They said as long as I didn't make trouble and voted with them, I could have it."

"If you're a spy, why do you shoot your mouth off?"

"Ever heard of a spy that came right out with it? My disguise is that I have no disguise. Everybody thinks I'm a fuckin' great guy. I got station four in one day, didn't I? Know why?"

"A fluke."

"Personality—that's why."

"Four's the best station at The Homestead. People request it. Right now they're waiting for bread. They may not have water. You've got to make a good impression, or they won't come back. Is anybody famous out there? I really need a big autograph."

"That's for me to know and you to find out."

"Be on the lookout for very famous literary or political types. Nothing's too big."

"Will you make it worth my while?"

"Sure, if you don't keep it a secret."

"That's not my style," says McDougal, winking and walking back through the swinging doors.

Zambrozzi won't lend me money. I try and make him remember the years we've worked together. He says times are changing. He tells me about his design for the new uniforms, the new menu, the new image. I ask him to buy my Homestead scrapbook. "That's old hat," he says.

I don't understand. Old history's good history.

The sinks are rumbling. The pots gurgle with steam. Victor and Anthony yell at each waiter as he comes in, "What's the story?"

"Veal *parmigiana!*"

"Spaghetti *alla matriciana!*"

"*Insalata rugola!*"

Temporary cook's help is no fun. Peel this. Carry that. Nothing steady. You wait to be called.

"What's the story?" Victor shouts to Tony Mendoza as he hurries in with his tray propped up on his shoulder.

"Where's the chef?"

"No story, no chef."

"Lady Bird Johnson's out there. She wants to congratulate Chef on the new specialities."

Victor walks over to Zambrozzi's table. When he gets the message, Zambrozzi takes a flower from the vase on his table and pins it to his coat. He puts on his white chef's hat, and holds a copy of the complete new menu. The whole kitchen goes silent as Zambrozzi steps forward, even the dishwashers stop banging the tubs.

Victor and Anthony give Chef the thumbs-up sign as he passes by. He tugs at his coat and steps through the swinging doors. The rest of us rush to the window to watch.

"Stir the soup, Walsh."

"C'mon, Victor. It's my chance. We both know the same show-biz types—Eartha Kitt, Carol Channing."

"Calm down, Benny. Do your job."

"She believes in giving people a head start."

"Don't fuck with me, Benny. Don't screw things up."

"I saw her husband take the oath. I saw her daughters get married."

"I don't care what you saw, you're staying by the stove."

"She'd make a great Christmas gift idea."

Victor and Anthony walk me back to the stove. "Stay here," says Victor. They go back to the window. All I can see is heads and elbows.

"What's happening?"

"Desi's kissin' her hand, pourin' on the charm," somebody calls back.

Zambrozzi's kissing the hand that has been kissed by kings and queens. Royalty kisses rings, not skin. Doesn't Lady Bird know about Italian men? "What's he doing now?"

"Still kissing."

"Watch out, Lady Bird!"

She won't listen to me, but I've got proof. On 42nd Street. The scientific exhibition. "A moral for all the family," it says, and if she saw it she'd beware. The facts and figures are under you know what? "Cancer. Leprosy. Accidents." It's horrible looking at the specimens, but it makes you stronger. If people realized what could happen to them when they touched others, they'd keep their hands to themselves.

McDougal pushes through the crowd at the window and comes over to the stove. "Some bigwig broad's out there. Did you get a load of Zambrozzi's flower? A *red* rose. The Big Shot's dress is the same *red*. It's fuckin' blatant. He gave her the flower! They've got the guts of burglars. I'm tellin' you, Walsh, I'm so fuckin' close to crackin' this joint wide open my fuckin' life's in danger."

"That's Lady Bird Johnson."

"I don't care if it was the fuckin' First Lady. Listen up here! The chef sent me out for special rolls. Does that make sense? I mean how special can rolls be?"

"There's Italian bread in the stove."

"He don't want me listenin'. He don't want me breakin' the code."

"Did you meet her?"

199

"I don't touch what I can't eat."

"She's a very smart lady."

"Fuckin'-A, she's smart. So's he. You got to be a genius to get away with this kind of thing in broad daylight."

"I know her."

"No shit? It figures. That's how it starts. They brainwash the dupe in the street. Man, your ass is grass. You're playing with fire."

"It's an emergency. Ask for her autograph."

"I'm not talkin' with the enemy."

"She's not the enemy."

"I know the enemy when I see him. I fought in two fuckin' wars. I killed seventy-five of them, and another twenty in peacetime. How many did you kill?"

"I'll write a message to her."

"No names. I don't want nobody fingerin' out McDougal. Blackmailers piss the hell out of me. And the Ruski fights dirty."

The rest of the staff are still staring out the window. McDougal puts the bread in the basket. He says he doesn't want to know what I'm going to write in case they catch him and try to torture him. I type it on Zambrozzi's typewriter so there will be no clues.

```
DEar LadyBird...I am trapped in the
kitchen,. please sixgn your name on the back
xxof this paper and give itto the man wxith
no nose. THIS IS AN EMERGWENCY. ThankingYOu
in adxcvance and WeLcome to Station @4.
A fan..
P.S. Be careful. Wash youxxur hands.
```

I slip the note under the bread. McDougal puts the basket on his tray.

"There's somethin' fishy about that P.S., Walsh."

"You said you didn't want to know."

"It's my business to know everything. You could have somethin' stashed in the ladies' room. The only place I can't go."

"I wouldn't double-cross you."

"People have made that mistake before."

"Think of it as *Mission Impossible*."

"Don't get the wrong idea, Walsh. I work solo."

Zambrozzi walks back into the kitchen, smiling but not talking. He goes to his desk, takes off his hat, rolls up his sleeves, and pulls out one of his old Italian cookbooks. He makes notes. Victor and Anthony pester him to explain. Finally, Chef says, "I kiss her hand, I wish her *'buon appetito'*—it's the custom. I show her the new menu and tell her of our struggle. She asks for lobster *fra diavolo* with linguini—as a special favor. Our first real test. It must be triumph!"

Zambrozzi stands over the stove discussing the sauce with Victor and Anthony.

I walk over to the kitchen window to get a look at Lady Bird. Garcia's standing next to her.

McDougal's serving the table behind them. He puts his tray down and walks quietly toward the kitchen. Ten yards from the kitchen, he starts to run. I hardly have time to dodge the doors.

"The fit has hit the shan, Walsh."

"What?"

"The fuckin' plot thickens."

"Did she sign? Do you have the paper?"

"All I got's the message."

"What did she say?"

"All I heard was 'What's the meaning of this?' "

"Maybe I can get that in writing."

"Your dick's in the sand, Walsh."

"I don't get it?"

"Garcia broke the fuckin' code. He knows who sent the message."

Chef and Victor are talking by the freezer. "I can't get my autographs."

"Scram, Walsh. Take your bongos and beat it."

McDougal's looking through the window. He sees what I see. Garcia's walking toward the kitchen.

"I think I'll get some air."

*　　*　　*

Riding shotgun on a stagecoach is like riding an Atlantic City roller coaster. You lean back, hold onto the bottom of your seat, and gulp the air that's pushing against your face. Rumsey's got the horses really moving. What a getaway!

The first stop's Screen Femmes down the road. All the way there, I try to dream up an excuse to get Gloria out of work the way I used to skip school. I told the teachers my father was dying of cancer. I'd lower my head. Tears would come to my eyes. But I wasn't sad. Mom was the only one in the house. Gloria might get upset. She remembers her father.

It's my lucky day. Gloria's walking out of Fascination when we drive up. She climbs up top and sits between us. I tell her about the Scotch. She squeezes close to me. "Your collection's going to be the best, Benny," she says. "I knew I could trust you."

Rumsey thinks we should celebrate. "Hell with work," he says. "Hell with The Homestead. Let's make tracks."

The stagecoach starts to rumble up the Avenue of the Americas. The wheels squeal and clatter. Rumsey's laughing as he slaps the backsides of the horses with the reins, and they trot faster down the road. He shouts to the traffic lights to change to green. They do.

"What about the money?" says Gloria. A warm wind flies in our faces. Glaria says something, but it's hard to hear. Her voice gets louder. "You can't waste time!" Passersby look at us and wave. We wave back. Cars slash past us, cutting in and out like Indians attacking a covered wagon. Headlights are flaming arrows, their honking war cries. We ride high into the battle. Nothing touches us.

"This is fun!"

"What?" shouts Gloria, brushing her hair out of her eyes.

"This ride's fun!"

She nods yes. She's smiling.

We outrace the Indians. They're stopped at a red light. The horses pull us ahead into the park. The trees are

202

black and spooky. The sky and stars are close to us. The trail zigzags. The coach slows down. Rumsey and Gloria are singing something into the wind. Their voices trail off behind them, floating backwards like the smoke from Rumsey's pipe. You don't light fires or make noises in Indian territory. We can't double back for safety. The trail's one way. Without warning, a whole pack of them's on top of us again, charging close enough to touch us and run us off the road. They surround the stagecoach on three sides. We keep moving. The light from their arrows just misses our heads, and disappears into the forest. "Pull the wagons into a circle!" Gloria and Rumsey are still singing. They don't realize the danger. "Pull them into a circle!"

The moon makes a path across the water.

In the morning, there'll be mists. The sun'll burn through by noon. Flamingos, rabbits, deer, cougars, buffalo—they'll be drinking at the shore. We won't disturb them, but they'll come near us anyway. They'll be our friends, we'll be theirs. It's good to be near water if you're building a house. We'll make ours of natural wood. Rumsey'll help cut and clear the forest. I'll gather and collect. Gloria'll cook. Together, we'll plant the fields in the spring and forget about them until October. Then, we'll harvest. There'll be too much of everything. Fish, meat, and flowers we never expected.

"Isn't it beautiful, Benny?"

"Let's explore."

"Are you kiddin'? This place's a jungle at night," says Rumsey. "Wanna get yourself killed?"

We'll be safe.

It's no Boardwalk, no Broadway. We'll walk only on land no man or animal has touched. We'll know by the sound—the snap like fresh carrots—that ours are the first steps. We'll be the first on this territory, and we'll make it beautiful.

"Don't you think it's gorgeous, Benny?" says Gloria.

"Fantastic."

"I've seen pictures of this in the ads."

"Not this."

"Maybe not, but almost."

"Giddyap," says Rumsey.

The clock on the Grand Central building is round and white. It stares at us. 11:00. It's not my fault it's late. It's not my fault we can't move. Riding the stagecoach through the park, an hour seemed like minutes. Now, standing still with cars bumper to bumper in front and behind us, minutes seem like hours. Fumes from the cars smell up the air. The buildings blot out the sky. The horses lift their tails and make number two in front of us. The other cars have air conditioning and radio, they can forget the traffic jam. We're out in the open. Shadows and stink are all around us.

Rumsey's stopped singing. There's nothing to think about but what's inside your head. This gives everybody the jitters. "I knew we shouldn't have taken this ride. I knew it," Gloria says.

"The clock's off."

"What are you going to do?" she says. "There's no time to waste."

"Why is it always my fault?"

Gloria won't look at me.

I wish we were moving, then I wouldn't have to think. I'm reliable. My collection proves it. I wish Rumsey would crack his whip, and Gloria would start singing again.

We're not the only people who are upset. Kids honk their horns. They leave their cars and sit on the pavement. Cabdrivers open their doors and pull themselves up above the hood to see if anything's moving.

"Ain't this a mess," says a driver to Rumsey.

"Terrible."

"They should make the Mayor take a cab, instead of a helicopter," the cabdriver says. "Every cab in New York should drive up to Gracie Mansion and honk him out of bed. Keep the lights on so he can't have his beauty sleep."

"The traffic cops should be out here."

"There's a thousand policemen at the Waldorf tonight."

"Where'd you get that?"

"Radio."

"It figures. They're all inside eating chicken and peas and listening to a speech."

"Shit, no. There's a convention of longhairs protesting the President."

Gloria turns toward me. "The President." She jumps off the seat. "C'mon, Benny."

"Hey!" Rumsey says. "We still got some celebratin' to do."

"Business," I explain.

Louis says he'll do it for a Judy Garland.

He takes an I.O.U.

This is where connections help. Without Louis coming to the garage door, Gloria and I could never have gotten inside the Waldorf. Louis says not to mention it.

"Did you get a load of those crowds?"

"It's a good thing Cole Porter's passed on—it would've turned his stomach to see so much hate stretched all the way around the block to the Waldorf Towers."

"Where's the President speaking?"

"The ballroom."

"Let's go."

"You don't want to go in there, believe me. You won't get near him."

"I've got to get him, Louis. It's do or die."

"Every two minutes, people are standing up, applauding. It don't matter what he says—wars, money, moon landings. They keep jumping up and down. You'd think he was hitting fungoes off the dais."

I hate talking to Louis after what he did to Judy. He's as cocky as ever. I pinch Gloria's arm to make her smile and be perky. You've got to get along to get ahead.

"The smart money's with Lena Horne upstairs at the Empire Room," says Louis. "She's breaking records. *Variety* said the b.o. was a socko fifty-two thousand last week."

"The President's more impressive."

"They say Lena wears such a tight dress they have to lift her onstage."

"But I need the President."

205

"If you saw Lena, she'd make you forget that old fart."

"Please, Louis."

"It's such a hassle. I can't take you through the kitchen."

"You just said—"

"I know what I said, Walsh. But I'm taking a big risk. I'll need more than a Garland. We've got to sneak up through the garage to Peacock Alley, where they're holding the press conference. That's worth a Sinatra."

"It's a holdup."

"At the Waldorf, you pay for the best."

"How do you know he'll be there?" says Gloria.

"My buddy set up the chairs," says Sypher.

"How do we get there?"

"Frank Sinatra, Juliet Prowse, and . . . Ava Gardner."

"Let's go."

"Because of you, Otto Preminger and I are quits."

"I'm in a hurry."

"Frank Sinatra. Juliet Prowse. Ava Gardner. Rocky Colavito."

"Okay."

Louis writes out the names on the I.O.U. He makes Gloria and me sign our initials over each one.

I'm very nervous waiting outside Peacock Alley. The microphones are there, the water and cups are in place. But nobody's around. Louis has taken us through so many doors and up so many stairs that the President could've given a quick talk and gone.

The Empire Room's past the elevators. Louis points across the lobby.

"Maybe I could just sneak over and get Lena while we're waiting."

"You stay right here, Benny Walsh."

"This guy could be all night," says Louis. "Lena's a pro. She knows when to stop."

"I can't go with you, Louis."

"Pussy-whipped," says Louis. He heads across the lobby. The elevator bells start pinging. Doors open. Men with thick necks and dark suits rush out and line the way toward Peacock Alley. "Move back there!" one of them says to us and pushes us off our spot.

There's so much whiteness, it's hard to see. Men hold gigantic lights above the crowd. I hear cameras humming. Suddenly TV men, strapped like astronauts with mechanical equipment, are walking slowly backwards towards us.

The President's smaller than he looks on television. His color's better. In a tuxedo, his skin's very white, not gray. He walks slowly. He's used to the light, he doesn't squint. He's speaking to a young man beside him. Reporters and photographers pester him, but he keeps on talking as if they weren't in front of him and at his knees. Gloria says she likes him better on television.

The young man's whispering to him as he passes us.

"These?" the President says.

The President stops and pushes by the two broad-shouldered men who've muscled in ahead of us. They get out of his way. The President touches our shoulders. He's smiling.

"Do you like football?"

"Thank you, Mr. President," says a photographer.

"We'd like your autograph," Gloria says.

He grins, not the way he looks in photos. His gums are salmon-colored. "I like the Jets and the Mets."

"Would you sign my book, Mr. President?" Gloria says.

"What a lovely comb you have in your hair, young lady. My mother had one just like it."

He puts his arm around Gloria. He asks her name. He writes in her pad.

"Over here, Mr. President!" somebody yells.

He stays with us.

"You're great, Mr. President," I say.

He turns to me for my pen and pad. I have the pen. But I forgot the paper!

I take Gloria's pad and turn the page to a new, white sheet.

"You don't change the game plan at half time, do you?"

"Benny Walsh, Mr. President. Sign something revealing."

"A great captain sees an opportunity and takes it. He never looks back. He never falters."

"You're doing a great job, sir."

"What should I write?"

"Us Mets fans stick together. Isn't that right, Mr. President?"

"Why do you think I'm great?" he says, looking up from the pad.

"Make it like a letter."

He puts his hand on my shoulder. "Tomorrow, I'm off on that three-week nonstop tour of Europe you've been reading about. The Cavalcade for Community."

"A personal postcard."

"It's the toughest job in the world. But you know, son, it's worth the twenty-hour days."

"To Benny—A Good Guy."

The young man comes up behind us. "Mr. President, we've got the *Times* deadline."

"It's great the way you make history, Mr. President."

He hands the pad back to Gloria and waves at us. "My pleasure," he says, and steps inside the Peacock Alley.

Gloria wants to get outside before looking at the President's autographs. We try the back exits.

"Didn't you feel funny being that close to the President, Gloria?"

"I felt at home."

"I don't think of him having nose hairs."

"He doesn't."

"People always joke about the President. They wouldn't if they met him. He's a great guy. You overlook hairiness."

"He put his arm around me."

"Some people say it's a sign of a he-man."

"His fingers were strong like my father's."

"He had hair on his knuckles. Did you see that? We root for the same teams. Did you get that? If he had time to spend, he'd be interested in my autographs. I could fly to Washington to show him. Maybe when he retires . . ."

"He's not retiring," Gloria says.

"When he does."

"He's not hairy either."

"He was wearing makeup."

"But he's a lady's man. I could tell by the look he gave me."

"Springer's going to pay through his Jewish nose for this one."

"The President's the most powerful man in the world," says Gloria.

"Don't I know it."

"He's got everything."

"Even free postage."

"His hands were smooth like a boy's. His eyes were deep and blue. He was affectionate."

"Let's look now, Gloria."

"Can't we wait?"

"Let's do it now."

She takes the pad out of her purse. "Let me look first. Alone."

Gloria walks to the florist's window. I hate silences. "What's it say?"

"It's beautiful." Gloria hands me the pad and turns back to stare at the flowers. "Poetic."

"The signature's a little small."

"It's the thought that counts, Benny."

" 'To Gloria—Keep a Good Thought.' Not bad."

"He's so generous," says Gloria.

"It's not what I call personal."

"I think it's intimate. Don't forget I've never seen a President before."

"If you'd have asked for something revealing, he might have done a whole page."

"Give it to me." Gloria grabs the pad.

"Okay. Read mine. Surprise me."

" 'To Benny Walsh.' "

"My whole name. Already that's historical."

Gloria shuts the book.

"I told him to be revealing. If it's embarrassing, they'll pay even more."

"Benny."

"Read the rest."

" 'To Benny Walsh.' "

"I've already heard that part. Now the good stuff."

"That's it, Benny. He didn't sign."

"I saw him write his name."

"It's not here."

"It has to be."

Gloria shows me the pad.

"He was right in front of me, wasn't he? He put his arm on my shoulder, didn't he?"

"What's wrong, Benny?"

"I'm not excited, Gloria."

"If you say so."

"At least he signed your pad."

"Yes."

"We can get good money for it."

"No, we can't."

"Oh, yes. Springer said he paid the highest prices. Of course, a letter'd be better. This still makes a good gift."

"I can't give away the President after all he's said."

"But you were the one . . ."

"He stood so close. He called me Gloria. We hadn't even been properly introduced."

"My collection's the best. You said so."

Tears roll slowly down Gloria's face. "I'm going to be faithful."

"But we're a team, Gloria. You helped me."

Gloria feels her cheeks, and looks at her fingers. "My mascara. I look awful."

"Give me the autograph, Gloria. I gave you Crawford."

"Don't ask me, Benny."

"Please."

Gloria runs down the hall. She disappears through the revolving doors. I'm too tired to run. I've got to sit down.

"Get up, mister," says the doorman, pulling me to my feet. "The Waldorf has enough trouble with protesters sittin' down. It don't need drunks."

"I'm not drunk. I'm all right."

"You were spread-eagled on the floor."

"I forgot. For a moment I forgot."

"This isn't a flophouse."

"I went blank. No buzzing. No vomit."

"Think about it in the street, mister. People pay top dollar here. They don't want to see the likes of you."

"I forgot how to breathe."

THE TV IS MY FRIEND. When *TV Guide* says that Humphrey Bogart and Lauren Bacall are on at 1:00 A.M., they show up. If it says *Samson and Delilah* with Victor Mature and Hedy Lamarr starts at 3:30, you can set your watch by it.

I sit very still.

I have one hand on the remote-control switch, the other on the arm of my chair. One cracked knuckle, one burp, one false move, and I'm done for. Bogie's been hired by Lauren Bacall's father to trail her other sister, Martha Vickers, who's a wild one. She's been hanging out with underground connections and running up a big dope bill. The old man sits in the greenhouse. It's hot and steamy, but the potted palms look familiar. Bogie has a few suspects. One of them's me.

I don't have time to explain. Bogie's gat has a hair trigger. He'd as soon shoot as hear my story. It's why I can't move. Bogie tried to get Mom to put the finger on me. He showed her a picture, me washing dishes. "That's not my Benny." He was stumped. Then Gloria tried to squeal to Bogie and tell him where I was. She said she wanted a straight $400 for herself. But when he got to the warehouse for his rendezvous with Gloria, she'd been poisoned by a rival gang. Tough titties.

Hiding out is harder than I thought. It's a big city—millions of people, thousands of streets. But the walls have eyes. You're never alone, especially when you're wanted. Maybe I should switch on the radio, too. Turn up the lights. In New York lights mean nobody's home. Bogie's from California. There'll be a knock on the door. I won't answer. Another knock. He'll push Bacall behind the bathroom door in the hallway. He'll fast-talk me. I'm not falling for it this time. I'm holding my breath. I'm squeezing my asshole tight. Nobody's getting it. I'm so quiet, I can't even believe I'm here.

Icy sweat dribbles from my armpits. I bite my lip.

I hear footsteps coming up the stairs.

The first gunshot is the worst. It knocks me back into the chair. The springs claw me. "You've got it all wrong." But Bogie won't stop. He's got a job to do. He's supposed to have six bullets in his gun. But they keep exploding—ten, twenty, thirty shots. Not the BLAM! of a .38 but the BOOM! of a sawed-off shotgun. It's worse than a shooting gallery. The noise is so loud I can't feel my head.

He's left me for dead. But I know I'm not dead, I'm not bleeding. Hedy Lamarr tries to sweet-talk me. I'm through with painted lips, perfume, the long-hair bit. She wants to get me hot. But I'm frozen. Victor Mature's a sucker for her come-on. "Keep your mouth shut and your eyes open, Vic." He won't listen. He can't see me in all this dark.

Delilah sets a fine table—goat's milk, dates, bread, assorted meats, fish, and wine. The napkins should be to the left of the silver plates. She wants me to sit down and have a bite. "Give your type an inch, and they'll take a mile!" That scared her. She goes back to Victor Mature.

Women are spoiled. Just because they are beautiful and have a hole, they think they can get anything they want. Hedy Lamarr wants Samson's hair. A piece of his coat, his arrow quiver—that I could understand. But hair? She complains. She pushes. She wants to know the secret to my strength, too. "Not telling, lady. You're not putting your clammy paws on my hair." She keeps after me. She thinks my secret's in my head. It's in my collection, and it's staying right here in this room. "It took a lot of hard work." Delilah doesn't understand this. She's never worked a day in her life.

They poke out Victor Mature's eyes with a flaming stake. He should've kept to himself. They're not getting me. My eyes are shut. What you can't see can't hurt you.

I can hear Victor screaming. I can hear the others laugh. After a while I sneak a look. Samson's in the stadium. Dwarfs are running around him, tripping him, pinching him, confusing him. He's bleeding. Samson asks God for revenge. God comes through. Samson puts his arms between two pillars and pushes. The stones start to rumble. Rocks fall fast. First, the dust and pebbles, then the big stones tumble down. There's no time to move. I put my hands over my head—it's too late.

I feel a thud.

Everything goes dark.

Feet—on the ground. Hands—holding the chair. Bladder—full up and aching. Eyes—straight ahead.

Samson got the little bastards. I survived. So did the collection.

The room's cold. The TV's running. That's lucky.

I slide the chair close to the screen. I lie my head on top of the set. It's warm. I hug it close. The tube shines white light on my belly. People run across my skin. The shadows itch. I feel warmer.

Hugh Downs talks like he owns the news. I press the control switch. I make Downs silent.

Soldiers on search and destroy. They must have guns, but I can't hear them. Bodies are moving, so they can't be dying. The jungle's full of traps, but not a twig breaks. No one screams. Marines are foxy.

Press.

The splashdown. My chest's flashing like a neon sign. It's the astronauts' way of saying, "Thanks, Benny." They're too tired to talk. Frogmen haul them into rafts. Nobody pushes.

Press.

The President talks to the nation from the Waldorf.

Press.

I feel honored and safe. The President's not shining on anybody else's body. His words are passing in through my pores. A whole letter. Maybe an electronic tattoo.

The Cubs are challenging the Mets for the pennant. Leo Durocher and Gil Hodges are talking together. Hodges keeps quiet, Leo's mouthing off. He says the Cubs are rested and they've got strategy. He says the Mets in first place is a joke. He says the Cubs are going to overrun New York and demolish them.

That's enough lip, Leo. I make him silent.

Press.

Hugh Downs says it's going to be a pleasant, cool Friday. He says it's a day to do all those things you've been putting off. He says to keep your fingers crossed for the Mets' crucial doubleheader with the Cubs. What does he know? I don't need him. When the news stops, I've got my autographs. They stick to your bones. They don't talk back. I'm sick of Mr. Downs anyway. I click him off. He starts to shrink. First to half the screen. Then a third. Finally he's only a white spot swallowed by blackness. "Good-bye, Hugh!"

I slide the armchair to the autograph table. They're all safe and sound. I lay the boxes on my lap. I run my fingers along the dividers. It feels good. I drop in on some of my collection at random.

JOE AMALFITANO, utility infielder. 1954–67.
REMARKS: "What the hell do you want me for?"

" 'Cause you're the best pinch-runner in the business, Joe." I should've told him that when we first met. I was younger and shy. After Dusty Rhodes would single to tie the game, Joe would run bases. He knew how to steal. He knew how to get the jump, even when the opponents were looking out for him. He slid under every mitt. He had a gift. He was always safe. He looked sharp, too, standing with both feet on the bag, dusting himself off after a slide. His liners were straight. The peak of his cap was pointed, the tongues of his spikes were turned down. He was professional.

GEORGE JESSEL, MICKEY ROONEY, OLEG CASSINI,
JENNIFER JONES, BURT BACHARACH,
RACHEL, JOHNNIE RAY

Everyone I ask has the same story. As kids, they knew what they wanted to be. No Delilah could stand in their way. They didn't come out smelling like a rose. But once they'd grabbed the brass ring, nobody remembered anything but the sweet smell of their success. All those years practicing alone in their rooms, then the big break. When they came in the open everybody knew them. There was no more silence.

Everything will be new and white. Everything will smell fresh.

Nobody'll see me.

Everybody'll see me.

First, white socks with rubber bands snapped around the ankles. Tops turned down, the socks fit smooth as cellophane. My feet feel special—light, streamlined, quick. Then the trousers. The pleats are stiff and straight. Bones. They hold up my legs. Ben Casey wears white pants, so does Bogie in *Casablanca*. It looks professional. These pants are brand new. The white jacket's as flat and hard as a shield. It's got a starched shape all its own. It fits over me snug as a turtle's shell.

I pin my union button underneath the Flying H. I'm leaving my Mets cap at home. I open the drawer and take out the white hat. This one's not stained. I place it on my head at a Jimmy Cagney angle. It's no cunt cap, it's a uniform.

The day is full of people. They stare at me.

I'm looking good.

My card's gone. I can't punch in.

There's an envelope in my slot. No letter, just money.

Leo said he'd punish the Mets, but messing with the fans is below the belt. The Mets need me. One word to Zambrozzi, and Durocher or anybody from his crowd will never set foot in this place again.

I'm in my Homestead whites. I'm loyal.

The kitchen's empty. The vegetables are out. The meat —tattooed purple—is on the block. The tiles are wet from mopping. I'm not scared, I've had this dream before. The hissing isn't snakes, it's steam. Keep busy. Act natural. Stay alert. Leo likes to hit and run.

215

The candles are still burning on Chef's birthday cake. Over his desk is a streamer—FIGHT FIERCELY DESI. On his chair is Durocher's picture, folded face up on the back page of the *Daily News*—Leo's calling card.

Leo has a great eye, but he didn't find any autographs. I stuff the paper bag in the front of my pants. My white jacket hides the bulge. I go about my business. I take two dozen bricks from the freezer and put the wire ladder on top and push—butter patties. I arrange them neatly six to a dish. Leo's a tough coach. He respects only one thing—results.

If the crew's in trouble, maybe I should help them. Leo's probably herded them into the cellar for a pep talk, which means a brainwashing. He's telling them "nice guys finish last."

The cellar's dark and damp. The door cracks when I open it. There are voices at the bottom of the stairs. *"Marrone!"* "Oh, no!" "Christ!" Leo belonged to the Gashouse Gang, he knows how to play rough. I've got to flush him out.

"What's the story?" I yell.

Everybody's silent. I scared him. I've got my back to the wall so he can't sneak behind me.

"Get down here and shut the door."

The voice means business. I do what he says.

Leo's a shrewd manager. He's making us look at films. He shows girlie movies. He wants us to beat off before the big game.

A man on the screen holds up a piece of paper to the camera—

FUCK FILMS PRESENTS
A Doctor's Dilemma

I don't get it. Three girls are wiggling in bed. A knock at the door. Three doctors arrive with black bags. The camera slowly moves up their bodies from their boots, to their belts, to their faces. "Victor! Anthony! Garcia!"

"I can't stand it," says a voice.

"I'm fainting," says another.

216

"Blackmail!" I yell.

"Shut up!"

The three men are impostors. I can prove it. Victor, Anthony, and Garcia work at The Homestead. They're family men. They've seen *The Big Sleep*. They'd never get suckered into a frame-up like this.

The staff's laughing. They're losing respect for the chain of command. No waiter's going to give an order to a pervert sauce chef. No chef will listen to a sexed-up maître d'.

The three impostors take off their clothes and get into bed. The sheets move up and down. The girls aren't satisfied with the cure. One girl reaches for the phone. She makes a call (probably the police). Next, a woman enters dressed in black leather. Except for her lipstick, the cape, the hat, the mask, and the whip are exactly like Zorro. She marches to the bed. The impostors are tangled up with the patients. They don't know what to do. She cracks the whip over them in bed. They bump faster and faster. The girls seem to be screaming. Their mouths are open, their tongues are out. The man playing Garcia pushes himself up with one hand and waves his cowboy hat to the camera. She whips harder. And faster. Her mask slips to her neck.

It's Gloria. "Turn it off!"

"More. More."

I can't trust anybody with this information. I've got to beat Leo at his own game. You've got to respect him. He knows how to undermine morale. The man's dangerous. But, if you get caught by him, you're getting it from the best.

I ask myself—why would he stoop to this? There's only one answer. After years of managing the Brooklyn Dodgers, Leo wants to move back to New York. He plans to beat the Mets, then take them over. He needs a hangout. He'll put Laraine Day behind the cashier's desk. He'll serve Michelob and hamburgs. He'll put pictures of the Old Gang around the room. He'll throw sawdust on the floor so his boys can practice their hook slides off season. This won't do. It's terrible. I'll fight to keep The Homestead great.

The door squeaks open. McDougal's voice. "Hurry fuckin' up, you guys! The customers are comin' in."

"Lights. Give me some lights."

"Shit."

"Lights, lights, lights."

"I'm looking, Chef."

I count to five. I sneak up the stairs and out the door. Downstairs they're still shouting. I've got to work fast.

McDougal sings loud, he's not hard to tail. At ninety-three bottles of beer on the wall he turns into the pantry. By eighty-five bottles he's down the hall and in the john. I catch up with him at seventy-nine. Smoke puffs out from the vents. He's flipping the pages of a magazine. With all that noise, he can't hear me. I turn the key in the john. I take it out. I hide in the broom closet and wait.

The air smells of soap and dust. It makes my nose twitch. The mop's slimy fingers fall on my face. I've got to stand still. Soon the bell's banging. Zambrozzi's voice is saying, *"Fai presto!"* Victor and Anthony are yelling. Everything seems normal.

You can only fool some of the people some of the time.

Buttons on. Check. Shoelaces tight. Check. Autographs in place. A-okay. Time to bail out.

On the way to the dining room, I knock on the john.

"Busy."

I knock again.

"Go shit in a hat."

"The jig's up, McDougal."

"You gotta earn the crapper."

"I'm wise to you."

"Back off, jack-off. All you guys in the cellar. I like a good time, too, ya know. Just 'cause I'm new here, don't mean you can stick me with all the punk jobs. I ain't missin' the next show."

"Stay right where you are."

"You bet your sweet ass!"

The dining room looks great. The tall green trees giving shade to the tables, the paintings of Western history on our stucco walls, the waiters' cowboy hats moving among the customers who talk and take their time. It's real atmosphere. It takes you back. It makes you dream.

Station 4's filling up. A man at table 25 waves at me. "Could we have some bread and butter?"

He looks familiar. He has cuff links made of gold nuggets. He's talking to a beautiful blond, whose earrings are also made of gold nuggets. They must be a team.

I fill the glasses.

"Bread and butter."

"That's inside. I can't go inside."

"Bread and butter. I don't care who gets it."

"I'll get it."

"Good."

"Aren't you famous? Haven't I seen you on TV?"

"Should we go somewhere else, darling?"

"The movies. That's where I know your faces."

"Let's go."

"Stay right here. It's station four—the longest history of service at The Homestead."

"I don't believe this!"

'Pictures are worth a thousand words." I take out my wallet and put three snapshots on the table.

"We're hungry."

Only the very famous pretend not to be famous. I go to table 36 and borrow the bread. "Hey, that's ours," says a lady who belongs in Schrafft's.

"Station four needs rolls, ma'am. There's a V.I.P. over there."

"Who?" she says.

I hurry back to my table. The rolls are still warm. I wrap a napkin around them to hold in the heat. I put the basket on the table. "Fast, huh?"

They open the napkin. They take rolls and break them. The smell of fresh dough is sweet and strong. The first whiff's the best. They start nibbling.

"Did you like the pictures?"

"Butter."

"Of course, in the famous crowd you two move in, you probably don't recognize Eddie Arcaro, the jockey.

219

He's not the special supplement type. A little man with a big heart. A big money winner, too."

"If I say I'm famous, will you leave us alone?"

"I've been at this station eight years, three months. I know famous."

"The butter."

"That's Levy. He was the best. Drove a Buick. Notice how jazzy our outfits were in the old days?"

"This is incredible," says the blond.

"I swear it's true. I wouldn't lie to stars."

Business is really picking up. Waiters bang through the doors with Zambrozzi's food on large steel trays. "Watch it! Watch it!" It's great to be outside on the floor. People excited about their meals, peeking toward the kitchen, looking at all the important people who are looking back at them. I sidestep two waiters. I grab the butter on table 36. "Hey, pick on somebody else."

"If you don't have bread, lady, you don't need butter."

I'm back with the butter in no time.

"What's your name?" the man asks. He takes out his pen.

"Call me twelve-sixty."

I'm looking good.

There's screaming at the reservation table. The customers are upset. They look up from their food. Screams are what you hear in the street, not in a restaurant with atmosphere. The waiters pretend nothing has happened. The screams continue. Short squeals. Outside, anybody'd guess this was a purse snatching and go about their business. I sneak close. This could be another of Leo the Lip's tricks. He likes a lot of noise when he plays.

"*Puta!*" Garcia shouts. A woman's shoving by him. He blocks her way. Finally he grabs her and lifts her to the door.

"He's in here! I know he is!"

"He no here. Get lost."

Garcia may be mean to me, but he's loyal to The Homestead. It's the real Garcia. He may need help. I step closer.

"There he is!" The girl's pointing over Garcia's

220

shoulder. She's putting the finger on me. It's Gloria up to Leo's stunts.

"I got it, Benny!"

"Throw her out, Mr. Garcia. Good riddance to you, Miss Lady Lash LaRue."

"I brought you luck."

"Don't fall for the sweet talk, Mr. Garcia. Those are 'Fuck Me' shoes."

Garcia spins around. "Jesus Christ!" The news shocks him, too.

"She's trying to frame us. I'm onto her game. You're no sex maniac."

Gloria puts her hands over her ears.

"What's the matter, you Cub kamikaze? Can't take the truth?"

Garcia stares at me. He doesn't say a word.

"She'll show you her credits. She'll try and snow you with her medical background. It's the flimflam, Garcia."

"Walsh, you never worked here. Understand?"

"It's me. Willie. Remember? Below the waiters. Station four."

"I count ten. You disappear."

"You've got The Homestead hat. The maître d' spurs. The greaseball accent. But you're not Garcia. I've worked here."

"I count five. Then I chase you out of here. One, two . . ."

"This clinches it, mister. Now I know you're a wooden nickel. There's no running in the dining room."

I'm running Joe's pattern—down and out. It works like a charm. I've got my balance. I feel strong. I see an opening and bull ahead. People are screaming from the sidelines. Opponents crash and curse behind me. I've seen this before. This is how it's supposed to happen. It feels as smooth as slow motion, but it's not. Swivel-hip fake. Change pace. I'm in the clear. Run to daylight, big fella. I'm golden.

The staff's yelling. "Block him! Block him!" I shove a table in front of the kitchen door. The impostor blitzes the front wall. He crashes through.

They try to stop me. My rip-away jacket fools them. I stay on my feet. My number's still on my chest. They can tell who's running the ball.

I pick up two white footballs from the bowl. I heave them at Garcia. My bullet passes explode on his chest. I knew he was chicken. He's bleeding yellow. "Get him! Get him!" My team's too slow. They want to be nice. They don't know how to win.

"Sonofabitch!"

He corners me by the freezer. I feel something heavy in my hand. "Stand back, Mr. Big. I'm turning you over to the proper authorities. The blackmail's stopping right here."

"You pussy, Walsh. You motherfucker."

"Keep my mother out of this!"

"Benny, put that down!"

"I'm winning, Desi. If you can't stand the heat, stay out of the kitchen."

"Walsh, you got your money. Get out. You're fired!"

"Nobody fires an eight-year man, jerk. They give him a watch. They call him into the Boss's office for a highball and handshake."

"You always trouble. You and those dumb autographs."

"You think it ends here, Mr. Frame-up. It doesn't. I got friends. They're not gonna let you get away with this."

I show him the bag. "These people could buy you and sell you."

"I call the cops."

"That's been tried before. These people are above the law. They could ruin you." I shove the bag under his nose. "I should make you eat them. But they're too good for you."

He grabs the bag.

"Give me that back!"

"Your friends, huh?"

"I'm warning you. They're right behind you."

"Fuck your friends!"

He rips my bag. He treats it like lettuce. He makes it into small pieces.

I can hear myself laughing.

I can see my arm moving.

Garcia opens his mouth. Red ribbons roll out.

The staff's lined up across the kitchen. They stand in silence. I wish Mom was here.

The honor guard, in blue, surrounds me. One man's writing me up.

"You have the right to remain silent."

"He was an impostor! It was some fight. I feel on cloud nine."

"Mr. Walsh, anything you say at this time may be held against you."

"I want this for the record."

"You're entitled to counsel."

"A cleaver's for your ribs and joints. Splitting, not chopping. It's a one-stroke tool. The power's in the follow-through. The wrist."

The man scribbles on his white pad. I watch him. He's got every word.

"Pen?"

He looks up from his writing. He hands me his ballpoint.

"What's your name?"

"Sergeant Anthony Ambrosi, Homicide."

I sign underneath my story.

TO TONY

KEEP THE FAITH

Benny S. Walsh